BRAHMO SAMAJ AND INDIAN CIVILIZATION

CULTURE AND CIVILIZATION SERIES

BRAHMO SAMAJ AND INDIAN CIVILIZATION

Edited by
Dr. R.K. Pruthi

DPH

DISCOVERY PUBLISHING HOUSE PVT. LTD.
NEW DELHI-110 002

Published by:

DISCOVERY PUBLISHING HOUSE PVT. LTD.
4383/4B, Ansari Road, Darya Ganj
New Delhi-110 002 (India)
Phone : +91-11-23279245; 23253475; 43596065
E-mail : discoverybooksindia@gmail.com
discoverypublishinghouse@gmail.com
web : www.discoverypublishinggroup.com

First Published: **2004**

Reprinted: **2021**

ISBN: 978-81-7141-791-9

Brahmo Samaj and Indian Civilization

Printed at:
Infinity Imaging Systems
Delhi

PREFACE

In the nineteenth century Christian religious ideas, modern, western rationalist and utilitarian thought brough about a ferment in the Indian civilization. A series of creative individuals started social reform movements to rejuvenate the Indian civilization. The Brahm Samaj inaugurated this new era of reform movements.

Attempt in this book has been made to examine and understand the teachings of this movement and to see how far and in what ways has the Brahmo movement influenced the Indian civilization.

In preparing this work we have incurred indebtness of the many authorities on the subject whose works we found of great significance and benefits to our readers and for its wider publicity.

We are thankful to friends and family members for their encouragement and support.

My publisher and his staff members have worked extremely hard. They deserve the love and patronage of my readers.

R.K. Pruthi

Contents

1

Indian Civilisation in Modern Period

India was a divided country when the British won the battle of Plassey and made Calcutta their capital. Little by little they moved inland from Calcutta, Madras and Bombay. All three of these places are situated on the sea coast. The entire sub-continent came under their domination. They failed to conquer Afghanistan, and they stopped short of annexing Nepal. But they took Burma, incorporating it in their Indian Empire. This was an anomaly. There were other similar anomalies.

The various East India Companies that came to India in the first, instance to trade also traded with Malaya, Indonesia, Indo-China and China. In their eyes India was only a part of East India, better known as Hindustan. Gradually the Companies added conquest to their activities. Each acquired an Empire. One was British India. Another French India. There was also a Dutch India and Portuguese India. British India did not take over the various kingdoms known as the princely states directly but the rulers acknowledged British paramountcy. The British sovereign was represented by a Viceroy whose authority extended to both parts of India, the Indian states as well as the territory known as British India. This unity was not established in a day. It took a long time to achieve. When it became an accomplished fact it was accepted by the Indian people as a natural and normal state of affairs. Indian nationalists took it for granted and denied the British credit for it. To them also it seemed a fact of nature. They looked upon the British as profit-motivated capitalists and imperialists whose object was exploitation. There was much more to it than that. Great cities grew up. Calcutta, Bombay and Madras became centres of a metropolitan culture that included the new, modern, Wastern culture. The man who was the first to welcome this development was Raja Rammohun Roy. He personally defied the ban on travel by sea, sailed to Europe and acquainted himself with English and continental culture at first hand. He was agreeably surprised to find that several of his books had preceded him and his work was known. It is symbolic that his tomb has become a place of pilgrimage for all Indians who venture abroad for he died in England.

Rammohun Roy was a man of religion. He was also a patriot. Yet culture was, for him, independent of both creed and politics. Culture, he felt, should be as modern as the age, on a par with the culture of other countries and, of necessity, cosmopolitan. He himself received his education in the time-honoured traditional institutions of both the Hindus and Muslims. In the absence of a western educational institution he studied English privately. He was fluent in both Persian and Sanskrit as well as Bengali. As the upshot of his experience he advocated a new system of education for India. The subjects he wanted to see on the curriculum were the subjects being taught in contemporary European schools, not those studied in the *madrasahs and chatuspathis*. This change was as epoch-making as the change that was wrought in Europe three centuries earlier by the Renaissance, the change from the old learning to the new.

The East India Campany, however, did not feel that Rammohun Roy's new system was either desirable or necessary. India was an oriental country. It should remain oriental. There were European scholars, deeply learned, who apprehended that the introduction of new-fangled western notions into India would have a deleterious effect. These scholars were orientalists with an enlightened appreciation of and respect for traditional Hindu and Muslim teaching. In Europe itself the debate between those who favoured a classical education and insisted upon its superiority and those who were trying to introduce science subjects and scientific methods into the schools was far from over. Sanskrit has affinities with Greek and Latin. For this and other reasons there was tendency to assume that the classical pattern of education in India was the same, or nearly the same, as the European. To them Rammohun Roy appeared exotic. They did not regard him as representative of his country's intellectual life. In India, however, a section of public opinion was on his side. The urban middle classes in Bengal, Hindus for the most part, were expanding rapidly and the inadequacy of the old system of education in the new circumstances was a matter of daily experience for them. They supported the demand for a new type of school on a modern, western model.

When the Hindu College was founded in Calcutta a number of Europeans were impressed. They began to see Rammohun Roy's point and to agree with him. Macaulay, by his famous Minute, made it the Government's policy to give encouragement to education on the English model in preference to the traditional Hindu and Muslim schools. Rammohun Roy won a posthumous victory. He had not suggested the abolition of the traditional subjects nor did he desire it. On the contrary, he had envisaged a Vedanta College. What he really wanted was that the people of India should have access to the knowledge being imparted to people of Western countries. They had a right to it. That this new knowledge had its uses was self-evident. It was intended to bring our people into line with the more advanced countries and to revise their sense of reality. The world in which they had been living so long had become unreal, having lost touch with actuality. They were three hundred years behind the times and seven thousand miles from the main currents of progress. Men like Rammohun Roy strove to diminish the distance both in time and space. They were not primarily interested in equipping middle class Bengali young men with qualifications that would land them jobs in the British establishment although clerks with a working knowledge of English were in great demand. Not did the promoters of the new education intend to widen the gap between the educated and uneducated classes. The gap was already there. The uneducated did not know Persian and even those who could read a little Bengali had no access to books. Books did not became available until the printing press made them so. Libraries did not appear until much later. The sudras, in the earlier periods of our history, were forbidden to hear a word of Sanskrit. It was an offence for them to listen. The gap between the Sanskrit-speaking Brahmans and the lower classes was enormous. English did not create a new division. It has never been an offence for anybody belonging to any caste to listen to English being spoken.

The cultural scene in India underwent rapid change. A new generation rose, a generation which was educated in western ways and equipped with a knowledge of science and scientific method. The printing press accelerated the pace. Its effects were in evidence everywhere. Newspapers, journals, magazines, books poured in a steady stream into the public life of the country. A critical mentality developed. Everything was scrutinized by the light of reason. Public orations reflected the change:

Henry Louis Vivian Derozio, of Portuguese extraction, was an inspiring teacher. Many of the young men who later became leaders were his students. Their lack of veneration for the merely old and time-honoured offended the traditionalists. What was, on the surface, a confrontation between Oriental and Occidental was actually a domestic confrontation between the old and the new. The intellectuals of India had done no original thinking for at least a thousand years. Their instructors were gurus to them, the relationship between teacher and taught being one of unquestioning trust and blind devotion. Authority had never before been questioned. It was unthinkable that a group of youngsters should have the audacity to challenge a learning and way of life that had stood the test of centuries. The rishis had handed it down to successive generations from their forest schools. The inexplicable impertinence of these young men was blamed on the new education, a *mlechchha* education.

This new generation was regarded as lien in culture if not in blood. The young men were *feringhis*. The difficulty of their getting a hearing was complicated by the presence of the missionaries. The missionaries were critical of things Hindu and their attitude disturbed the traditionalists. They suspected the Derozians were halfway to Christianity and would soon begin to leave the Hindu fold. They did not know and could not be expected to know that an Age of Reason had set in or that the eighteenth century Enlightenment was in any way different from the preceding Age of Faith. The Derozians were rationalists. They did not believe in an infallible religion. But missionary influence was strong for many reasons and some eminent Hindus did become Christian converts. The old guard of Hindu Society felt that their fears were justified. Many features of liberal Christian practice and belief were incorporated in the constitution of the Brahmo Samaj, a religious body founded upon the teachings of the Upanishads by Rammohun Roy. It formed a kind of bridge between Hinduism and Christianity, uniting the best features of both. The Brahmo Samaj became a kind of Church, not unlike the Unitarian sect. Those for whom Christianity had a strong attraction found all they needed in it. Vedic and Brahmanic authority also gave place to the authority of the Upanishads.

The main body of the English-educated Indians remained inside the Hindu fold, acting as a leaven from within. The mythological approach to life was slowly replaced by a critical, scientific and historical attitude. Theology was separated from philosophy and Western philosophy was given precedence over Eastern even at the Calcutta Sanskrit College, Vidyasagar himself insisted upon it. Bankim Chandra Chatterjee was deeply influenced by Comte, the great French philosopher.

The Hindus did not doubt that theirs was the oldest and the best of cultures but they were less confident than formerly of their power to subdue their conquerors through it. The Muslim Arabs and Turks and Moguls had not succumbed. On the contrary, the appeal of the ancient and traditional had no hold over them; they resisted it with complete success. The Hindus developed a defensive attitude in the centuries following their appearance on the Indian scene. They sought a way to live and let live on mutually acceptable terms. An alien creed and a different culture alarmed them instinctively. There were some, however, who became familiar enough with Arabian-Persian culture to be able to distinguish it from Islam. They admired it and adopted many features of the elegant and beautiful Persian way of life, making it their own. To these connoisseurs the new culture of the West presented no difficulties. With gracious urbanity and a polished sophistication they were able to accommodate it without jarring incongruities. Europeans, in their turn, yielded to their environment and Persianised their ways to a great extent. Yet people of this kind were feared by the orthodox Hindus almost as much as Christian missionaries. They were regarded as equally impure and dangerous.

The Hindus had known the Arabs and Turks before the rise of Islam. When, inspired by the proselytising zeal of their new faith, the Arabs and Turks appeared in the role of invaders, former acquaintance stood both parties in good stead. They shared attitudes that belonged to their period of history such as the feudal mentality. The same was not the case with the newcomers from England and France. The people from these countries were utter strangers for there had been no previous contact. They did not belong to the same period of history nor did they share common attitudes. Both the British and the French were two or three centuries ahead of the Hindus and Muslims. They belonged to the modern age and feudalism was a long-discarded phenomenon. The Industrial Revolution had begun; and the French

Revolution with its revolutionary aftermath, had taken place. The English and the French were concerned with capitalism. A policy of live and let live was possible for the Hindus with the Turks and Arabs for their ways of thinking were nor radically different but with the English and French it was another proposition altogether. Threats to religious belief were nothing new but threats to established social order could not be lightly dismissed. Science and technology were entirely outside the range of traditional Hindu thought. Traditionalists could not understand them and few made any effort to do so. The changes that were coming were far-reaching in their social consequences and not at all reassuring.

The Hindus were therefore divided as never before. In Russia, where Western European culture prevailed among the elite, there were Westernisers and Russophils. In India there were Westernisers and Indophils. The Muslims were in a separate category. They detested Christianity with a passion left over from the Crusades. They hated the *feringhis* for having, as they believed, deprived them of their empire by trickery. They still dreamed of a day when Allah would restore the throne of India to its rightful owner. Of what use would an English education be to them? They clung to their *madrasah* without any qualms. English classes were introduced into the Calcutta *Madrasah* but few students were attracted to them. Modernism was just as incomprehensible to the Muslims as it was to traditionalist Hindus. They regarded it with alarm. It was a menace to their social order.

The British rulers and their Hindu and Muslim subjects formed a triangle. The Hindus were grateful to the British for not putting them under Muslim authority. They were freed from an irksome subjection. The Muslims were wholly unreconciled. They resented having lost their supremacy and they resented having Hindus put in higher positions, second only to the British who, of course, occupied the top posts. This triangular configuration could not be broken unless India's former rulers formed and alliance with the Marathas and Sikhs and drove the *feringhis* into the sea. Another alternative would have been to invite Islamic powers like Turkey, Iran and Afghanistan to do this for them. A Pan-Islamic solution appealed to orthodox Muslims more than a Pan-Indian one. To liberal Muslims the Pan-Indian alternative made better sense. They wished to live in amity with the Hindus and participate in a common culture.

The installation of Queen Victoria as the Empress of India and the deportation of the last Mogul emperor marked a turning point in Indian history. It ruled out for all time any possibility of a Muslim restoration. The Pan-Islamic brotherhood continued to dream of the glorious days of the Arab conquest of Spain and the Turkish conquest of the Balkans, hoping against hope for a grand alliance that would defeat Britain on every front. The more realistic and far-sighted leaders rejected the idea however. They also rejected the idea of a powerful alliance between Muslims and Hindus that might ultimately lead to a joint victory. Their attitude to the British was changed. They now regarded them as friends and patrons if not equals. This was a volte-face that was to lead inexorably to separate electorates for Hindus and Muslims, separate quotas in the public services and ultimately to a separate Muslim state. By the withdrawal of the British the triangle was broken into two parallel lines. The two lines, India and Pakistan, may or may not meet in infinity.

There were differences between Hinduism and Islam no doubt but it had never occurred to anybody that these differences would lead to a complete separation, a division into watertight compartments inevitably accompanied by an unofficial exchange of population on a tragic scale. The secular policy of the Indian leaders was the only ameliorating factor in this exchange, preventing an even greater holocaust than that which took place. The British connection was the only link that remained between the two separated territorial units. Both India and Pakistan stayed in the Commonwealth. Yet the British presence was constantly decried as a wedge driving Hindus and Muslims further and further apart, in order better to subdue them both. Cultural ties were broken also and the only link that remained was English. India chose Hindi. Pakistan chose Urdu. The two communities had not been so hostile to each other since the twelfth century. Eight hundred years of a common development was forgotten for the moment. To all appearances the continuous and unremitting efforts of well-wishers on both sides to achieve a viable synthesis had failed.

The modern period of Indian history is a time of conflict and reconciliation between East and West, old and new. Never before had India been ruled from a base outside its territory. Never before had Indians been subject to the authority of a less-than-sovereign government in India. The British Government in India was subordinate to a superior Government in England that was directly responsible to the British electorate, not to the Indian people. Never before had Indian interests been subsidiary to those of a foreign power. The needs of British capitalists and industrialists were given priority. Never before had Indian soldiers been forced to fight people with whom they had no quarrel. Never before had Indian labour been sent as indentured labour to work on plantations in foreign lands and been treated as inferiors. In his own country the tallest Indian was humiliated with impunity by the lowliest Tommy.

On the positive side India was united for the first time from Kashmir to Cape Comorin and from Baluchistan to Burma. The unity was real. A railway system was laid out that enabled a man to travel from Peshawar to Dibrugarh without a passport, without a change of currency, and without customs formalities. Goods moved without let or hindrance over the whole surface of the land. Post and telegraph services facilitated and speeded up communication between far-flung and hitherto isolated areas. Books began to circulate in the mails. Ideas travelled faster than people. The Punjabis and Bengalis, the Marathas and Malayalis found themselves thinking the same thoughts. And same feelings stirred in their hearts to an extent that never before happened in history. The same laws applied to all and were administered through a network of law courts to appeal to. The administrative system was the same everywhere with a few local modifications in the princely States. Internecine wars came to an end. There were no more invasions. Pax Britannica saw to that. Newspapers voiced the grievances of the people. The people were unified as never before. Unifying also was the experience of standing on platforms and giving voice to discontent. Associations of many kinds were freely formed and permitted to function without hindrance, even the Indian National Congress. Constitutional changes were suggested, fought for, and granted.

Careers were opened to the middle classes that had never existed before, The middle class itself was a product of British rule. It began to prosper. By a dialectical process thesis created antithesis. Indian nationalism was generated by British imperialism. Indian nationalists wanted to replace their rulers but they did not want to do away with British institutions. These they wished to retain, all of them, the administrative, judicial and legislative. An Indian city on Indian soil should be the capital instead of London. Moderates and extremists differed not over ends but over means. What means were to be used to achieve those ends? This was the picture before the First World

War. India had telescoped into a single century three major European transformations, passing through a Renaissance, a Reformation and an Enlightenment.

When World War I broke out there were only two parties that did not rally around the British Crown. Pan-Islamists saw in the possibility of a Turkish victory the revival of their dream. And those nationalists who believed in terrorist methods sought assistance from the enemy, expecting Germany to help them achieve their objective.

During the Mogul era the Banias had a large share in the wealth of the country and the Rajputs enjoyed a large measure of power also. Indian princes and large landowners or zamindars enjoyed a large measure of power under the British Raj and Banias retained a considerable share of the wealth. The ascendancy therefore was not altogether White, Anglo-Saxon and Protestant. It was also Hindu Muslim Bourgeois Feudal. In times of trouble the latter made common cause with the former and all differences were forgotten.

After the War a change took place which was comparable to that ushered in by the introduction of Western education. It was as subtle and as far-reaching. In the course of fighting Germany Indian soldiers overcame any sense of inferiority they might have had. They could not be expected to display the same degree of servility as before. Demobilised army men were among the agitators who protested against the Rowlatt Act. Unfortunately men like Dyer and O'Dwyer had learnt nothing. They resorted to repressive measures harsh in the extreme. In 1919 India was seething with discontent, a veritable volcano. The British bureaucracy however showed no signs of regarding India as anything but a permanent dependency. The press and the Bar, both of which had fostered the political advancement of the people with a fair degree of freedom, giving voice to grievances and advocating remedies, sharpened their criticism by degrees, moving steadily towards an extreme position. Two of the new professions, the Law and Journalism, attracted men who were of an independent turn of mind and were capable of giving the country leadership. They favoured parliamentary institutions and when they had these, looked beyond to their logical extension in a cabinet responsible to the parliament not immediately, of course, but as soon as feasible after the War. It was at this point that the unrest seething below the surface erupted at Amritsar. Civil disobedience became unavoidable.

Gandhi took the initiative. The nation had to be mobilised to fight a war, a non-violent war. The initiative remained in his hands until the withdrawal of the British in 1947. The Indians. became a fighting people, something they had never been before in history. The common people had always been passive, leaving the fighting to the military castes. Wars had been conducted by professionals according to a professional code, in a prescribed style. The sole exception had been the Sikhs who fought as a single body under the leadership of their gurus. Gandhi conjured up mass civil disobedience, a technique without precedent in the annals of war. He drew upon the ethical teachings of the Buddha and of Mahavira as well as other great spiritual teachers in his efforts to give shape to a new political order, and order with a moral code. This too, was something that had never been done before. He was hailed as a Mahatma both in India and the West. A man of his stature could not remain content with political objectives only and he placed before his countrymen a new set of goals, suggesting a new set of institutions to achieve them. His call to purge Indian society of age-old abuses to make the country fit for independence appealed to the sense of purity and the aversion to ritual pollution which characterized both Hindus and Muslim. The response was phenomenal.

Novel also was the attitude he took up in regard to the industrialization of India. He insisted that science, no matter how wonderful, must be kept in check by ethical considerations, This could be done, he said, only be developing decentralized civilisation and by limiting the size and scope of industrial projects. He wanted industry to be controlled by the workers. Capitalists should, he persuasively argued, act as trustees for the public good.

The initiative in cultural matters was retained by the westernized intelligentsia until the last decade of the nineteenth century. At that time the Indophils brought forward their proposal for resisting the cultural subjection of India. By extolling all things Indian and ancient and denouncing all things foreign and modern they hoped to revive the glory that was India. Materialism was condemned and identified with the West: the spiritual tradition of India was exalted and identified with the East. This Revivalism applied to intellectural matters, arts and crafts and ways of living in general. The new learning and all that went with it was discredited. The Indian Renaissance, Reformation and Enlightenment were decried as materialistic and foreign-inspired. India, it was said, must go her own way without imitating others. The only place she could go, in the circumstances, was to the past. The Vedic ashram ideal was vaunted. National schools were established. India was told to discover her own soul and live according to her own truth. The call was non-political but the response soon took on a political colouring. The Swadeshi Movement identified itself with the boycott of British goods. This was followed by the cult of the bomb. From start to finish the entire movement was Hindu. The British turned to the Muslims and began to favour them. A weapon for more powerful than the bomb was manufactured in the laboratories of the rulers: separate electorates for Hindus and Muslims. Hindus confronted Muslims in small electoral squares all over the country.

The Westernisers were liked by nobody, neither the revivalists nor the political activists nor the communalists. Did the British like them any better? No, the British were not at all sure that India was ready for either freedom or democracy. They doubted whether an Indianised civil or military service could cope with the problems that were certain to arise. Nor did they think Indians equal to the task of developing technology and industrialization wisely. The only visible alternative was reversion to oriental despotism. Short work would be made of Westernisers if that happened.

The Westernisers were on their way out before the Non-co-operation Movement began. The essential tenet of Indian nationalism was that India contained within herself all that she required, spiritual, intellectual, moral and material. Nothing need be imported from outside, not even science or technology. Even the sincerest nationalist demurred. He felt it would be sufficient for science and technology to be infused with the Vedanta spirit and a mystic element added to them. Science and technology had to be accepted and this formula satisfied India's self-respect. It also left some scope for co-operation with the West and some areas in which Western influence could act beneficially. The Westernisers were also modernisers and could not be rejected outright. They were not traitors to Indian nationalism. But Gandhi put them completely in the shade. Tagore protested against cultural non-cooperation. He invited the whole world to come and make its home in India Sri Aurobindo did the same as he outgrew his early fiery nationalism. And a religious organization had been formed that spread all over the earth for the second time in India's history, carrying the spiritual message of a great saint, Sri Ramakrishna. The order founded in his name by Swami Vivekananda has established itself in the world at large as only the Buddhist Sangha succeeded in doing centuries earlier.

As for art, it was too late in the day to expect poets and artists to draw inspiration from Indian sources alone. Some artists who did do so initiated what is known as the Bengal School of Painting in the wake of the Swadeshi Movement. They did their best to revive the spirit of Ajanta and Ellora. When these efforts reached a dead end Jamini Roy turned to folk art and opened up a rich vein of vital and vigorous promise. Folk tradition could be taken advantage of only if artists went back to the village and lived there. Most of them felt a compulsion to live in cities. Their patrons were in the cities. Folk art produced in urban surrounding is like homespun khadi made in palaces.

Mahatma Gandhi was a man with a mission. He was the world's only specialist in Mass Civil Disobedience, a moral equivalent of war and revolution. He had a message for the world, all of it, not excluding the West. His quarrel was not with Westernism as such as with certain deleterious aspects of Modernism. He was not opposed to all things Western on principle. What he took exception to was criticised also by Tolstoy, Ruskin and Thoreau. A democracy controlled by wealthy industrialists and militarists through mass communication media seemed to him to be a contradiction in terms. He opposed the proletarianisation of whole classes of skilled craftsmen and agriculturists; he opposed compulsory militarisation; he opposed large-scale industrialization and urbanization. He opposed the multiplication of material wants and the neglect of the starving spirit. Gandhi was one of the great rebels who regarded the British as the carriers of a deadly disease, a disease from which they themselves were suffering without knowing it and with which he did not want India to be infected. He wanted to protect India and at the same time cure England. He claimed to be the friend of both. He hoped to help both to maintain a healthy society by withholding co-operation from the forces which were the cause of a dangerous imbalance in the metabolism of the state. He questioned the so-called benefits of British rule, including the railways and the law courts, hospitals, parliamentary institutions and the educational system, turning the tables on the modern West and those who saw only good in it. What he stood for was, actually, a new social order based on truth and non-violence. All that was conducive to health found a place in it. The roots of the Indian tree of life remained deeply buried in antiquity while new branches enriched the foliage of the times.

Few of his followers thought as he did. His Khilafatist allies certainly did not. The majority of the nationalists were revivalists and their gaze was fixed on the long and glorious past. They cast their eyes back to the Vedas. What they wanted was to revive this past, resuscitate Vaisya affluence, Kshatriya power and Brahman diplomacy. The Gandhian cult of non-violence, truth and brahmacharya had little real appeal for them. Moreover, they considered industrialization a desirable way to get rich quick, militarisation a way to get strong quick, and parliamentary elections a way of gaining control of the government machinery, including the instruments of coercion like the police and jails.

The Khilafatists were still dreaming of the past glory of Islam. They wished to recapture their ancient eminence and extend it from the Atlantic to the Pacific. How could such a brave dream be realized without a modern army and large-scale industry? They did not believe in parliamentary democracy for in India the Muslims were a minority and would be at a disadvantage. They were, however, willing to give it a trial provide the Hindus agreed to a pact that would ensure equality of representation. They were more concerned over the fate of the holy places in the Middle East than of India's enslaved and impoverished millions. Gandhi's leadership was accepted because they needed a champion to defend the holy places. There were of course some who did share his concern for the poor and they also shared his non-violent and patriotic ideology. They were true Indophils. They remained with Gandhi after the Khilafatists took their departure, asking for no safeguards in the context of a free and independent India. The Khilafatists, in the course of their journey, finally arrived at a half-way house, somewhere between Pan-Islamism and Indian nationalism. This half-way house was a Muslim homeland in the Indian subcontinent and to win it they were prepared to fight their old allies, the Hindus, rather than their old enemies the British.

A spirit of non-cooperation in the cultural field preceded Gandhi's Non-cooperation Movement in the political. The Indophils stood for the boycott of Western education and for a scheme of national schools and colleges. This scheme made a concession to the times by accepting English as a subject but it was heavily encumbered with Sanskrit, Vedic practice and Puranic lore. At Varanasi the traditional learning went its traditional way. The spirit of the West was accommodated only superficially. In many other parts of the country, however, and particularly in Bengal, that spirit exercised considerable influence over literature. In Bengal an English-educated middle class elite cooperated with the English ruling class in all matters except religious. Because of this co-operative attitude Bengalis were able to spread out over Northern India and Burma. Everywhere they set up educational institutions, practised law and medicine and opened schools and colleges. Many were in Government service and some in journalism. Bengali influence in India was at its height towards the end of the nineteenth century. Their close contact with the British had an adverse effect also. British exclusiveness, arrogance and snobbery, the humiliating way they treated the 'Babus' gave rise to a hatred that was deep and deadly. The Babus turned against the Sahebs, terrorism was born. Thesis created antithesis.

Religious reformers like Keshab Chandra Sen arose, who felt no hesitation in adopting elements of both Christian and Islamic teaching. To translate the Qu'ran into Bengali was a daring thing to do. No Muslim would touch the translation but the Brahmos did. They read the Qu'ran as they read the Bible and the Upanishads. Some Brahmos studied Hebrew and Greek. The same catholicity was shown by the followers of Sri Ramakrishna who used both Christian and Muslim disciplines in the search for spiritual enlightenment. He summed up his conclusions by saying: The ways to God are as many as there are faiths. This was also the message of Theosophy which Madame Blavatsky gave to the world. The Theosophists made Adyar their international headquarters. Empires could come and empires could go. That Christianity and Islam should have been brought to Indian soil to join the fraternity of great religions already existing there was looked upon as an act of God.

All men of culture who had thought about this problem felt the same way. If the Indo-Aryan roots were the deepest the Dravidian roots were the oldest. The Indo-Persian had a limited but nonetheless important appeal. It was not confined to the Muslims in the North and the Deccan. There were Hindus and Sikhs and Christians who both spoke and wrote Urdu. Hindustani music was and is common to all without distinction of caste or creed. In music it was no longer possible to revert to a purely classical Hindu idiom, The South tried to preserve the old and succeeded in a large measure but much diversification took place in the North. During the Modern Period diversification spread widely. Western influence was absorbed and made the basis of new variants. In the course of her long history India has assimilated many and diverse elements. One more did not make too much differencc. The Tagores discarded all barriers, experimenting endlessly. Why should political status interfere with communication between people, or peoples, or place obstacles in the way of their understanding one another? The theme of Tagore's great novel *Gora* is the plight of a child whose Irish parents have died, leaving him to be brought up by Brahman foster parents. He was a *mlehcchha*. Would India take this orphan to her heart and make him her own or cast him out? Anandamayi, the foster mother, is prepared to forfeit her caste if need be rather than deny the child. Anandamayi symbolises Mother India to whom all children are her own, Christian, Muslim, Hindu, brown, white or yellow, Orthodox. Hindu society rejected Gora but the Brahmo Samaj welcomed him. India accepts the West in the same way. Tagore composed an inspiring poem in which he calls India the 'shore of humanity, where all rivers flow into the sea,'. He goes on to say: 'Come, O Aryan, O Non-Aryan, O Hindu, O Mussalman, O Christian, O Englishman!' The poet invites them all to take part in the synthesis that is India. This poem was written long before Tagore was awarded the Nobel Prize and India was accepted into the comity of the nations of the world as an equal. Twenty five years earlier, in 1885, the Indian National Congress. adopted what this poem affirms as the truth by which it stood. The founder-secretary was Mr. A. O. Hume, a Scotsman, who retired from the Indian Civil Service to devote his life to the cause of the Indian nation. Among the founder members of the Congress were Parsis, Anglicised Hindus and Muslims, lawyers and journalists, and some businessmen. All of them were loyal to the Crown and all of them were also patriotic Indians or friends of India. Lord Ripon, a former Viceroy, speaking at Edinburgh, urged England to recognize and guide the Indian people in their efforts to establish their freedom of self-expression and natural development. He spoke of the justness of these aspirations and advised against resisting or ignoring the movement developing around them. The makers of free India did not design an exclusive nation. They were the architects of a country patterned as in Tagore's great poem, an inclusive country, a country that could and did take into its ample bosom Muslim and Englishman as well as Hindu.

Thus the culture of India is a comprehensive culture. In what language could all the diverse constituents converse? Sanskrit was not modern enough, nor was Persian. The only alternative was and is English. Without any encouragement Indians in every part of India have done and are doing a considerable amount of creative thinking and writing in English. Many of them, such as Sarojini Naidu or Aurobindo Ghose, were ardent nationalists. They had to write in English or not at all; they had no choice. Their subjects were Indian. European writers like Sister Nivedita, Sir Edwin Arnold and Annie Besant also wrote on Indian themes. The Indo-English literary tradition began to evolve as early as the time of Sir William Jones and Rammohun Roy, at the point of time when Western and Eastern minds met for the first tentative exchanges of thought and sentiment. Indologists have been communicating constantly ever since and English has been the medium through which they have made contacts and expressed their conclusions. There is no question of rejecting the many and great contributions that have been made to the Indian heritage on the grounds that they are contained in the English language. Halhed was the first to write a Bengali grammar. He wrote it in English in the eighteenth century. No Bengali grammar at all existed at that time, not even in Bengali. The Sanskritists did not even believe there was anything that could be called grammar in Bengali, They had scant regard for their own language. As a language distinct from Sanskrit, with a character and beauty of its own, Bengali won recognition in the nineteenth century. The pliancy that was required to embody that Renaissance was found in it after persistent cultivation. It responded to the new ways of thinking and speaking with a flexible and nuanced richness that met the needs of the great thinkers of the Modern age and creative writing as well.

While Indians took to writing English, Europeans took to writing Indian languages. Christian missionaries were the first to articulate these languages in a modern context. The growth of Bengali prose has been traced to Portuguese initiative. Englishmen developed it further and their example was followed by pandits and munshis. The pandits often overloaded Bengali with Sanskrit baggage and the munshis often overloaded it with Persian baggage. The English-educated gentry tried their hand at writing Bengali too and adopted it to English models. They looked to English or French for essay forms, the novel and the short story, For lyric and epic poetry they continued to turn to Sanskrit and Medieval Bengali but finally settled for English. Sanskrit drama gave place to Shakespearean and contemporary English. Even the great Sanskrit scholar Vidyasager, the father of Bengali prose, was seen translating Shankespeare's *Comedy of Errors*. The first Bengali play was performed under the direction of a Russian on a European-type stage towards the close of the eighteenth century. The European community in Calcutta had their own theatre. It interested the Bengali elite so much the Bengali theatre of the nineteenth century was modelled on it but, as it catered to a Bengali audience, it developed in its own way, acquiring a distinct character that persists to this day. The tendency to Sanskritise remained and resulted in the creation of a stilted and artificial style known as 'high' or *sadhu bhasa* or polite speech. Colloquial speech was introduced into literature slowly, at first in the drama and later in the dialogue of novels and short stories. The speech of the people has now become standard for creative writing, yet Sanskrit is still drawn upon when a difficult thought requires precise expression. And in such cases Sanskrit is given preference over English. The first Bengali novel was written for Bengali Christian women by a certain Mrs Mullens. The first Bengali journals were published by Christian missionaries. After the Mutiny in 1857, however, European literary activity in Bengal ceased.

The Mutiny, it seems, came as a deep shock to all classes of Europeans: public servants, businessmen, missionaries. They became apprehensive lest another, similar outbreak occur without warning. Elaborate arrangements were made for the protection of the lives and honour of Europeans. The policy of Divide and Rule was deliberately adopted and conscientiously applied. All Indians who had anything to do with Europeans were hurt by the sudden coolness in a hitherto warm relationship. Converts were in a dilemma. If they aligned themselves with the Europeans their Indian compatriots looked askance at them. They lost status. They were mistrusted. If, on the other hand, they held themselves aloof from the European community they lost contact with the only people upon whom they could rely. Ties with their Indian kinsmen were broken by the act of their changing faith. They became isolated. Culturally they continued to be Indian and their fate was finally decided by that fact.

The relationship between Indians and Europeans became perfunctory and formal after the Mutiny. Indians who travelled abroad found a welcome contrast in the way they were received. They developed a preference for European civilisation and culture but British clubs in India remained closed to them no matter how high their rank or how wealthy they might be. How could there be any meeting of minds in such an oppressive atmosphere?

Westernised Indians lost what little voice they had had. Their detractors quoted Kipling: *"O East is East and West is West and never the twain shall meet."* Inronically they agreed with him. Those who believed in the possibility of an East-West synthesis as an ideal were out of favour. Tagore went bravely ahead with his plans to provide a place and an atmosphere where the best could meet the best freely, without fear or favour. Santiniketan was and is such a place although by creating it he exposed himself to the suspicion of narrow-minded parochialist nationalism. His own people doubted him and so did the foreign rulers.

Then the Muslims began to look upon the nationalists with doubt in their eyes. In their struggle for freedom hundreds and thousands of Indians had found in inspiration and courage in Bankim Chandra's famous anthem, *Bande Mataram,* "Motherland, to thee we bow." This song was now discovered to be offensive to Muslims in the Congress camp. Ultimately it was replaced by Tagore's *Jana gana mana adhinayaka* "Thou art the ruler of the hearts and minds of all the people". This song, celebrating the unity of Hindu and Muslim, East and West, became India's national anthem. India, in the greatness of her vision and the wide sweep of her loving embrace, accepted all comers.

Yet it failed to win over the separatist Muslims. They did not want to lose their identity as Muslims, as an identity which cut across frontiers and made them a part of the Islamic fraternity over which the Caliph presided. They did not want to merge themselves with Indian nationalism to the exclusion of what they regarded as a higher loyalty. Had they not fought for the Khilafat? Like the British they were in India but not of India.

Jinnah and his Muslim League followers decided to quit India at the same time as the British. Thus the country broke apart. India surrendered her unity for the sake of her freedom. The Indo-British question was solved, to everybody's relief. The Hindu-Muslim question still defied solution and nobody was satisfied, it looked as if a thousand years of sharing of homeland and living side by side had gone in vain.

The Hindustani culture of which I have spoken had the ground cut away from under its feet. The same thing happened to both the Bengali and the Punjabi cultures. After 1947 there was no common ground between the Hindus and the Muslims who had shared Hindustani culture. Gandhi gave his life in the effort to subdue the frenzy that swept over the country. His funeral was held on the day the last British soldier left India's shores. The departure of the British was the measure of the Mahatma's success in the application of his Non-violent methods. He had aimed at a change of heart in the British, not their defeat, The people of England showed their good will. So did their Parliament, their Government and their Viceroy.

Those who dedicated their lives to the effort to achieve Indian Independence little knew that freedom, when it came, would undo the work of two centuries of sustained effort by the people of two countries, two continents and two historical backgrounds. The Indians belonged to the Medieval Period and the British to the Modern. India reverted to disunity, in spite of the co-operative spirit which had presided over its development in a manner unique in the history of the world. Two centuries are a brief period in a history covering fifty centuries. The good accomplished outweighs the harm done. While the struggle for freedom lasted the dust of battle often blinded us to this fact.

A new dimension was now added to the battle. Tagore never said, 'Come, O Marxists! O Proletarians!' But they came. Some came from outside the country. Others came from within, from below. Many of the terrorists who had been forced to flee the country and were seeking arms and allies abroad came back Communists. They dreamed of staging a revolution on the Russian Model. Books and pamphlets poured into the country. These were more dangerous than arms. The heads of the younger generation were filled with social revolutionary ideas.

The literature their writers produced was subversive to a degree. It aimed not only at undermining the state but society as well. The Indian social order was shared by Hindus, Muslims and Europeans. Gandhi did not favour class war. He laboured to the last day of his life to build and strengthen a non-exploitative society, His followers were committed to a democratic form of socialism, a controlled measure of industrialization and a modicum of military defence. By these means Gandhi hoped to eliminate the iniquities of the social set-up and of unjust caste and class discrimination. He went further than his followers in his advocacy of non-violence and would have chosen death for himself rather than death for an enemy. His ideal state was a state without an army and he recommended mass civil disobedience as the best menas of defence. Living on the produce of one's own hands, self-reliant and self-contented labour, went with it. He believed in manual work.

In a country like India, criss-crossed with divisions vertical and horizontal, it can never be an easy task to rise above casteism, communalism and regionalism. It is not easy for the individual nor is it easy to persuade others of the necessity. These things have been with us since ancient times. They are so deeply embodied in the mental make-up of the people sustained and unremitting effort to alter them must be kept up for a long time yet. We are no longer under foreign rule. Our government is our own. Our laws are our own. The administration of justice is also in our hands. How gratifying that is! Yet we are not at peace either inside our frontiers or outside them. Peace has yet to come. We have not won it. The problem of Pakistan is still with us: Pakistan to the West and Bangladesh to the East. For a nation to split apart as India and later as Pakistan has done is not unprecedented in history. The Holy Roman Empire of the German nation was at first under a hereditary Emperor, then under an Emperor elected by autonomous Catholic and Protestant princes and prelates. Finally it split into Protestant-majority Germany and Catholic-majority Austria. At an earlier stage Protestant-majority Switzerland broke away. At a later stage West Germany became separate from East Germany. The grounds were ideological. Pakistan and Bangaladesh separated for linguistic reasons.

Although divided the Germans have a common culture that still distinguishes them from others in the world. All who possess it are identifiable as Germans. In cultural matters there is still so much we have in common as inhabitants of the Indian sub-continent it cannot but be to our mutual advantage to be given the opportunity to welcome poets, singers, dancers, instrumentalists and artists from Pakistan and Bangladesh. We shall surely welcome the opportunity to send our cultural ambassadors to those countries also. A sense of the unity in diversity we still share can be revived in this way and our consciousness of a common heritage re-invigorated.

Political division does not mean cultural division. The cultural heritage of all three independent nations on this sub-continent, India, Bangladesh and Pakistan is still undivided. Fundamentally it is indivisible. Culture, as I have said, is independent of religion and nationality. The culture we speak of as 'Hindu' is the culture of a geographical area known in history variously as Hind, Hindustan and India. Now that it has been divided into three political units no single world can be used to describe the culture of all three. One or the other is sure to take offence. I, therefore, make bold to suggest a term of my own coinage, Indo-Pak-Bangla. It includes 'Hindu', 'Hindustani' and 'Indian.' The new name will ensure the continuity of the composite culture of this sub-continent in each of its several parts.

Let it be clearly understood that our cultural heritage is indivisible and that it includes the legacy of the West also even though the British Raj is no more. It is not possible to eliminate this legacy from our heritage any more than it is possible to efface what the Turks and Moguls contributed to it also. A politically inglorious period can be a culturally glorious one. Our cultural heritage has been diversified and enormously enriched by peoples of all races and religions and languages, Eastern and Western. It may be that we have been enslaved politically, emasculated militarily, and ruined economically but it cannot be said we have suffered a set back culturally. Left to themselves none of the literatures of India would have become as great or greater than they have as a result of the additional waters of the many cultural streams that have poured into the riverbed of the mighty Ganga on its way to the sea.

Conflict is often conducive to growth, sometimes essential to it. Contacts cannot be dispensed with without impoverishment. The old diehard policy of avoiding contacts, to evade confrontations that might result in conflict, resulted in a barrenness on the eve of the Turkish invasion. It came again on the eve of the British conquest. The only way to overcome this sterility was through cross-fertilisation. If India had not withdrawn into her shell in the Early Medieval Period but gone out to meet the new world of Islam boldly it would have certainly been much better for all of us. It would have been better if she had gone out to meet the new world of the European Enlightenment in the Late Medieval Period. By doing so the humiliating situation which followed in both cases might have been avoided. But that would have required the discarding of inhibitions concerning *jati* and *varna* that had enslaved the Hindus even more surely than any alien rule and emasculated the bulk of them. And the Muslim likewise lived in a prison of the mind into which no light from the world of advancing knowledge penetrated. To him the Quran was the last word, the holy word, on every subject of importance to man. The conquerors of half of Europe were themselves conquered by a handful of Western islanders. Could there be anything more shameful than the Battle of Plassey? It was measure of the degradation produced by obscurantism.

We had to learn the lesson history had in store for us with sweat and tears. I do not add the word 'blood' because comparatively little blood was shed in India. In Europe of the same period much more flowed. For us to forget these lessons would be, on the part of our intellectuals, a betrayal. Others may play to the gallery. We cannot. If we have learned anything at all it is that the mind must be kept alive and alert in every generation and in every country. It must be honed and whetted every single day. Nothing has been thought out once and for all by some sages who lived thousands of years ago. No savants have made final formulations of solutions to all problems in all circumstances, nor have any law-givers done so no matter how great. Nor have saints, prophets or *avataras*. What they have taught us should not be allowed to circumscribe our efforts to explore Reality further. No community and no nation can make any progress or contribute anything new to the human family as long as it lives in an unreal world. Pre-occupation with the nation or with the community is as harmful as obsession with considerations of *jati* and *varna*. These groupings have been made to serve worldly purposes. Truth is above and beyond such things. The same applies to the Marxists' emphasis on class division and preoccupation with proletarianism. A social revolution may be facilitated by them to some extent but the higher truths will not necessarily become any easier to attain in a society whose mental and spiritual horizons are circumscribed by dogma. Sterility in creative activity in the arts of literature, painting, sculpture, dancing, music and thinking is the consequence of State control over the horizons of human vision. Science and technology may thrive but the Ultimate Reality remains as distant as ever, eternally elusive. Literature and philosophy had reached a dead end just before the Renaissance and were, as we all know, revived and invigorated by the influx of hitherto unknown treasures of the mind that were made generally available by the fall of Constantinople and the migration of scholars to Italy.

Contacts do often lead to conflict but conflict often brings out the best in a man or a country. If no conflict with the British had developed the people of India would not have found the strength to resist, nor would a new and powerful weapon have been discovered by the great soul whose leadership they had the wisdom to follow. The name of the weapon was satyagraha. It is a credit not only to India and the Modern Age in particular but to every human being alive that a man of Gandhi's caliber emerged and gave the world a weapon more powerful than any atom or hydrogen bomb for it changes man from within and helps him to become a better representative of man-kind. The liberal democratic traditions of England helped to make a peaceful confrontation workable no doubt but to India goes the honour of providing Gandhi with the Non-violent tradition he drew upon in forging his methods. And how different has been the subsequent peace from that wrought by the bomb dropped at Hiroshima! But India, while it attained for a time a moral height far above that of the free nations of the world, later plunged into fratricide of a squalor that, at a single stroke, effaced all it had won. But the message survives. People at least know that it was possible to reach such moral heights and resolve a mortal conflict peaceably, without butchery. What was done successfully once, can be done successfully again. The atom of hatred was split.

The British and the Moguls ruled India for approximately the same length of time. The legacy of both is impressive but the British left nothing comparable to the Taj Mahal or other monuments of the Moguls. These have permanently enriched India. British architecture is more utilitarian than beautiful. The churches and palaces they built tended to be replicas or imitations of similar structures in Europe. The impressive High Court Building in Calcutta. for instance, is a copy of a Belgian town hall. The architecture of New Delhi is European in its origin likewise. No attempt was made to adopt or modify Mogul or Rajput or ancient Hindu buildings to modern purpose. The British were probably prompted by a desire to create or recreate an environment with which they were familiar in India and leave a little bit of England behind. What they achieved was perhaps more of a hybrid than a synthesis. But the British were terrified of hybridization. They were determined never to make India their home as the Moguls had. They come to spend a few years working at a job, preaching or trading or administering and them retired to their English homes. England was always home to them. Their wives came from there and their children were educated there. What they were able to earn during their time in India went to England and provided for English families there. Nevertheless there are some examples of Colonial architecture from the time of the Company which show a mixture of styles. The Victorians were nothing if not practical and the cost of construction had risen considerably since the early days of the Company when the new capital in Delhi was planned. Its lavishness was much criticised. Lord Hardinge called it a waste of resources, imposing a drain upon a poor country that needed many other things much more urgently. The British conscience pricked where the Mogul conscience did not. No distinction between personal income and public expenditure was made by the Mogul Imperial Treasury. Work on the Taj Mahal was not suspended when famine occurred. Shah Jahan was determined to complete it in all its splendour, cost what it might in terms of human suffering. Many or most of the Rajput or older Hindu monuments were also built by forced labour for that matter. What price glory? This is a question that is never asked by those who live in a dream of a Golden Age of long ago. The autocrats or aristocrats of the Ancient and Medieval periods never lacked cheap labour, sometimes free, sometimes forced. Those of us who have been brought up in princely states have seen how such systems work with our own eyes, even in the Modern period.

The utilitarianism of Britons is to be found in other spheres of art as well wherever, in fact, they had a hand in its shaping. Few of the sculptures they left are of much artistic merit. The figure of Outram on horseback which was set on the Calcutta maidan is probably as good as any. As for the Moguls, they left no sculpture. The Moulvis forbade the representation of the human form. Even the taking of photographs was regarded with horror for a long time. So whatever treasure India possesses in the way of sculpture is due to the Hindu-Buddhist-Jain practice of idolatry. Utilitarianism has laid its deadening hand upon temples and temple figures also today. These are built and paid for by Banias. Patronage has passed into their hands. The princes are, if not defunct, no longer forces to be reckoned with. The Banias differ little from their British counterparts. Utilitarianism is the prevailing doctrine in all walks of life, including art. It too came to us with the British part of our heritage, in a mixed bag of good and bad.

The number of Europeans in the three metropoltan cities of India was always small. The British lived in an exclusive social enclave. These, with a few hill stations which they frequented, could not possibly leave a lasting imprint on Indian life and culture. But the English language had a wider range. It was propagated mostly by Indian teachers and its content passed through their hands. In another twenty years or so no trace of the British presence will remain. The institutions they founded or introduced are already on the wane. The entire milieu will be forgotten when the English-educated middle classes are superseded. A few landmarks will be the only exceptions. They will vanish as completely as the Persian-educated Hindu gentry of the Mogul period and the impress of liberal democratic ideas will be eventually effaced. These ideas were, in fact, the best that Britain had to give. By her example at home and by putting them to use in India so successfully through her liberal-minded administrators, educationists, journalists, lawyers and judges Britain passed on a treasure no previous ruler had even bestowed upon this country.

The significance of what they did is becoming clearer as the British phase of our history passes out of our sight. It will soon be out of our minds also. Its meaning is clear. India needed Britian as much as Britain needed India. Britain wanted prosperity and power. India required unification and modernisation. It was not and could not have been a permanent relationship. It was fitting that an honourable partnership within the same Commonwealth of nations should replace it. What appeared to the casual observer to be a long period of degradation was actually a short period of national regeneration, through contact and conflict. The cultural gains of this brief interlude outweigh its material losses. But neither the losses nor the gains should be exaggerated. We could never attain our full stature with others sitting on our backs, approving or disapproving silently or aloud. In such a situtation no nation could have done better. Many have done worse. While we should not exaggerate our achievement we should also be careful not to underrate it. It is doubtful whether India would have fared better during the past two hundred years without the British connection. Neither the Arabs or the Chinese have had such a connection. How have they fared? To imagine that either the Mogul or the Mahrattas would have voluntarily stepped aside in favour of a united and independent India governed by an educated middle class composed of both Hindus and Muslims through democratic institutions with a leadership responsible to a joint electorate ranging from Peshawar to Shillong and Srinagar to Trivandrum is sheer nonsense.

No less an illusion is the attitude that does not regard the Turks and Moguls as historically determined rulers according to the circumstances of the times. The Arabs were ruling Spain during the same period of history, the Turks were ruling Greece and the Mongals were ruling China. India's was not an isolated case. We shall do greater justice to the Turks and Moguls if we think of them as foreign rather than Muslim rulers just as we speak of British rather than Christian rule. The Turks and Moguls held India together and defended it against worse enemies, protected its industries, instructed its troops to keep away from cultivated fields, and patronised poets, musicians and scholars irrespective of community to which they belonged. The policies they followed were state-centred, not dictated by religious considerations. But in the Medieval period policy and religion were inseparable, in Europe as well as India and if the British successfully separated the two they did it because they belonged to the Modern Period. As instruments of history all India's foreign rulers served certain necessary purposes not otherwise realisable. In each case India was in need of a revitalizing change and the change came. We are all the better for these changes.

Our culture now contains strains attributable to European, Middle Eastern, Central Asian and Tibeto-Burman contacts. It is a cosmopolitan culture, very nearly universal in its scope. The Tibeto-Burman elements were added by the Ahoms who invaded Assam from Indo-China and Thailand, in the Late Medieval Period. The Tibetans ruled the territory now known as Arunachal. It is apparent that our culture is not destined to be static. Again and again it has been forced to play a dynamic role in the life of the people, overflowing eastwards, westwards, northwards and southwards. One must know how to receive graciously in order to give. One who is destined to give must also take. This explains the entire course of India's cultural history. It has been a tale of giving and taking on a wide scale as any in the history of any country. Periods of decadence have interrupted the process but not for long.

Sixty years ago when I was a child I often heard my elders say India has a genius for synthesis. The leading thinkers of the day all thought so and I began life with the firm belief that it was true, that India would arrive at a synthesis between East and West and a synthesis between Hindu and Muslim also. Sixty years is not a long time in the life of a nation and although I have been partly disillusioned by what I have seen. I have not lost all hope that these two dreams will come true in course of time. A third dream is the hope of peaceful outcome to the conflict between Marxian thesis and antithesis. Nothing less can avert a class war in India and perhaps a revolution followed by a counter-revolution. Both may be violent.

I was also told in my childhood that India is characterized by her unity in diversity. Now I find an effort being made to do away with diversity in the name of unity, replacing it by uniformity. India is more like a continent than a single country however and the various parts of it are as different from each other as the nation-states of Europe; France, Germany, Spain and Italy. Maharashtra, Gujarat, Tamil Nadu, Karnataka, each has its own language and literature and these are as strongly marked as French and German and Italian. The histories of their literatures are distinct. All these distinctive cultures are held together by a central Government which we owe to the Moguls and their British successors. In each consciousness of nationality is coupled with consciousness of a manifest individual character. There is a possibility of this developing into a separate national awareness in course of time if one's mother tongue is made to feel less important than Hindi. These languages and literatures are not less important to their own people. Nationalism in modern Europe is based upon language. While there is still time they must be accepted and given full scope in the cultural field as equals among equals. A national consensus wholly in favour of Hindi and wholly against English is not yet possible. Meanwhile both link languages must be maintained and cultivated each using it according to his convenience while regional language and cultures develop side by side. Two of our regional languages—Bengali and Urdu—are the national languages of Pakistan and Bangladesh. Tamil is one of the languages recognized by the state in Sri Lanka. Malaysia and Singapore. Marathi, Gujarati, Telugu, Kannada, and other regional languages are no less developed and no less national whatever their numerical position may be. Malayalam is one of the smallest, yet it has the highest circulation of books and periodicals per head of the population. The first Jnanpith Award went to a Malayalam poet, Sankara Kurup. If numbers were so important English would not occupy the position it has in the world today. Many of the Indian literatures are being taught in Universities abroad and are given parity with Hindi and English. UNESCO recognises this parity. The Nobel Prize for Literature went to Rabindranath Tagore and remains with Bengali.

As medium of instruction Indian languages may be weak in science and technology but this cannot be a permanent disqualification. It can be remedied. There was a time when European Universities were reluctant to abandon Latin for regional European languages like French, German and English. The German Universities took the lead and others quickly followed. Something similar is sure to take place all over India in the not too distant future. In a few places the process has already begun. Our Knowledge of the world is however expanding at such a rate Indian languages cannot yet cope with it as English can. English is therefore destined to remain indispensable. Learned research papers can enjoy an India-wide and world-wide circulation only in English. But for emotional expression the Indian languages are better suited to the needs of the Indian people in the hands of the poets and story-tellers. A few swallows do not make a summer. Indian writers of English have their limitations. They cannot reach the hearts of the Indian public in the same way or with the same depth as writers in Indian languages. A reading public that is modest in size and unremunerative financially has proved no obstacle.

Delhi now ranks third among Indian cities. Hundreds of other cities, large and small, have sprung up all over the country. Urbanisation is proceeding apace. Industrialisation is the order of the day. Vast industrial complexes that are cities in themselves are spreading over the countryside. The life lived in these new environments differs radically from the traditional Indian way. Almost all our artists and writers now live in one or the other city. The change is certain the be reflected in their work, The rural scene is portrayed less and less and with diminishing authenticity. The sophisticated public takes little interest in it. *Yatras,* plays performed in rural areas by travelling players, have come to the city and are undergoing modernisation in much the same way as Japanese Kabuki drama and like their Japanese counterparts enjoy a popularity undreamt of by the theatre proper.

As we take a panoramic view of our culture over a streatch of five thousand years one thing becomes clear. Not until the twentieth century did the common people of India come into the picture in a significant manner. They responded to Gandhi as the masses, in Russia responded to Lenin, and the Chinese people to Mao. The gap between the commoner and the elite is in urgent need of being closed, as speedily and as gracefully as possible. There is no other way of forestalling a cultural revolution. And standards should not be lowered. Vulgarisation and falsification are not desirable.

Meanwhile we must retain our hold on the wisdom garnered down the ages by our sages and saints and poets and seers. Truth and Love and Beauty and Justice and Courage are not platitudes or abstractions we can afford to dispense with. No life devoid of these eternal verities can ever be worth living. Without life there is no wisdom and no culture to cherish. It is therefore to these that we must turn to find renewal.

The time is long past when we could think of each nation as an isolated unit and assign a separate culture if not a separate civilisation to it. We now face the same vital problems everywhere. The world is drifting towards another war, a nuclear war this time. If the resources of the world are wasted on war preparations there is bound to be underfeeding and overbreeding. Inflation without meaningful production and distribution will lead to an impossible situation ending up in revolution or worse. As the crisis deepens from year to year humanity lives or survives by means of an instinctive faith that all will eventually be well. Hope that a fresh beginning can be made is undying. To faith and hope let us add charity or the love that Mahatma Gandhi practised in the midst of wild violence. He exemplified the best in India's culture today and the best throughout the four or five thousand years of its history.

As I meditate on the renewal of our culture I regard Reverence for Life as the first imperative. The second is an insatiable curiosity, the desire to *know*. It is in this the West excels. We have need of it, free though we are from its domination. The third is our traditional dedication to Beauty which has made Indian culture so wonderful. No renewal will be complete without Liberty, a fourth element. From it follows Democracy and with Democracy Equality, a fifth ingredient which leads to Social Justice in its turn. We have to look far and wide for their interpretation and application. Other countries started earlier and have gone farther than we have. They are ahead of us. We must learn from their mistakes and do better. we cannot re-live the past. Nor can we duplicate the West. Independence means independence from one's own ancestors as well as independence from foreign masters. Without this two-fold independence there can be no renewal of culture. To it we may add a third: the common people's independence from every form of ascendancy over them.

When I speak of the common people of India I include those who are known as tribals. We have owed them a debt of justice since the dawn of our history. Their claim takes precedence over that of the proletarians. It is not less pressing than our debt to the so-called untouchables. They are the descendants of the Pre-Aryans and their very presence in our midst is a constant reminder of our Early Ancient Period. Ours is a country where all historic periods exist simultaneously, side by side. No account of Indian culture can be complete without paying due regard to the contribution of each.

A. S. Ray

2

Society and Religion

STATE OF SOCIETY AND RELIGION IN THE EIGHTEENTH CENTURY

Society and religion in India have passed through numerous phases of change. In her long and chequered history, there have been periods of progress, regeneration and reform, as well as periods of decay, dissolution and degeneration. The eighteenth century witnessed the latter tendencies. While in Europe it was the age of enlightenment, in India, it was a period of stagnation.

With the death of the last great Mughal Emperor, Aurangzeb, in 1707, there began the speedy disintegration of a political fabric with ominous results for the whole country. In brief, the fall of the Mughal Empire inaugurated an era of unlimited political chaos. For considerable times and over vast areas there there was no authority, no administration, no law and no security. There were prolonged struggle and conflicts among numerous small powers who were striving to make capital out of the decline of the Mughals. Society had to pass through a period of instability and insecurity, and suffered within itself from the stupefying effects. The strong prevailed over the weak, the poor suffered oppression, wayfarers endured plunder, and anarchy became the order of the day. Accounts left by eighteenth century foreign travellers and Indian writers present the picture of such a sad state of affairs.

Of course, Indian society as a whole remained detached from and indifferent to the political developments. The innumerable village communities over the length and breadth of the land led their self-contained and more or less secluded life as before. They endured the impact of the bad political times in a fatalistic mood and continued to remain unconcerned as far as possible. But their unconcern had unfortunate results, for the village communities became more and more isolated and closed, and their social life became more and more stagnant and static. Social institutions, customs and practices began to assume a rigid and petrified from.

Social rigidity and irrational social practices became conspicuous features of eighteenth century India. The disease was more aggravated by the outer aspects of contemporary religions which became even more dogmatic. In the fifteenth and sixteenth centuries India produced a number of seers and saints, preachers and religious reformers who played a vital role in rationalizing medieval religions. But the eighteenth century was a dark period in her religious history. There was no great religious, spiritual or moral preacher to preach enlightenment to the ignorant. Thus the eighteenth century religious outlook harked back to the out moded practices and beliefs of bygone centuries. The echo of the social philosophy which the great medieval Bhakti reformers like Kabir, Nanak, and Chaitanya had preached, was not heard again for two centuries.

Religion, the pivot of Indian life, had always exercised great influence on the people in their social ways and habits. That being the case, the condition of the society depended on the condition of its religion. The epochs in which religion stood for deeper philosophies in quest of the Absolute, were the epochs when society represented vitality and tolerance, vigour and elasticity. At other times, when religion meant only the outer form and rituals, the pattern of social outlook became stereotyped. In the eighteenth century, for most men, religion meant rigid rules and restrictions regarding what to eat and what not to eat, whom to touch and from whom to keep apart, in which pot to cook food and where to cook it and eat, how far to go, where to take one's bath, and which temples to visit. To maintain religious purity, people became intolerant of others and developed excessive sectarianism. Extreme dependence of people on the priestly class and of the priestly class on irrational practices made religion synonymous with bigotry and orthodoxy. It was a paradox of Hinduism that, while it tolerated all external religions with quiet indifference, it was intolerant within its own orbit towards anything which did not conform to established ritualistic details. Yet, Hinduism within itself was hydra-headed. It was amorphous enough to mean anything to anybody. It was complex and composed of numerous forms. Each form was subservient to a number of hard formalities. Deviation from formalities was unpardonable, though the meaning underlying them remained ever unintelligible and was seldom questioned or understood.

In the eighteenth century, idolatry and fetishism had been extended to extremes. Believers in monotheism and pantheism were there, but the mass of people were believers in sacrificial rites, witchcraft and sorcery, various pujas, festivities and ceremonies. In certain areas like Bengal, *tantric* rites and *sahajiyanist* practices were widely prevalent, and in some places, certain religious practices were dreadful. There was no escape from superstition, and surprisingly enough, there was hardly any protest even against inhuman practices.

Islam, too, had become an intolerant religion. In the heyday of Islamic glory, the Sufi preachers preached tolerance. But from the latter part of the seventeenth century the Muslim rulers assumed religious bigotry as a part of their state policy. In fact, the fall of the Mughal Empire was due to the struggle of the Rajputs, Marathas, Sikhs and others against the oppressive laws which the orthodox Aurangzeb unwisely introduced. The bitterness between Muslims and Hindus became a legacy of the seventeenth century which continued into the eighteenth. The earlier understanding between the two communities had almost vanished with the consequent result of their indifference and antipathy towards each other. The days were gone when Muslim liberals like Akbar and Dara Shikoh had tried to appreciate the spiritual doctrines of the Hindu scriptures. Instead, religious animosity pervaded the mind of the Muslim ruling class. Instead of understanding between the two major communities in their socio-cultural life, there was more and more of separation. Muslim society withdrew inside its own orthodox shell as Islam in India detached itself from other spiritual streams.

With religions attaching more importance to external form than to inner reality, religious superstitions began to pervade all aspects of social life. The more numerous the superstitious practices, the greater became the dominance of the priestly class. The bulk of that class seldom understood the scriptures, and cared little for spiritual values. But they practised the ceremonies in all earnestness and society obeyed them faithfully. Amid ignorance and blind belief, dangerous social customs appeared as religiously sound. Priests could explain any social vil as holy, with the apparent sanction of the scriptures behind it. nfanticide, child marriage, polygamy, the burning of widows, and ther social evils, were all interpreted as scripturally and religiously alid, and hence there was no qualm of conscience even before the iost horrible performance. Similarly, such social systems as caste, ntouchability, seclusion of women and slavery were all considered s sanctified by the *shastras,* and therefore, absolutely valid and stimable.

Thus the eighteenth century was an age of intolerant institutions nd irrational customs. In the following lines a brief reference is made) some of these social institutions and socio-religious customs.

CASTE

Hindu Society was a caste society and the caste system was as d as Hinduism, if not as old as Rig Vedic Aryanism. Through the enturies, the history of the caste system was a record of ups and owns, of rigidity and liberalism. There has been periods of extreme iste exclusiveness, when the shadow of a Chandala was abominable the Brahmin. Equally there were periods when the Chandala and e Brahmin embraced each other in emotional delight. In sixteenth ntury India, in the days of Chaitanya and the Bhakti preachers, caste gidity had slackened greatly and God had been brought nearer to e Sudras through personal devotion which did not require priestly ediation. But the eighteenth century saw the reversal of the sixteenth ntury social ethics. In the nineteenth century there began the reform ovements to liberalise the caste structure and rationalise the religious ictices. Since there were no such progressive movements in the hteenth century, the caste prejudices were at their height. In a sense, rigidity of the caste system attained its strictest form in that epoch l continued to be dominant till the reform movements began in the eteenth century.

It is difficult to determine the actual number of castes and sub-es which existed in the society. There are different estimates, some vhich even suggest the existence of two to three thousand castes sub-castes. While such numbers might include all possible social sions existing all over the subcontinent, in any particular area the ber might only be a few. The merits and demerits of the caste em have been debated since the days of Buddha, but without any lusion. It remains, therefore, one of the most controversial social institutions of human history. Its greatest demerit was that it divided the society into water-tight compartments, Without social unity, the country had to suffer many consequences including foreign domination. Much before the eighteenth century, the French traveller, Tavernier, described the great disadvantage of caste in the following words: 'The idolators of India are so numerous that for one Mahomedan there are five or six Gentiles. It is astonishing to see how this enormous multitude of men has allowed itself to be subjected by so small a number of persons, and has bent readily under the yoke of the Mahomedan princes. But the astonishment ceases when one considers that these idolators have no union among themselves, and that superstition has introduced so strange a diversity of opinions and customs, that they never agree with one another.'

The advantage of the caste system has been ascribed to its economic implications. An occupational function was allotted to each caste or sub-caste, however small it might have been. There was means of livelihood for everyone in the society and inside every group there was a place for every individual. It is this aspect of the caste system which has prompted even some modern thinkers to justify the system in that it preserved Hindu arts and craftsmanship, besides religion and morals. In the words of Monier Williams: 'Caste has been useful in promoting self-sacrifice, in securing subordination of the individual to an organised body, in restraining vice and in preventing pauperism.'

Its merits or demerits notwithstanding, the caste system stood on certain social formalities. It was a ladder from the highest to the lowest. While the highest caste contained God's men and claimed the utmost reverence, the members of the lowest groups were so inferior as to remain secluded, while of course doing their duty by society. Between the highest and the lowest, there existed numerous grades depending on the nature of caste profession. In such a system, the individual's life and occupation were determined at his birth irrespective of his inborn qualities. Thus a dullard born in a Brahmin family was accepted by the society as a sacred man, supposed to be well versed in the *shastras* and laws, whereas a genius born in the house of a Sudra had no opportunity for recognition, and society regarded him as nothing more than a washerman or tanner or scavenger. In the periods of liberalism, men from lower ranks had won recognition and distinction, but at other times, talent lay buried beneath the caste. Intercaste marriage was unthinkable. Eating with other castes was equally forbidden. Even to take water from the hands of many castes was a sin. Restrictions were so strictly enforced that any one who broke the rules, even unknowingly, faced social excommunication. The fear of losing one's own caste was great. The upper castes assumed greater and greater pretensions regarding caste purity. The practice of touch-me-not was an austere mode of maintaining personal purity.

On established forms, the caste system remained rigid. To the Hindus, it was a sure and settled way of existence, sanctified by time and religion. In the eighteenth century, the caste system was no problem to the society. But in the eyes of the Europeans of that time, as in the eyes of the Hindu rationalists of the nineteenth century, caste appeared degrading. The modernism of the nineteenth century became synonymous with a crusade against caste, and the most degrading evil of the caste system, untouchability.

UNTOUCHABILITY

Had the caste structure been merely an economic system of the division of labour, it could have been justified as useful. But the society was divided into touchables and untouchables in the most irrational way. The concepts of human equality, upheld by religions and preached by prophets, were valueless in the context of social relations. Untouchability was itself the supreme example of social inequality. But, more than that, there was the problem of injustice associated with it. The untouchables were denied certain basic privileges of living. They could not use tanks, wells, inns or schools meant for upper caste people, not to speak of places of worship or public institutions. In the eighteenth century, the old injunction of the *Tantra* dominated Hindu society. "Avoid the touch or the Chandala, and other abject classes. Whoever associates with them undoubtedly falls from his class; whoever bathes or drinks in wells or pools which they have caused to be made, must be purified by the five productions of kine."

The only redeeming feature of untouchability was that the untouchable belonged to a class of his own, Inside it, he was accustomed to the traditional ways of his forefathers and did not feel, or was not conscious of, the injustice to which his class had been subjected through the ages. In the words of Horace Hayman Wilson who was an admirer of Hindu ways of life: 'The lowest native is no outcaste, he has an acknowledged place in society; he is the member of a class; and he is invariably more retentive of the distinction than those above him.... The veriest Chandala, who is one of a community, is less miserable, less unhappy, than many of the paupers of the civilized communities of Europe, with whom no man owns companionship or kindred; they are the true outcastes—not the Pariah or Chandala.'

Be that as it may, the eighteenth century society retained untouchability in its extreme form. That was the last great epoch of social inequality in India. With the impact of western ideas and the rise of Hindu reform movements in the subsequent century, caste was assailed and there began a slow slackening of rigid attitudes towards untouchability. However, in spite of reform movements, throughout the nineteenth century the caste inertia continued without any spectacular improvement in the position of the untouchables.

SECLUSION OF WOMEN

The position of women in the eighteenth century was far from being satisfactory. It was their total seclusion which brought about their physical and mental degeneration. In many parts of India, especially in the north and east, the *purdah* had long become an established system both among Hindus and Muslims. The general insecurity and lawlessness which prevailed at that time made the seclusion more tight. The freedom and status which the Indian women enjoyed in ancient times were beyond the range of imagination. For centuries under Muhammaden rule there had developed an apathy towards the lot of the women. The climax of that tendency was perhaps most marked on the eve of British rule.

There was hardly and opportunity for girls to attend educational institutions. Among the Rajputs, the girls belonging to richer sections received some kind of elementary education. Among the Vaishnava sects in Bengal, too, there was some inclination to educate girls so that they might read religious books. But apart from a few exceptions, as a general rule Indian women remained unlettered and ignorant.

Women in South India were not so much subjected to *zenana* as their counterparts in the north. Similary, mainly for economic reasons, the women belonging to the lower classes of society did not lead such a secluded life. They were called upon to work in their caste professions or in agricultural fields. Women in cities and towns were more confined to their homes than women in remote villages.

It was the complete dependence of women on men which reduced their position to one of abject surrender. 'Their fathers protect them in childhood; their husbands protect them in youth; their sons protect them in old age'—such was the ancient saying which dominated the Hindu mind through the centuries. Protection in this case meant making the female dependent on her father, husband and son in childhood, youth and old age respectively. It was the system of denying Hindu women any right to paternal property which made them economically completely dependent on men. Their economic status was a vital cause of their misery and suffering.

Much before the eighteenth century certain abominable socio-religious customs had entered Hindu society which affected Hindu women in the most horrible manner. The most iniquitous of these customs were five,—infanticide, child marriage, polygamy, forced celibacy of widows, and last but not least, the burning of widows on the funeral pyre of their husbands. In eighteenth century India, the above mentioned customs were, if not universal or widely prevalent, yet prominent enough to catch the attention of the new rulers. They survived through the eighteenth century, but were challenged in the nineteenth century both through legislation and reform movements. A brief reference to those customs is made below.

INFANTICIDE

Destruction of female children at their birth was not a common custom. But its worst aspect was that it was practised secretly. Surprisingly, it was more prevalent among the wealthier and upper sections of the people in certain areas. In 1789, Jonathan Duncan, at that time the British Resident at Benares, discovered the practice among the Rajkumars of that place. It was also discovered among the Jadejas of Kathiawar and Kutch. Subsequently it was seen that the custom was familiar among the Kuchwah Rajputs near Allahabad. The Chauhan Rajputs and the Pathak Ahirs of Mainpuri were addicted to the crime. In the Punjab, too, it was widely practised. The Bedis of Jullundur were so accustomed to it that anybody among them who kept a daughter was excommunicated. Certain Muslims of the Rat tribe also practised it.

The reasons for infanticide varied. Among the Chauhans it was primarily due to economic causes, vailed by ignorant pride. They killed their infant daughters as it was imperative to spend large sums of money for the marriage of a daughter. Among the Bedis, it was a matter of social pride not to give a daughter to an inferior caste. The practice was first enjoined upon them by Dharm Chand Bedi, the grandson of Guru Nanak. It arose out of a fit of temper of that religious leader, and consequently took on a superstitious colour and continued into posterity as a social custom. In Rajputana, the chief cause was the determination of the chiefs not to allow their daughters to remain unmarried beyond the age of ten. This feeling induced the fathers of the boys to demand heavy bribes for their consent. Hence it became a common custom to kill daughters to avoid difficulties in getting them married. Among Munha Rajputs, infanticide became a means of preserving the purity of their race.

Whether it arose from pride or poverty, superstition or ignorance, the custom was a crime. That the society tolerated it was itself a proof of the degradation to which it had stooped. The methods of killing the infants were extremely barbaric. At many places the child was destroyed immediately after birth by filling the mouth with cowdung or by immersing the head in cow's milk or by coiling the umbilical cord around the face. At certain other places, the infant was buried alive. Another method was to administer a small pill of opium. In the Kangra area, the juice of the Madar plant was administered, or death was brought about by causing injury to the navel. Such were the cruelties associated with the custom.

CHILD MARRIAGE

There were times in ancient India when girls selected their own husbands, if they were considered sufficiently grown up to exercise due discretion. Indeed, for a considerable period in ancient Hindu history, there was perhaps no system of early marriage, though there were probably exceptions to the rule. But by the time of the *Manusamhita* the custom had already become so familiar that the marriageable age for girls had been prescribed as twelve or even eight. Gradually, early marriage became an established custom. Various social factors operated to make the system popular. The influence of climatic conditions being what it is, social systems became regulated in the light of such influences. Maturity comes earlier in hot climates, and society, over-anxious to uphold its moral standards, laid particular emphasis on the chastity of girls. By giving them in marriage before they were of proper age, people felt assured that society would retain its moral purity. There were economic factors as well. To the poorer people a girl was as much a burden to her parents as of use to her husband's family where she was required to remain in charge of the kitchen. The Hindu joint family system was no less responsible for encouraging the custom. The desire of the grandparents or even great grandparents to see the younger ones marry was a strong factor.

Whatever be the causes, child marriage was a widely prevalent system during the medieval period. Hindus and Muslims alike practised it. The Emperor Akbar, as already mentioned, tried to abolish the custom, but in vain, and by the eighteenth century it had become more deep rooted than ever. The growth of the population and the physical degradation of women proceeded side by side. Motherhood at the tender age, with numerous sickly children around her, made the Indian women the epitome of misery and distress.

Child marriage produced many side evils. In the lowest and most ignorant stratas of society, according to the depth of their economic misery, parents would sell away their child daughters as brides to those, who could afford to meet their demands. The bridegrooms, or their guardians, ran into debt in purchasing the brides. There was no concept of a proper match as is understood in modern times. The difference in age between the bride and the bridegroom was of no account.

The greatest evil arising out of child marriage was the growing number of child-widows. Without the economic means by which to sustain themselves, without benevolent treatment from their immediate relations, and being subjected to suspicion, social stigma and superstition, the girl-widows lingered through their unfortunate existences. In the upper stratas of society, some of them escaped misery through the custom of *sati* or self-immolation. But to the vast majority of widows in all stratas and castes life was one long misery.

Polygamy was an old social evil. It pervaded both the Hindu and Muslim societies. But the evil crossed all limits in course of time. It was confined mostly to the richer and higher sections of society. With their affluence and wealth, the rich could afford to become polygamous and licentious. It was neither a matter of shame nor sorrow to maintain a harem and to keep many wives. Rather, it was a matter of personal pride and social prestige if one could afford it.

The worst example of polygamy prevailed in eighteenth century Bengal, and that, too, among the highest classes of Brahmins. As early as the eleventh century, the king of Bengal honoured a few Brahmins for certain excellent qualities of head and heart, Their families ultimately came to be regarded as superior to the rest and became famous as the Kulin families. In course of time, the descendants of the original Kulins had nothing to do with the virtues associated with Kulinism, yet they remained superior in the caste ladder. Out of that superiority complex, a few social evils developed. It was undesirable on the part of a Kulin to marry into inferior Brahmin families. It was equally a strong temptation for inferior Brahmins to give a daughter to a Kulin. To achieve the purpose, the inferior Brahmins offered a large dowry and much money to Kulin bridegrooms. The latter found it difficult to resist such material temptations. Eventually, the Kulins married into Brahmin families of lower rank and thus fell from their original rank. Yet, though fallen and styled as the broken Kulins, they enjoyed a great demand for their hands in the marriage market. The lower Brahmins competed among themselves to offer daughters to Kulins and the latter made marriage a means of livelihood, a business or a profession of profit through many marriages.

By the eighteenth century, such an absurd system of polygamy assumed monstrous proportions. On a single day a Kulin could marry two, three or four wives. In his lifetime he could marry dozens of wives even a hundred. There were parents who offered all their daughters to a single Kulin. There was no upper age limit for the Kulin; he could be of any age. Similarly, the brides of the same man could be as tender in age as possible.

Still more absurd was the system that the Kulin husband was not required to maintain his numerous wives. The so-called wives remained in the houses of their parents. But now and again the husband would come to collect some money from the unfortunate father-in-law. The result of such a system was dangerous. It encouraged social immorality and vice. Without any sanction of religion, Kulinism developed into a social superstition and ruined the lives of innumerable women while causing degradation to the society as a whole.

Elsewhere, polygamy created various social and domestic complications. The upper class Hindus and Muslims, when polygamous, suffered family unhappiness and economic hardship.

Among the Muslims, polygamy made the *purdah* system more stringent. The only happy feature in regard to it was that it did not become a common vice among the general population.

CELIBACY OF WIDOWS

While widow-marriage prevailed among the Hindus in very ancient times. gradually it was abandoned and came to be regarded as a sin. The forced celibacy of widows become a strict social custom which few could dare defy. Society imposed the duties on widows as prescribed in the *Manusamhita*: 'Let her emaciate her body by living voluntarily on pure flowers, roots, and fruits, but let her not, when her lord is deceased, even pronounce the name of another man, let her continue till death forgiving all injuries, performing harsh duties, avoiding every sensual pleasure, and cheerfully practising the incomparable rules of virtue which have been followed by such women as were devoted to only one husband.' It was one of the most severe codes of conduct which the widow was required to observe in accordance with semi-religious injunctions. Society paid its habitual regard to the widow who remained above suspicion. Her life was adjusted to a formal routine of fasting, devotion, prayer and pious works. Through the centuries, such became the lot of the Hindu widow.

In normal cases, the austere celibacy of the widow was no social evil. But the real trouble arose with the spread of the evil of child-marriage and with the consequent increase in the number of child-widows. Little girls, who while marrying knew nothing of their husbands, became widows on the death of those unknown or even unseen persons. For them, the laws of widowhood constituted a code of tyranny. Even in the days of the *Manusamhita,* virgin windows were permitted to marry a second time. But, as time advanced, the practice fell into disrepute and was abandoned. Among the lower castes, widow-marriage was permitted. But in the higher castes, it became impossible. There were widows under the age of five years, not to speak of other age groups, such as, five to ten and ten to fifteen.

The treatment of widows varied from place to place, and also according to their age. Old widows had an established place in the Hindu joint family. They commanded respect and played the role of counsellors in domestic matters to their younger relations. It was the younger widows who suffered ill treatment so frequently. People regarded their persons as inauspicious or even ominous. They deserved neither sympathy nor pity from men since God had shown them no mercy. Extreme ignorance also led people to believe that young widows were responsible for family misfortunes. They were denied many privileges in day-to-day life. They could not take part in many ceremonies and functions. In essence, the life of young widows, especially in places like the Bombay Presidency, was mostly unbearable.'

In 1756, Raja Rajballav of Dacca wanted to give his daughter in remarriage. She became a widow at a very early age. The Raja gathered the opinion of the most learned pandits of Benares, Mithila and of the south to learn if the Hindu *shastras* actually did not sanction widow-marriage. The learned men gave the unanimous opinion that, 'women are at liberty to marry again if their husbands be not hard of, die, retire from the world, prove to be eunuchs or become outcastes'.

Even if the *Shastras* had not closed the doors against widow-marriage, the convention was too firmly established to change. So, against Raja Rajballav there stood Maharaja Krishna Chandra of Nadia with his band of orthodox priests. The time was not ripe in the eighteenth century to bring about a social change of so great an importance. Thus, the non-marriage of the widows continued for yet another century without any formidable body of opinion against it.

SATI

Among many irrational social customs, the most unnatural was the custom of sati or the immolation of the Hindu widow on the funeral pyre of her dead husband. The custom appeared revolting to the Europeans who had the occasion to discover it. The Danes at Serampore, the Dutch at Chinsura and the French at Chandernagore did not allow sati to be practised within the jurisdiction of their authority. The English East India Company at Bombay, during the period from 1770 to 1780, tried to stop the custom in the territories under their control. Elsewhere, the English rulers in the eighteenth century showed a timid approach towards the rite in fear of general Hindu discontent.

Much before the Europeans, some Muslim rulers in India like Akbar had attempted to abolish sati. Even the Sikh Guru, Amardas, and the Maratha Peshwas tried to stop it in their spheres of influence. But the custom was so much a matter of blind faith among the orthodox that its eradication was only a remote possibility.

The origin of the system remains a mystery. At some unknown time in ancient days it began to take shape through some kind of misinterpretation or misrepresentation of a passage in the Rig Veda. At least that is what Max Mueller believed.* Once the rite gained recognition as a virtuous action of the widow, the priestly class made the best of it for their own advantage. Towards the end of the Hindu period, the custom was fairly well established. Alberuni described it in the eleventh century: 'If a wife of a Hindu loses her husband by death, she cannot marry another man. She has only to choose between two things, either to remain a widow as long as she lives or to burn herself; and the latter eventually is considered the preferable, because as a widow she is ill-treated as long as she lives. 'The purpose of the superstition which inspired the widow to die voluntarily, or prompted her near ones to engineer her death, has been vividly described by the sixteenth century expounder of Hindu Law, Raghunandan. The following are the prescribed words to be recited by the victim herself before entering into the fire: 'I,... desiring to attain the glory of the heavens to be obtained by acting like Aroondhatee, to dwell in the religions of bliss, rejoicing with my husband as many years as there are hairs in the human body, to purify the three families of my mother, father, and father-in-law, to be glorified by the *Apsaras* as long as fourteen Indras last, to enjoy the company of my husband and to purify my husband from sins..., do ascend the flaming funeral pyre of my husband.'

It was the hope of attaining heaven which originally led the widows to experience the supreme ordeal. In the same superstitious faith, the society and its leaders did not suffer any revolt of conscience when the custom was celebrated. Superstition blinded the fathers to persuade their little daughters to burn themselves with the dead body of their old husbands. Sons pleaded with their old mothers to sacrifice themselves. Many satis died willingly. But for many others, death in the fire could only have been torture. It was more or less forced on them by society. However, such inhuman performances were mostly confined to the upper classes, including Brahmins, and never become universal among all castes of Hindus.

---

* A passage in the Rig Veda referring to widows contained the word *Agre,* while describing her position in the front. But when the word *Agre,* through some mysterious process, become *Agne,* it meant her position in the fire.

The campaign against the sati system began in the British occupied territories in the last quarter of the eighteenth century. Christian missionaries began the campaign. Some lone English officers, too, in their remote stations came across the horrid rite and felt moved to raise their voices against it. But the Company's Government was unprepared to offend Hindu sentiment by interfering their religious customs. So, it continued.

OTHER SUPERSTITIOUS PRACTICES

In eighteenth century India, quite a number of superstitious rites of doubtful antiquity or origin, were practised in different parts of the country. They were neither very common nor even widely known. Mostly they were superstitions of individual preference. The rites represented in certain cases an inner urge of the individuals to give up the best in them and suffer the most. One could sacrifice his own life, or a child, or inflict on himself the most severe physical pain. As far as self renunciation was concerned it was one thing; but the tragedy of such rites was that they were practised blindly without any rational thinking.

Human sacrifice can be described as first in the series of superstitious practices. Not to speak of the human sacrifice practised by the Khonds in their remote hill fastnesses, it was the upper class Hindus who on very rare occasions resorted to it. It was the legacy of the Sakta cult which prevailed in some form or other. The goddess Kali required human blood or heads and, for the gratification of the *devi*, a human victim was slaughtered. The ceremony was celebrated in the utmost secrecy. Even as late as the second half of the nineteenth century, there were instances when human heads were discovered in some Kali temples of Bengal in sacrificial forms.

In the eighteenth century, self-immolation was yet another form of human sacrifices. Instances are related of a person drowning in the sea or particulary at the confluence of the Ganges with the sea. Instances of such sacrifices were described by Europeans. In some cases, in order to escape disease, one could drown himself in a river. In other cases, life could be taken by way of mortification and penance. The references of the early Europeans to death under the wheels of the chariot of Lord Jagannath (whom they called Juggernaut) came in extremely exaggerated forms and lacked substance.

Among other forms of human sacrifice, there was the sacrifice of one's own child. Parents, under peculiar conditions, used to take a vow to offer their first born child to the river Ganges. In due time, when the child was born, in order to keep that sacred promise, they used to carry the child to the Ganges and throw it into the water. This was a rare custom, and was abandoned as soon as people became aware that the Government viewed it with great disfavour.

Self-torture was yet another superstitious rite. The familiar form of this was usually observed in the *charak* festivals in the month of *chaitra*. Quite a number of devotees used to perform the painful practice of piercing their tongues and arms with pointed rods. On the final day of the festival, the still more painful custom of hook-swinging was performed. This was not practised by many but only by those few persons who could endure such pain. The devotees were suspended from a beam fixed on a high pole with hooks piercing the muscles of their backs and they remained swinging in that horrible manner. Such barbarous rites were practised in the belief that good results, either for the individual or the community, followed such self torture.

Among the women in the eighteen century, specially in Bengal, the offer of drops of blood from their own bodies to some goddesses was a not uncommon custom. Usually, when a husband or a son developed a serious illness, the woman took a vow to offer her own blood to the goddess Durga or Kali on the recovery of the patient. Such vows were fulfilled in due time. Blood-offering was practised among men on rare occasions. To propitiate the goddess, a man could cut out his own tongue and offer it at her altar.

Irrational as all such practices were, fortunately for the society they could neither be universally adopted nor widely acclaimed. They were bad, nevertheless. No society could have tolerated inhuman customs for the sake of pleasure. It was a wrong faith, followed through ignorance. In an era of mental stagnation, the prevailing abuses continued without affecting the conscience of thinking men. But when the time came, society showed an eagerness to abandon these pernicious systems.

THE STATE OF SOCIAL MORALITY

Socio-religious superstitions and ignorant ways of life no doubt rendered the eighteenth century one of the dark epochs of Indian history, but yet the society was not devoid of social ethics or virtues of a higher order. The traditional ethical standards were habitually maintained by all sections of people, irrespective of the standard of consciousness or enlightenment. People in general followed established codes of moral conduct. They cherished the higher values of life against the background of an ephemeral existence. The most ignorant as well as the highly learned knew in a definite manner what was right and what was wrong, what was virtue and what was vice. Absolute faith in fate, in the doctrine of *karma*, the cycle of birth and rebirth, and in other such religious concepts, kept the people on the right path. Even when one practised a wrong custom, the intention was never bad. Everything passed in the name of religion and virtue. Its merit was that in day-to-day life, one remained pure, pious and virtuous. Its demerit was that in the name of religion one subscribed to what the priests prescribed by way of irrational customs.

The Europeans who criticised Hindu superstitions in vehement terms were greatly prejudiced in their understanding of real conditions. Undoubtedly the society was full of unnatural customs, but yet there was a brighter aspect to the people's character and manners. Some distinguished Europeans who spent a part of their lives in eighteenth century India left a glowing testimony to Hindu character. It is worth-our while to take note of their estimates.

While giving evidence before Committees of both Houses of Parliament in 1813, Warren Hastings described the national character of the Indian people in the following words: 'Great pains have been taken to inculcate into the public mind (in England), an opinion, that the native Indians are in a state of complete moral turpitude, and live in the constant and unrestrained commission of every vice and crime that can disgrace human nature. I affirm, by the oath that I have taken, that this description of them is untrue, and wholly unfounded.... In speaking of the people... the Hindoos... are gentle, benevolent, more susceptible of gratitude for kindness shown them than prompted to vegeance for wrongs inflicted.... Gross as the modes of their worship are, the precepts of their religion are wonderfully fitted to promote the best ends of society, its peace and good order; and even from their theology, arguments may be drawn to illustrate and support the most refined mysteries of our own.' According to Thomas Munro: 'If a good system of agriculture, unrivalled manufacturing skill, a capacity to produce whatever can contribute to either convenience or luxury, schools established in every village for teaching, reading, writing, and arithmetic, the general practice of hospitality and charity amongst each other, and above all, a treatment of the female sex, full of confidence, respect, and delicacy, are among the signs which denote a civilised people—then the Hindoos are not inferior to the nations of Europe, and if civilisation is to become an article of trade between the two countries, I am convinced that this country (England) will gain by the import cargo.' John Malcolm described the Hindoo character in upper India thus: 'They are brave, generous, humane, and their truth is as remarkable as their courage.' To Captain Sydenham: 'I think the general character of the Hindoo is submissive, docile, sober, inoffensive, as long as his religious prejudices and habits are not violated: capable of great attachment and loyalty, as long as they are well treated by their governors and masters; quick in apprehension, intelligent, active, generally honest, and performing the duties of charity, benevolence, and filial affection with as much sincerity and regularity as any nation with which I am acquainted.' With an experience of twenty-five years in distant parts of India, Graeme Mercer described the people as 'mild in their dispositions, polished in their general manners; in their domestic relations kind and affectionate'.

Such observations of eminent Europeans early in the nineteenth century go a long way to show that in spite of political turmoils and general confusion, the society retained many moral and ethical values as well as the norm of civilized conduct.

IMPACT OF THE WEST

In the eighteenth century, Indian society was rigid within itself, but not closed to external influences. Though the general mental horizon of the people was limited, yet the intellectual horizon was kept open to receive enlightenment. The newness of the West was therefore quickly felt when Western contact became definitely established. From the days of Vasco da Gama at the close of the eighteenth century, the European contact began to touch the Indian society at its outer fringe. But by the first half of the eighteenth century, the Europeans had become a definite factor in Indian politics. By way of a historic accident the eighteenth century was an age of enlightenment in the history of Europe and it was during that age of unusual mental and physical activities that Europe came nearer to India. The impact became inevitable. During the second half of the eighteenth century and the early decades of the nineteenth century the effects of that impact became manifest.

European influence operated in three spheres—economic, religious and political. The trade and commerce which the Europeans carried on in different parts of India had no direct bearing on the social life of the people. With the growth of their political domination, the economic impact of the West proved disastrous. As will be discussed later, in her economic relations with Britain India was destinated to suffer badly. Her traditional economic structure in agriculture and industry fell to pieces.

It was through their religious and political activities that the Europeans, of necessity, came very close to the Indian ways of life. Or, more precisely, they broke through the seclusion of the Indian society for the purpose of preaching their own religion as well as of introducing their own political and legal systems. In that process they had to understand India. India, too, had to understand the West. The impact was not merely an imposition. It was also in the nature of an accommodation.

It was the religious activities of the European missionaries which brought Christianity to a direct confrontation with Hinduism. Earlier, the Portuguese authorities, in their various pockets of influence, had combined religious with political activities. They converted their conquered subjects. The Dutch, too, believed in conducting both activities together. It was the French who paid primary attention to politics. The English Company, in its earlier days when they were traders, thought of preaching Christianity. But when they became rulers, its was thought prudent to abandon their Christian zeal in order to avoid rousing popular antipathy against their rule. But if the Company avoided it, Christian missionaries in their private capacity took up the work with zeal. For a time, the Company did not view missionary activities with favour and tried to discourage them. But that did not stop the missionary work. In the last decade of the eighteenth century, men like William Carey, Joshua Marshman and William Ward began their missionary activities from Serampore, which at that time was a Danish possession. Their influence spread to Calcutta.

To the missionaries many things in Hinduism appeared abominable. They forgot that Christianity itself was not free from irrational dogmas. Even towards the close of the seventeenth century, 'Shrieking Scotch Covenanters were submitted to torture by crushing their knees flat in the boot ; women were tied to stakes on the sea-sands and drowned by the slowly advancing tide because they would not attend Episcopal worship, or branded on their cheeks and then shipped to America.' Similar fanatical customs elsewhere in Europe were tolerated in the eighteenth century. Even greater barbarities were committed in name of Law. In England in the eighteenth century, a man could be hanged for stealing a fish, writing threatening letters, stealing five shillings from a store and pick-pocketing. A Hindu rationalist would have felt shocked to witness many of the customs in eighteenth century Europe, just as European rationalists felt shocked to witness some of the Indian customs.

For India it was a blessing in disguise that the Christian missionaries felt so strongly against some of her socio-religious customs. Practised through ignorance they were required to be exposed by an external agency. The missionaries, in order to convert India, condemned Hinduism in the most vehement manner, affecting every aspect of Hindu belief and practice. From polytheism and idolatry to smaller rituals, nothing missed their observation. Two results emanated from their campaign. Directly, they gained converts to Christianity and created a small but new class inside the existing socio-religious frame of India. Indirectly, the Christian crusade against Hinduism inspired in higher Hindu minds a sense of inwardness to discover in the inner core of their own religion concepts of monotheism, and all other higher philosophies to feel proud of. Thus the impact of Christianity led to external and internal change.

It should not be forgotten that while the precepts of Christianity had their socio-ethical impact, the conduct and character of the English rulers in the eighteenth century did not prove that the newcomers were the representatives of a higher type of society. They became famous for their violence, rapacity, greed, corruption and licentiousness. A European associate of Sir Thomas Roe, writing in the seventeenth century, described what the Indians thought of the Christians thus: 'It is a most sad and horrible thing to consider what scandal there is brought upon the Christian religion by the looseness and remissness, by the exorbitances of many, which come amongst them who profess themselves Christians, of whom I have often heard the natives, who live here near the port where our ships arrive say thus, in broken

English, which they have gotten, *Christian religion, devil religion; Christian much drunk; Christian much do wrong, much beat, much abuse others.'* In the eighteenth century, the conduct of the East India Company's servants and merchants was little better. In several among them, their lawless conduct, debauchery, vices, malice, crime and cruelty rendered the name of white men in general disgraceful. Hastings, Francis, Impey and some others, who occupied the highest position among Englishmen in India, were by no means pillars of virtue with the highest ethical standards.

However, it was the freshness of a new religion which counted, not the conduct of its adherents. Moreover, some of the missionaries set a good example in matters of religious sincerity and in devotion to their cause. They began to learn Indian languages for religious propaganda, and at the same time encouraged Indians to learn English. Men like William Carey possessed a wide vision regarding Anglo-Indian relations. In Bengal, he laid the foundation of English education. Bengali literature, too, began to develop under the patronage of the missionaries. In 1801, Carey published his Bengali grammar. Simultaneously, J. C. Marshman wrote a history of India. A printing press was established at Serampore by the missionaries. Though it was meant primarily for printing religious literature, yet its role in spreading knowledge was significant. The press also caused the birth of journalism. While the ground was thus prepared for the spread of the Christian religion and Western ideas, the Company's opposition to missionary activities came to an end. The Charter Act of 1813 granted to the missionaries freedom of action in India.

Christianity spread slowly at first. On account of various factors, Hindus and Muslims did not feel encouraged to abandon their religion and embrace Christianity. For the upper class Hindus, conversion was inconceivable, and on rare occasions only some of them changed religion. The strong bond of caste, Hindu laws regarding right to property, the hold of the joint family, and the natural aversion to abandon their faith on the part of Hindus, were some factors which stood in the way of missionary success. However it was the spread of Christian ideas rather than the Christian religion which influenced the traditional Indian society to take a fresh look at their own set of values.

The impact of the West was also felt politically. The ladder of the new administration could not, of necessity, have been composed only of Englishmen; it lower rungs had to be filled with Indians. The people, long accustomed to dealing with foreigners in trade, felt attracted to join their administration. There was the necessity for them to learn English. For intelligent young people who wanted jobs in commercial firms or government offices, knowledge of the English was a desirable objective. Early in the nineteenth century, Calcutta led the way in the new desire to acquire knowledge of the English language. Surprisingly enough, the demand for the new learning came from leading Hindus. In other parts of India, a similar desire was awakened. At Jhansi, its Maharastrian governor, Hari Damodar, learnt English in order to understand Western science and he actually established a laboratory on the Western model. At Benares, Bombay and Madras, the demand for English education came from leading minds among the Hindus. In their humble way, they began to establish English schools.

Thus as early as 1808, an English school began functioning at Calcutta under an Armenian Head Master. In 1816, Rammohun Roy established another school in the city for English education. In 1817, the famous Hindu College was founded in Calcutta with encouragement from David Hare, the Chief Justice, Hyde East, Rammohun Roy and Radhakanta Dev. In 1818, some Christian missionaries, with the help of some influential Indians, established an English school at Benares.

The authorities of the East India Company at first remained indifferent towards English education. In 1824 they established in Calcutta a school for Sanskrit education and another for Arabic and Persian. It still took some time for the Company to officially inaugurate Western education through the English medium. In any case, the greater impact of the West was bound to percolate through education, with far reaching consequences.

There was yet another platform on which the West-East understanding took shape. At first, to the leaders of Indian thought, Englishmen, either as traders, rulers or missionaries, were enemies of Indian culture, religion and traditions. But such an antagonistic attitude began to subside because of the unique role of some notable Englishmen who dedicated their Indian careers to discovering India. William Jones founded the Asiatic Society of Bengal in 1784. With earnest compatriots like Charles Wilkins and H.T. Colebrooke, he initiated the great movement of discovering India. The history and literature, and many facets of Indian civilisation, began to emerge steadily out of the limbo of oblivion. The more Western scholarship threw light on India, the greater became the attraction of Indian scholars towards research and learning.

The impact of the West began to operate through perceptible and imperceptible ways. It had its positive and negative aspects. Through actions and reactions, antagonism and assimilation, Western ideas began to penetrate into Indian thought and habits. The orthodox revolted outwardly, but searched inwardly for a change. For the intellectual, there was the need to rationalise the traditional society. To the learned, Hinduism, Islam and Christianity had common grounds on which to meet, the essence of all religions being the same. A wave of unrest swept over the thinking minds during the early years of the nineteenth century. Out of that unrest, the Indian renaissance began to take shape. In the wake of that awakening there also emerged the socio-religious reform movements. The nineteenth century in the history of India possessed the same characteristics which the eighteenth century possessed in the history of Europe. It was an age of enlightenment and awakening, of renaissance and reforms, of rationalism and progress, which all ultimately culminated in a growing consciousness of the need for liberty and unity.

Throughout the nineteenth century there followed phase after phase of various reform movements in India to renovate the society and rationalise religious thoughts. The first in the series was the movement initiated by Raja Rammohun Roy.

RAMMOHUN ROY AND THE BRAHMO MOVEMENT

Rammohun Roy born in 1774 in the district of Hooghly in Bengal. Those were the days of chaos and confusion following Clive's irresponsible government and the great famine. Born in a notable Brahmin family in an era of orthodoxy, he grew up amid social evils and religious prejudices. At the age of nine, he had to marry two times, and subsequently once more, because it was impossible for him to escape the privilege of Kulinism. As a grown-up man he saw the burning of his brother's wife a sati, a sight that shocked his conscience.

A prisoner of society and religion, he nevertheless enjoyed certain advantages which even that dark age provided. Rammohun's predecessors had held high offices under the Nawabs of Bengal.

Because of the family status, he was sent to Patna to study Persian and Arabic. After acquiring adequate knowledge in those languages, he proceeded to Benares to study Sanskrit. From his knowledge of Persian and Arabic he understood the essence of the Koran and Sufi philosophy; from Sanskrit, the deeper philosophies of the Hindu Upanishads. The inner meaning of Hinduism and Islam drew him to monotheism and created and aversion in him towards idolatry. For reasons not clearly understood, he took to a life of wandering for some time. He saw many parts of India and even, so it is said, visited Tibet. Their, instead of finding the inner spirit of Buddhism, he saw endless idolatry and, feeling unhappy, returned.

Finally there began his acquaintance with Christianity. On return to Bengal he was required to spend time at Calcutta where English officials and Christian missionaries abounded in those closing years of the eighteenth and the opening years of the nineteenth century. Rammohun came in to close contact with the scholars of Fort William College and next entered the services of the East India Company under John Digby. He learnt English and acquired so much mastery over it that Jeremy Bentham congratulated him, saying: 'Your works are made known to me by a book in which I read a style, which, but for the name of a Hindu, I should certainly have ascribed to the pen of a superiorly educated and instructed Englishman.' It was not the language, but the ideas which he got from that language which really mattered.

Thus it was that Rammohun grew up to his future role. With profound knowledge of Sanskrit, Arabic, Persian and English, and with a deeper understanding of the philosophies of Hinduism, Islam, Buddhism and Christianity, he became a rare intellectual of his time. He was in search of rationalism and felt resentful towards the prevailing socio-religious customs around him. From 1805 to 1814, he was in intimate association with John Digby. The latter left India on leave in 1814, and Rammohun too left the Company's service. Next year he settled in Calcutta to devote his life to the work for which he was mentally preparing.

Rammohun's vision was broad enough to encompass various aspects of Indian life. His movement covered religious, social, economic, educational, political and national issues. A brief reference to his approach to the above noted issues will show the nature of his thought and mission.

In religion, Rammohun pointed to a universal inner spiritual synthesis, far from the external forms represented through meaningless practices. A Brahmin himself, he peeped into the inner substance of Brahmanical Hinduism to discover the existence of One Omnipotent Being. The refined ideals of the *Vedanta* were forgotten and lost in ignorance, but they were, the eternal source of Hindu spiritualism. The ideal of monotheism was itself a supreme force in Hinduism, as it was in Islam and Christianity. To turn the mind of India to the truths of *Vedanta* became the prime motive of Rammohun. It meant a crusade against the outer forms of Hinduism, notably, polytheism, worship of images, ritualistic ceremonies, and superstitious rites. 'Belief in one Almighty God is the fundamental principle of every religion,' he said. And, the union of hearts, with mutual love and affection for all fellow creatures irrespective of colour or creed and religion, was the pure devotion acceptable to God. He established his theories from the *Vedanta*, the Bible and Koran.

In pursuit of his religious objectives, Rammohun thought of a concerted action by a band of true reformers. In 1815, he formed a society of friends, or the Atmiya Sabha, with a number of distinguished men including Dwarakanath Tagore. The society began to discuss religion and theology, ethics and truth. Reformist propaganda was initiated through books, tracts, articles and translations from the Upanishads. Rammohun declared: 'My constant reflections on the inconvenient, or rather injurious rites, introduced by the peculiar practice of Hindu idolatry, which more than any other Pagan worship destroys the texture of society, together with compassion for my countrymen, have compelled me to use every possible effort to awaken them from their dream of error: and by making them acquainted with their Scriptures, enable them to contemplate with true devotion the unity and omnipresence of Nature's God.'

His crusade against Hindu modes of worship roused in the orthodox a fanatical reaction against the reformer. He was exposed to great risks. But nothing could discourage him. Christian fanaticism was equally directed against him when he ventured to write and publish in 1820 his work entitled. *The Precepts of Jesus, the Guide to Peace and Happiness*. It was a liberal interpretation of Christianity, with emphasis on the spiritual principles of Jesus without the miracles. But the Serampore missionaries, including Marshman, attacked him strongly.

Amid these deep religious controversies Rammohun marched ahead. Finally, on 20 August 1828 he founded the Brahma Sabha which became famous as the Brahmo Samaj in 1830. The Samaj stood for the 'worship and adoration of the Eternal Unsearchable and Immutable Being—who is the Author and Preserver of the Universe but not under or by any other designation or title peculiarly used for and applied to any particular Being or Beings by any man or set of men whatsoever.' It admitted 'no graven image, statue or sculpture, carving, painting, picture, portrait or the likeness of anything'. It further stood for the 'promotion of charity, morality, piety, benevolence, virtue and the strengthening of the bonds of union between men of all religious persuasions and creeds'.

Thus Rammohun began the first great religious reform movement of the nineteenth century. Since religion was the dominating force in Indian society, reform of religion meant also reform of society. The Brahmo movement was thus a socio-religious reform movement. Rammohun raised his voice against the social abuses which rendered incalculable harm to society. The caste system appeared to him as the greatest obstacle to national unity. It also kept the bulk of the population in regarding conditions. Rammohun proceeded even beyond the frontiers of caste. He adopted a Muslim boy and gave the most daring example of human equality. Besides caste, the Hindu society suffered from other social evils, such as, polygamy, degradation of women, and, above all, the horrible sati system. Rammohun's endeavour to rouse opinion against those customs marked the beginning of an era of social change. If ultimately the sati system was abolished, it was as much due to Rammohun as to the Governor-General Bentinck in whose time it was effected.

A pioneer of modernism, Rammohun realised the value of Western education. He established two English schools and showed the way to new and liberal learning. He was not afraid to oppose the orthodox who believed that Sanskrit was the source of all knowledge and wisdom. Instead, he pleaded with the Government to give India the benefit of 'a more liberal and enlightened system of instruction embracing Mathematics, Natural Philosophy, Chemistry, Anatomy, with other useful sciences'. He negotiated with the missionaries to procure able teachers for Western education. In 1830, he obtained the services of Alexander Duff in the cause of English education.

Though Rammohun's primary concern was socio-religious reform, yet the economic misery of the people touched his conscience deeply. Bengal was passing through two economic evils. A series of revenue experiments culminating in the Permanent Settlement put the peasant at the mercy of the landlord. The second evil was the perpetual drain on the country's economy. The Company's commercial and economic policy, backed by their political power, had brought devastating results. Rammohun raised his voice in support of the poor, though at that time it was a voice in the wilderness.

He also pioneered the political awakening in India. Those were the days when a modern press was emerging as a potential force in public life. A prolific writer on various subjects, Rammohun became a patron of the free press and constructive journalism. His Bengali weekly, *Sambad Kaumudi*, established in 1821, began to discuss political matters, besides religious and moral affairs. His Persian weekly, *Mirat-ul-Akhbar* established next year, discussed national as well as international problems. But then came the Government's Press Ordinance in 1823 to restrict the freedom of the Indian press. In Rammohun's movement against that harmful law there began the modern method of constitutional movement supported by political consciousness. He inspired the intelligentsia to oppose the autocratic measures of the Government with a united voice. He also opposed the harmful Juri Act. Before the Company's Charter was renewed in 1833, he was busy with his campaign against many of the Company's harmful rights and privileges.

Finally, it was Rammohun's patriotism which made him one of the earliest nationalists in India in a modern sense. He advocated liberal humanitarian nationalism. Emancipation of man from the bondage of ignorance, and social tyranny, his freedom of thought and conscience, and his equality with other fellow men were considered as the fundamentals of liberalism. Such free and emancipated individuals, with feeling towards their motherland, could create national unity. The crusade of Rammohun to free the individual from social degradation and to abolish the caste system was for the purpose of building up a nationhood. It was also through a spiritual and mental revival that Rammohun wanted to regenerate the Indian people and unite them into a national fraternity.

In 1830, Rammohun had occasion to proceed to England. He was sent by the titular Mughal Emperor of Delhi, Akbar II, to place his grievances before the British Government. He was also required to give evidence before the Select Committee of the House of Commons on the judicial and revenue systems of India. At the same time he wanted to convince the British Parliament of the validity of the abolition of the sati system. He was the first Indian, the first Brahmin, to cross the oceans and land in Europe, breaking the fantastic Hindu orthodoxy against voyages across the water. Rammohun died at Bristol on 27 September 1833.

History has acknowledged Rammohun Roy as the herald of modern India and his time as the dawn of Indian renaissance. The Brahmo movement continued after him. It was not the Brahmo Samaj as an institution which hammered at the root of medievalism, but the original ideas associated with the movement which broke through superstitions and opened avenues for rational thinking.

LATER PHASES OF THE BRAHMO MOVEMENT

The death of Rammohun was no doubt a great tragedy for the Brahmo Samaj since he was the centre of the entire movement. But the mission of the master was taken up by other daring souls. From the beginning, the movement was confined to the intellectually advanced and educationally enlightened minds who believed in reforms. It was not their aim to make it a mass movement, though the purpose was to educate the masses. The Brahmos themselves did not abandon traditional religious ceremonies root and branch. But there was a changed outlook. At least, a challenge had been thrown against formalities and superstitions. The legacies of Rammohun could not die after him as they were in consonance with the requirements of the time. The movement, thus, destined to grow.

For a time after the death of the founder, the leadership of the Samaj was enjoyed by Dwarakanath Tagore, a close compatriot of Rammohun. In 1843, Devendranath, son of Dwarakanath, took over the leadership. Devendranath was born in 1817, and was educated in the Anglo-Hindu School of Rammohun and in the Hindu College. A product of the new spirit, he believed in reforms. A leaf from the Upanishads revealed to him the grandeur of monotheism. With a profound curiosity to discover and preach truth, he established the *Tattvabodhini Sabha* which played a prominent role in the moral awakening of Bengal. Some notable men of nineteenth century Bengal, like Rajendralal Mitra and Ishwar Chandra Vidyasagar, were members of the Sabha. The members turned their energy towards searching for the lost and forgotten values of the culture of the country.

Devendranath introduced into the Brahmo Samaj the famous Brahmic Covenant. This included the vows to worship through love the One God, without a second; to worship no created object as the creator; to perform righteous deeds; and to abstain from vicious deeds, etc. He organised a group of preachers to popularise the Brahmo doctrines in the remote countryside of Bengal and established branches of the Samaj at various towns. His *Tattvabodhini Patrika* became the mouthpiece of the movement. Devendranath took up a bold stand on two fronts. Inside Hinduism, his was the reformist movement on the ancient moorings of religion as embodied in the Vedas. Outside, his was the ruthless opposition to the Christian missionaries for their criticism of Hinduism and attempts at conversion. It was in fact a confrontation between Alexander Duff and his band of missionaries on one side and Devendranath and his Brahmo followers on the other. For the time, even orthodox Hindus paid veneration to Devendranath for his faith in the Vedas and opposition to Christian activities.

But before long, a crisis appeared in the core of the Brahmo thought. Were the Vedas infallible? Were they the fountain source of all truth? The more progressive minds among the reformers began to doubt and question the theory of Vedic infallibility. Devendranath himself, after a great deal of mental exercise on the scriptures at Benares, doubted many fundamentals of the Vedas. But the Brahmo movement was based on faith in the Vedas and it was thought unwise to shake that foundation. Amid doubts, Devendranath selected those portions of the Upanishads which advocated monotheism and published them as the Brahmo Dharma. The 'Seed Principles' of Brahmoism were also propounded. Thus the movement was undergoing a philosophical transformation. The rejection of Vedic infallibility made it more radical. The younger members began to advocate more radical social changes. Child-marriage, polygamy, and Kulinism were severely denounced, whereas emancipation of women, and widow-marriage were strongly advocated.

When such were the developments, Keshab Chandra Sen joined the Brahmo Samaj in 1858 at the age of twenty. Though born in an orthodox family, he had received an English education and had imibed Western ideas. His study of the Bible and Christian ethics drew him nearer to a greater understanding of Christianity. After joining the Brahmo Samaj he brought into it a new sense of confidence and purpose. His personal dynamism, vigour, capacity, and, above all, his eloquence proved great assets to Brahmoism. Many intellectuals and young men felt attracted to the Samaj. Keshabchandra established a great hold on the rising generation of progressive intellectuals. Within his close circle, he encouraged free religious discourses and study of Christian literature. It was apparent that he was nearing a new approach.

From its inception, the Brahmo movement was confined mainly to Bengal. But Keshabchandra wanted to make it an all-India concern. In 1864-65, he proceeded on a missionary campaign to Madras and Bombay. Wherever he went, he received encouraging responses from progressive quarters. The Brahmo Samaj was about to assume a much wider dimension.

But, as in the case of many religious movements, a schism confronted the Samaj. Keshabchandra's radical lines of thought and action appeared to the more conservative as too radical. His Society of Theistic Friends became a forum for bolder programmes. Even inter-caste marriage was advocated. To Devendranath Tagore, Keshabchandra's policies appeared aggressive. The culmination came in 1866 when Keshabchandra delivered a lecture on Jesus Christ with the remark: 'May the world appreciate him and fellow his precepts.' It created misgivings among others that he was on his way to embrace Christianity. But Keshab's intention was not to leave Brahmoism but to make it more revolutionary. Whatever was his real intention, the schism between the conservatives and the radicals came in 1866 when Keshabchandra with his followers left the parent body and formed the Brahmo Samaj of India. Therefter the parent organisation came to be known as the Original or the Adi Brahmo Samaj.

With the rise of radicalism, the original Brahmo Samaj lost its earlier glamour and began to decline. On the other hand, the new organisation of Keshabchandra began to grow for some time with more pronounced zeal. Instead of remaining a mere reformist sect within the Hindu fold, it aimed at assuming a universal character on its religious platform. On the social platform, it rejected the caste system in any and every form. Keshab introduced devotional elements into Brahmo prayer to stir up religious emotion in men. The *samkirtan,* or the devotional singing of the type of the Bhakti religious movement of medieval days, became a feature of the new Brahmoism. The movement appealed to the heart and gained popularity.

But a transformation was going on in Keshabchandra's personality which affected the movement adversely. In their emotional devotionalism, the close disciples of the master regarded him as an incarnation. To his progressive followers, this seemed an excess of human pretensions. Keshab's popularity waned because of it. In 1870, he visited England for a brief period and lectured there on various aspects of his thought. He met Max Mueller, John Stuart Mill and Gladstone. He observed closely the striking aspects of Western culture.

By the last quarter of the nineteenth century, Indian liberalism had progressed. Even Keshabchandra appeared conservative to many for his followers, Moreover, Brahmoism, which stood for religious liberalism, found in Keshab's person elements of authoritarianism as he interpreted his own words as divine will. Thus a second schism in the Brahmo movement became inevitable. And, it came on a relatively small issue. In 1878, Keshabchandra gave his eldest daughter in marriage to a Hindu orthodox family. The bride was less than fourteen and the bridegroom, who was the Maharaja of Cooch-Behar, was just fifteen, both being not strictly of a marriageable age. The occasion was a triumph of Hindu conservatism over the reformer himself. It shocked the conscience of the Brahmos to such an extent that many withdrew from the Samaj of Keshabchandra and formed a new organisation named Sadharan Brahmo Samaj.

After the schism of 1878 the Brahmo movement lost much of its earlier novelty and purpose. The consciousness of educated Indians had developed enough to rationalize much of the social and religious thinking. A reform movement to condemn traditional Hinduism was losing ground. Instead, a Hindu revivalism was taking the place of crusades against Hinduism. Revivalism also aimed at rationalism. Thus, within the forces of these new developments the Brahmo movement passively folded itself down within its own orbit. In its doctrinal aspect, Brahmoism maintained its universal approach and upheld its faith in the synthesis of all faiths. Even after the schism, Keshabchandra announced his New Dispensation with the message that 'It recognises in all the prophets and saints a harmony, in all the scriptures a unity, and through all dispensations a continuity. His faith in God and

Providence became so intense that the latter phase of his life was moulded in the pattern of the true saints of any religion. Meanwhile, the Sadharan Brahmo Samaj was still working for social and educational improvements.

On the whole, the Brahmo movement, from Rammohun to Keshabchandra, covered the greater part of the nineteenth century. In India's mental resource in the modern era, the role of the organisation and its pioneers had been outstanding.

—M. N. Das

3

Brahmo Samaj

While Sikhism was the result of contact between Hinduism and Islam, the Brahmo Samaj was inspired by Christianity and the civilisation of Europe. The founder of Brahmo Samaj was Raja Rammohun Roy, a Bengali Brahmin, who is now known as the "Father of Modern India." Most of the reform movements that have revolutionized Hindu society can be traced to this great son of India." He was himself the victim of social evils, and throughout his life he worked indefatigably for the social and religious uplift of his community. In his childhood he was married to two wives, and all his life he fought against the evil of child marriage. He saw has own sister mounting the funeral pyre of her husband, and it was through the agitation started by him that Lord William Bentinck abolished by law the institution of Sati. The idolatry, caste tyranny and animal sacrifices of Hinduism filled him with disgust. He was much attracted by Christianity and was a constant friend of the European missionaries of Bengal. A Study of the *Vedas* and the *Upanishads* made him realise that idolatry, caste and other well-known features of Hindu society had no foundation in the *Vedas* and were accretions of a later age.

Rammohun Roy was deeply imbued with the culture of the West and East, and was a scholar as well as a reformer. He was a nationalist but had profound contempt for narrow-minded nationalism. In his days, the controversy regarding the adoption of English education in India reached a heated pitch, all orthodox Hindus and Muslims and even some Englishmen opposing it. The following extract from a letter Rammohun Roy wrote to Lord Amherst expresses his views on the subject: "If it had been intended to keep the British nation in ignorance of real knowledge, the Baconian philosophy would not have been allowed to displace the system of the Schoolmen, which was best calculated to perpetuate ignorance. In the same manner, the Sanskrit system of education would be the best calculated to perpetuate ignorance if such had been the policy of the British legislature. But as the improvement of the native population is the object of the Government, it will consequently promote a more liberal and enlightened policy of instruction." Raja Rammohun Roy was the first high caste Hindu to defy the taboo prohibiting sea voyages, and visit England.

In 1828, this versatile genius founded the Brahmo Samaj "A Church open to all sorts and conditions of men for the 'worship and adoration of the Eternal, Unsearchable and Immortal Being, who is the Author and Preserver of the Universe." The Islamic attitude towards idolatry was adopted by the Samaj, and any kind of images at places of worship was considered an offence. All great religious leaders like the Buddha, Jesus and Mohammad were to be venerated and Hinduism was to be interpreted in the spirit of the *Vedas* and the *Upanishads.* In the congregation of the Brahmo Samaj, 'no sermon, preaching, discourse, prayer or hymn be delivered, made or used but such as have a tendency to the promotion of the contemplation of the Author and Preserver of the Universe, to the promotion of charity, morality, piety, benevolence, virtue, and the strengthening of the bonds of union between men of all religious persuasions and creeds."

Such a teaching, it can be easily seen, lacks the dogmatism of a popular religion, and the Brahmo Samaj could not reach the peoples of India. But it appealed to all enlightened members of the Hindu community, and in Bengal, in spite of the antagonism and petty persecutions by the orthodox, all great leaders in the political, social and religious field were inspired by the spirit of the Brahmo Samaj. Rammohun Roy, died in England in 1833, and on his death the affairs of the Brahmo Samaj fell in a bad way, due to luck of funds and proper leadership. In 1842, the Bengali saint Devendra Nath Tagore joined the Samaj and assumed its leadership. During his time an effort was made by some of the leading members of the Samaj to establish the new religion on a purely Hindu basis and to accept the *Vedas* as infallible. Opposition to this was very strong and the arguments between the parties began to affect the unity of the Samaj. On an effort being made to reconcile this quarrel, it was found that neither the adherents nor the opponents of the *Vedas* had an adequate knowledge of these ancient texts. Debendra Nath Tagore, therefore, immediately sent the most noisy of the disputants to Benares to study and scrutinize the *Vedas*. These men were so lost in the wranglings of the learned pundits of Benares, and they took so long to study the *Vedas* that most of them died before coming to a definite agreement on the subject.

The third great figure of the Brahmo Samaj was Keshab Chandra Sen, also a Bengali. Even in the time of Devendra Nath Tagore, Keshab showed an independent and original spirit, but the personality of the great saint restrained him from independent action. In 1905 Tagore died, and Keshab Chandra Sen became the leader of the Brahmos. He was an impetuous genius, impatient of the slow progress of the Samaj. He wished to organise a universal religion, known as the New Dispensation Samaj, with himself as the prophet of the new faith. He had a remarkable personality and a convincing voice, but failed to convert all the members of the Samaj to his way of thinking. Those who adhered to the old school, then came to be known as the Adi Samaj or original Samaj. Keshab was a man of indefatigable energy and in his time, the Samaj became widely known all over India. But his overbearing attitude and claims of prophetship created many dissenters, and these founded the Saddharana Samaj of extreme views. Keshab died without being able to achieve anything like unity in the Samaj.

An offshoot of the Brahmo Samaj was the Prarthana Samaj (society of prayer) of Bombay. Keshab was the inspirer of this Theistic movement and its most distinguished leaders were Mahadev Gobind Ranade, Sir Ramakrishna Bhandarkar and Sir Narayana Chandravarkar.

The Brahmo Samaj may be said to have paved the way for the success of the Theosophical movement started by Dr. Annie Beasant. The theosophists accept all religions as true, believe in the message of all the prophets that have lived in the world irrespective of caste, creed and colour, and celebrate, their birthdays. Some of the beliefs of the theosophists are curious. Their acceptance of the spirit world and the like is an enigma to many intelligent people. The world Messiaship Theosophy wished to confer on J. Krishnamurti, a Madrasi gentleman adopted in his childhood by Dr. Beasant for the purpose, was rejected by him on his coming of age. He bluntly declared that he was no Messiah. But an ordinary human being possessing normal human faculties and nothing more.

The greatness of the Brahmo Samaj is not in its religious leadership but in its pioneering spirit in social reforms. Through the efforts of its members, the Brahmo Samaj has been able to give expression to those forces which abolished Sati, prohibited child marriage and other social evils, and brought home to the Hindus a sense of the shortcoming of their institutions. In the religious sphere it could only provide a sanctuary to those enlightened Hindus who hated the superstitions of their countrymen yet wished to be known as Hindus. Hence the Brahmo Samaj has at present more leaders than followers, and its influence on the popular religion of the Hindus is not very considerable.

—P. Thomas

4

Influence of Renaissance and Reformation

The battle of Plassey (23 June, 1757) sowed the seeds of British political supremacy in Bengal, which was extended throughout India during the hundred years following it. *The expansion of the British dominion in India, and the development of an Indo-British administrative system as a corollary to it, naturally conducted India through manifold process of transition,—political, economic and social. This, for diverse reasons, generated fumes of discontent among various sections of the people in different parts of India, which burst into flames in the movement of* 1857-59.[1] The Movement of 1857-59 was no doubt suppressed by the government. But it produced significant consequences for India and its memory recalled in the subsequent years certainly worked against British imperialism.

The post-1859 period was marked by the development of some new forces in India destined to effect transformation in the various phases of her life. *Cultural renaissance and the Reformation movements in India during the second half of the nineteenth century were then producing a new awakening in Indian minds. The political development of modern India has been an aspect of a general renaissance pervading different spheres of life,—religion, society and culture—and producing mementoes consequences in each.* The inevitable penetration of its spirit into the field of politics generated there a commotion which gathered an irresistible momentum defying all the weapons of an aggressive imperialism.

It is true that growing acquaintance, through the medium of western education, with the progressive political thought of the West and the stirring achievements of the revolutions of modern Europe resulting in the triumphs of nationalism and democracy saturated the minds of some educated Indians with the ideas of liberalism, civic liberty and freedom. But this by itself could not have produced and fostered a truly Indian national movement if there had not been at the same time a *genuine urge from within, a spirit of renaissance aiming at the revival of what was noble and elevating in India's past and also at the redemption of her people from the crushing load of unreason, social abuses and political servitude.*

Indeed, discovery of India's past through the honest endeavours of scholars, poets and social or religious reformers proved to be a highly fertile source of inspiration generating in the minds of many a feeling or regard for the motherland. Indian nationalism has been, remarks Ramsay Macdonald truly, "the revival of her historical tradition and the liberation of the soul of a people." *"Indian Nationality is," in the words of Annie Besant "not a plant of mushroom growth but a giant of the forest with millennia behind it"*[2]

The establishment of the Asiatic Society in Bengal was significant landmark in the history of cultural renaissance in modern India. The researches of many zealous anti-quarians, Indian as well as European, revealed the majesty and glory of India's old civilisation, which served to inspire generations of people in this land. No doubt the pioneer workers in this respect were a number of European scholars like Jones, Prinsep, Wilson, Colebrooke, Rosen, Roth, Burnouf, Schelegel, Bopp, Max Mueller and some others. But it is highly gratifying to note how for this supremely important task of rediscovering and reinterpreting India's past we owe a heavy debt to our distinguished countrymen like Rammohun Roy, Radhakanta Dev, Rajendra Lal Mitra, Vishwanath Narayan Mandlik, Mani Shankar Jata Shankar, Bhau Daji, Bhagwan Lal Indraji, M.G. Ranade, B.G. Tilak, R.G. Bhandarkar, K.T. Telang, R.C. Dutt, Manmohan Chakravarty, Haraprasad Shastri and some others.

At first "the new wine of Western learning" went to the heads of young Bengal producing" denationalising tendencies"[3] in the minds of many of those who tasted it. But the Indian religious and social reform movements did much to arrest the evil effects of the blind imitation of what was apparently glittering in an imposing exotic civilisation and to maintain the dignity of our national culture. Rajnarain Bose, a progressive Brahmo who had drunk deep of Western education, stood undauntedly to uphold the superiority of our culture at a time when some of our countrymen, receiving new education, were growing prejudiced against it. To check denationalisation, Rajnarain started in 1861 a Society called the *Society for the Promotion of National Feeling Among the Educated Natives of Bengal* and issued a prospectus for it in the form of a pamphlet containing its aims and objects.[4] Bipin Chandra Pal writes that Rajnarain's lecture in Bengalee on *Hindu Dharmer Shresthata* or `the superiority of Hiduism' was 'really first public protest of the age-long Nation-spirit of India against the threatened domination of our thought, and life by the aggressive and colour-proud civilisation of Europe"[5]. This view was more emphatically and fruitfully expressed in subsequent years by men like Ranade and Vivekananda to nourish our early nationalism.

We should also note how a galaxy of inspired geniuses produced literature of highly creative nature, marked by a marvellous fusion of the old and the new, a grand intermingling of the best literary traditions of old India which the good features of the culture of the modern world outside by feelings of deep adoration for the motherland, and by profound emphasis on the virtue of patriotism. Influence of literature of this kind in stimulating dormant in souls can hardly be overestimated. R.W. Freezer very significantly observes: "Men such as Rammohun Roy, Keshab Chandra Sen, Machael Madhusudan Dutta, Bankim Chandra Chatterjee, Kashinath Trimbak Telang are no bastard bantlings of a Western civilisation; they were creative geniuses worthy to be reckoned in the history of India with such men of old as Kalidas, Chaitanya, Jayadeva, Tulsidas and Shankaracharya and destined in the future to shine clear as the first glowing sparks sent out in the fiery turmoil where old and new were fusing".[6]

In 1860, Dinabandhu Mitra produced in his work, entitled *'Nila-Darpan' (Mirrors of Indigo),* a seathing satire on the indigo-planters of Bengal, whose dealings with the local ryots form a tale of unspeakable tyrannies. Hem Chandra Banerjee (1838-1903) 'voiced in his national lyrics the sense of impotence of his people to assert their legitimate rights and self-respect against their British master.'[7] Bipin Chandra Pal thus describes Hem Chandra Banerjee's influence upon him; "Hem Chandra, however, was our special favourite. The intense patriotic passion that breathed through his poems captured our youthful minds in a way which no other Bengalee poems had done. The new generation of English-educated Bengalees had already commenced to advance themselves to positions of trust and responsibility in the new Administration. In the learned professions of law and medicine also, they were gradually asserting themselves as against the British members. A new spirit of independence and self-assertion was increasingly manifesting itself in the conduct and conversations of the English-educated Bengalee. All these had already commenced to provoke a racial conflict in the country Hem Chandra was, in a special sense, the poet of this new conflict and of the racial self-respect and sensitive patriotism, born of it".

Hem Chandra expressed in one stanza of his *'Bharat Sangeet'* or the *'Song of India':*

"Sing, O my clarionet ! Sing to these words:
Every one is free in this wide world.
Every one is awake in the glory of science,
India alone lieth asleep."

We read also in the same song:

"China and Burma, and uncivilised Japan,
Even they are independent, they are superior,
India alone knowth no waking".

Another national song contained the following heart-rending note:

'O, India, weep, weep Thou,

As long as thy polluted atoms have not been washed away into the waters of the ocean,
So long weep thou, so long weep'.

Ranglal observed in his ode to Liberty: "Breathes there the man, who would like to live, though shorn of liberty".

Govinda Chandra Roy, a nineteenth century Bengalee student of Agra, gave expression to his feelings of patriotism in some of his most touching songs. In one of these he said:

'How long will it take there, Oh Bharat,
to swim across this ocean of misery?
Or, sinking and sinking in depression,

Wilt thou enter the nether regions for ever?
Having gladly offered thy jewels to the
Stranger, thou carries now only an iron chain on thy breast!

There are rows of light in thy cities (owned by the stranger)
But thou art in darkness all the same'.
In another song they author pathetically noted:
'O India, gloomy is the face, beautiful that was as the moon;
Day and night tears flow from thy eyes'.

The writings of Bankim Chandra revealed remarkably the inward spirit of Indian life and thought'.[8]

Their lessons penetrated into the hearts of our country-men and stirred them to their very depths. He was not only a 'prophet'[9] of Indian cultural renaissance, but also, as Shri Aurobindo puts it, 'a seer and a nation-builder' and one of the 'Makers of Modern India'[10]. It is well-known how greatly stimulating has been the influence of the famous *Anthem 'Bande Mataram'* recorded in his classic work *Ananda Math*. The *'Bangadarshan'*, which began to be published as a weekly paper in Calcutta from April 1872, proved to be a very effective organ in contemporary Bengal for the expression of thoughts of her educated youths on the varied problems of life and society, and this facilitated the growth of our early nationalism. We read as follows in the Hindi drama *'Bharat-Darshan'* written by Harish Chandra in 1880:

'O brother Indians, come and let all of us weep;
Alas, alas, the misery of India is not to be witnessed.

The one whom God granted first of all wealth and power,
The one who was made civilised by the Creator first of all,
The one who bathed first of all in beauty, colour of *rasa*
And the one who first of all caught the fruits of learning,
Is now seen last of all.
Alas, alas the misery of India is not to be witnessed.

The British Government has arranged all big comforts:
But that this wealth goes away to foreign land is pricking,
And even then dearness, famine and diseases are spreading.
Oh, oh, God gives troubles doubly day by day:
And over all the catastrophe of taxation is come.
Alas, alas the misery of India is not to be witnessed.

A powerful dramatic literature coming out of the pen of D.L. Roy and some others also contributed to stir national feeling. For about half a century Rabindranath's works interpreted in a unique way the true spirit of Indian culture and civilisation. "Tagore's Poetry," remarks Ramsay Macdonald significantly," is India. It is the product of his devotion to Indian culture. It is the soul of a people, not merely the emotion of a man; a systematic view of life, not merely a poetic mood; a culture, not merely a tune."[11] A mighty stream of inspiration has flown out of the stirring speeches and writings of Sarojini Naidu, Sarala Devi, and some other highly gifted ladies of India.

Spiritual idealism has been also a highly potent factor in promoting the progress of nationalism in modern India. *The Indian social and religious reform movements of this period have undoubtedly exercised much influence on the course of our national development.* Referring to India's new awakening, Rev. C. F. Andrews wrote about 1912: *'But this awakening would have been wholly insufficient to usher in a new era if it had not been combined with a second and even greater change. A religious reformation has been advancing side by side with the new renaissance."*[12] Rammohun Roy, Devendra Nath Tagore, Ishwar Chandra Vidyasagar, Keshab Chandra Sen, Dayanand Saraswati, M.G. Ranade, Bal Gangadhar Tilak, Ram Krishna Paramahansa and his great disciple Vivekananda and Shri Aurobindo impressed on the minds of our countrymen the profoundness and sublimity of our ancient thought and created therein an indomitable urge for national regeneration on the basis of the best in Indian culture. Rammohun Roy was not only the "first earnest-minded investigator of comparative religion and truth" and the pioneer social reformer in modern India, but also an ardent champion of freedom. William Adam, a Baptist Missionary associated with his for some time, remarked: 'He would be free or not be at all.... Love of freedom was perhaps the strongest passion of his soul'. In his letter of Buckingham, dated the 11th August, 1821 Rammohun expressed his strong conviction in the following words: *'Enemies to liberty and friends of despotism have never been and will never be ultimately successful.* Particularly significant in this respect was the influence of the reforming activities of India during the second half of the nineteenth century and the early years of the present century. Famous Theosophists like Colonel Olcott and Mrs. Annie Bessant, who were themselves great admirers of India and helped the cause of Indian nationalism through their writings and speeches, tell how Swami Dayanand exerted 'great nationalising influence.'[13] In his numerous speeches and writings Swami Vivekananda impressed upon his countrymen as well as upon some foreigners the capacity of India's inborn spiritual genius, her rich cultural heritage, taught them self-confidence and trust, and thus immensely stimulated Indian Nationalism. "The queen of his adoration," says Sister Nivedita, his brilliantly gifted Irish disciple, "was his motherland." "Oh India! Wouldst thou Attain," he exclaimed, "by means of thy disgraceful cowardice, that freedom deserved only by the brave and the heroic? Oh India! forget not that the ideal of thy womanhood is Sita, Savitri, Damayanti, forget not that the God thou worshipest is the great ascetic of ascetics, the all-renouncing Shankara, the Lord of Uma; forget not that thy marriage, thy wealth, thy life are not for sense-pleasure, are not for thy individual personal happiness; forget not that thou art born as a sacrifice to the Mother's altar; forget not that thy social order is but the reflex of the infinite Universal Motherhood; forget not that the lower classes, the ignorant, the poor, the illiterate, the cobbler, the sweeper are thy flesh and blood, thy brothers. Thou brave one, be bold, take courage, be proud that thou art an Indian, and Proudly proclaim: 'I am an Indian, every Indian is my brother'. Say: "The ignorant Indian, the poor and destitute Indian the Brahman Indian, the Pariah Indian, is my brother'. Thou, too, clad with but a rag round thy loins proudly proclaim at the top of the voice; The Indian is my brother, the Indian is my life, India's gods and goddesses are my God, India's society is the cradle of my infance, the pleasure garden of my youth, the sacred heaven, the Varanasi of my old age. Say, brother: 'The soil of India is my highest heaven, the good of India is my good, and repeat and pray day and night; 'O Thou lord of Gauri, O Thou Mother of the Universe,. vouchsafe manliness unto me. O Thou Mother of Streangth, take away my weakness, take away my unmanliness, and make me a Man."

The thoughts and activities of Bal Gangadhar Tilak, Shri Aurobindo and some others richly fed this current of inspiration. The conception of India as the 'Mother' originated with Bankim Chandra, who, in a moment of inspiration, first 'uttered' in his *Bande Mataram* the '*Mantra* of an awakened nationalism.' To Shri Aurobindo India was the eternal and infinite Mother, and love of her was a spiritual experience. 'Patriotism', he wrote, cannot be anything sort of a desire to redeem one's country. It cannot bear to look upon the country as a sepulchre though it may seem so. It feels the immortality shining beneath these ruins with which subjection has overspread the country. It feels the pulsations of the immense eternal life of the country through the artificial crust with which the great sleeper has been covered as with a shroud."[14] He once wrote in the paper, *Bande Mataram:* "The work of national emancipation is a great and holy *yajna* of which boycott, Swadeshi, national education and every other activity, great and small, are only major and minor parts. Liberty is the fruit we seek from the sacrifice and Motherland the goddess to whom we offer it; into the seven leaping tongues of the fire for the *jajna* we must offer all that we are and all that we have, feeding the fire even with our blood and lives and happiness of our nearest and dearest; for the Motherland is the goddess who loves not a maimed and imperfect sacrifice, and freedom was never won from the Gods by a grudging giver."[15] The new nationalism of the early years of present century was characterised by an intense religious conviction as Shri Aurobindo expessed in this passage. Another prominent Indian leader of the time, Shri Bipin Chandra Pal (one of the trio *Pal-Bal-Lal),* Significantly refers to it in the following words: "All those old and traditional gods and goddesses who had lost their hold upon the modern mind have been reinstalled with new historic and nationalistic interpretation in the mind and soul of the people. Hundreds of thousands of our people have commenced to hail their motherland today as Durga, Kali, Jagadhatree. They are no longer mere mythological conceptions or legendary persons or even poetic symbols. They are different manifestations of the Mother. The Mother is the spirit of India."[16] In an article entitled *The Age of Gita again in India,* Barindra Kumar Ghose expounded the gospel of their movement by writing: "Shri Krishna has said in *Gita* that whenever there is a decline of righteousness and a rise in unrighteousness there shall be a reincarnation of God to rescue the good, to destroy the wrong-doer, and to establish righteouness. At the present moment righteousness is declining and unrighteousness is springing up in India. A handful of alien robbers are ruining the lore of the people of India by robbing the wealth of India. Through the hard grinding of their servitude, the ribs of their countless people are being broken to pieces.... Fear not, oh Indians, God will not remain inactive .... He will keep his word. Placing firm reliance on the promise of God, invoke His power.... When the lighting of Heaven flashes in their hearts, men perform impossible deeds."[17] Mahatama Gandhi's own conviction in this respect was thus expressed by him; To see the universal and all-pervading Spirit of Truth face to face one must be able to love the meanest of creation as oneself. And a man who aspires after this cannot afford to keep out of any field of life. That is why my deviation to truth has drawn me in to the field of politics; and I can say without the slightest hesitation and yet in all humility that those who say that Religion has nothing to do with politics do not know what religion means." [18]

References

1. Sashi Bhusan Chaudhuri, *Civil Disturbances During the British Rule in India* (1765-1875); K.K. Datta, *The Santal Insurrection of* 1855-57.
2. Annie Besant, *How India Wrought for Freedom*. L.
3. Ronaldshay, *The Heart of Aryavarta*, p.47.
4. For Full Test of It, vide *Modern Review, January*-June, 1994.
5. Bipin Chandra Pal, *Memories of My Life and Times*, I., p. 262.
6. Frazer, *Literary History of India, pp. 416-447.*
7. Bipin Chandra Pal, *Memories of My Life and Times*, I, p 252.
8. Frazer, *op, cit.*, p.420.
9. Bipin Chanra Pal, *Memories of My life and Times*, I, p. 226.
10. Shri Aurobindo, *Bankim, Tilak, and Dayanand*, p. 9.
11. Ramsay Macdonald, *Government of India*, p. 245.
12. C. F. Andrews. *The Renaissance of India*, p. 11.
13. A. C. Mazumdar, *Indian National Evolution*, p. 23.
14. Quoted in Sri *Aurobindo and Indian Freedom* by Sishir Kumar Mitra, pp. 47-48.
15. *Ibid*, p. 49.
16. Bipin Chandra Pal, *The Soul of India* (1916), pp. 187-188.
17. Quoted in Chirol, *Indian Unrest*, pp. 90-91.
18. *Autobiography*, p. 615.

5

Brahmo Samaj Inaugurates a New Era in Religion

ONE AGE MAKING ITS EXIT

As in many other spheres, in the religious reform movement also Raja Rammohun Roy was the pioneer. He inaugurated the modern age in India. In the words of his biographer, Sophia D. Collet: 'Rammohun stands in history as the living bridge over which India marches from her unmeasured past to her incalculable future. He was the arch which spanned the gulf that yawned between ancient caste and modern humanity, between superstition and science, between despotism and democracy, between immobile custom and a conservative progress, between... polytheism and... theism. He was the mediator of his people, harmonising in his own person, often by means of his own solitary sufferings, the conflicting tendencies of immemorial tradition and an inevitable enlightenment... He embodies the new spirit which arise from the compulsory mixture of races and faith and civilisation... he embodies its freedom of enquiry, its thirst for science, its large human sympathy, its pure and sifted ethics, along with its reverent but not uncritical regard for the past. and prudent... discrimination towards revolt.'[1]

Referring to the characteristics of that period in history another author rightly observes: 'The essential circumstance of the new age is the coming together of diverse peoples and cultures, the frequency, the intensity and the variety of their contacts being ever on the increase. The need that arises out of this situation is one of synthesis, universalism and unity, to enable men to rise superior to the limitations of localised, parochial, isolated life of the preceding ages. In the India of Rammohun's youth the past was making its exit, leaving on the stage unrealised ideals of Hindu-Muslim synthesis, and growth of the Indian renaissance and reformation, and a social and political fabric torn by reactionary conflicts... The synthesis of the Hindu and Moslem reformers of the 15th and 16th centuries had for various reasons ceased to be operative for more than five generations, being clogged with the mud of the return tide of medievalism in the 17th and 18th centuries. On the other hand, the future was drawing apart the curtains for entry on that wreck-strewn stage. Following upon growing Indo-European trade and commerce, a true and abiding Indo-European state had come to be formed, strangely combining Indian and European elements of law, polity and civilisation, and this was steadily breaking the fragments of the past and absorbing them. The Sunni-Muslim Padshahi had become a haunting shade after suicide, the rival Hindu Padshahi had missed its purpose and ended in a fiasco; the Sacheha Padshahi of the Sikhs had by disunion and narrowness become untrue and limited to inaction; while the new Inglistani Padshahi was acquiring stability and form.'[2]

Naturally, Western ideas and institutions made a strong impact on Rammohun. These ideas were primarily those of the seventeenth and eighteenth centuries, the age of enlightenment and of rationalism. Christian theology and philosophy also strongly influenced him.

NEW IDEAS CHALLENGE RELIGIOUS ORTHODOXY

He was the first cosmopolitan religious thinker of Modern India. ...He had brought...by his pioneer studies in comparative religion to universalism—and, what is more, to a universal scripture, a universal authority as underlying all historic scriptures and all historic authorities. He had proceeded from the sweeping negation of his *Tuhfat-ul-Muwahhidin* to the universalistic position of his prefaces to the Vedanta abridgement and translations. But he now perceived that the universal truth was stressed in different ways, and different accents in its different historic utterances. The Vedanta, which had restored him to faith, he always considered as strongest in *Jnana,* the knowledge of the unity of all souls and of the world in Brahma; Islam, which had given him his early iconoclastic zeal, he considered as strongest in the sense of divine government, and a militant of man with man; and Christianity, which gave him the Divine Exemplar, he considered as strongest in the ethical and social guidance to peace and happiness in the path of life.'[3]

Roy's theological and religious studies did not convert him to a new religion, but only made him cosmopolitan and universal in outlook. He was 'no more chained to orthodox Christianity than to orthodox Hinduism, although he believed that he had discovered its real meaning. He remained an independent theist, essentially a rationalist and moralist. He extracted from Christianity its ethical system, but he rejected the divinity of Christ just as he rejected Hindu incarnations. As a passionate unitarian he attacked the trinity no less than polytheism; hence both Brahmins and missionaries were united in enmity against him.'[4] As all the established religious institutions were closed to him, he had to found one of his own to preach his ideas. The first one he created was the *Atmiya Sabha* started in 1815, and the second, and most important one, was the Brahmo Samaj, which came into being in 1828.

Rammohun and the organisations he founded made a direct attack on many aspects of orthodox Hinduism. Some of his early undertakings in this field were the publication of a Bengali translation of some of the source literature of Hinduism and his studies on the Upanishads and Vedanta (1815-1819). Since then the sacred books of the Hindus have ceased to be a secret preserve of a priestly class.

The contents of his religious writings were no less significant. He called his countrymen to discard idolatry and to come to the worship of one true God. He wrote: 'My constant reflections on the inconvenient or, rather, injurious rites introduced by the peculiar practice of Hindu idolatry, which, more than any other pagan-worship destroys the texture of society, together with compassion for my countrymen, have compelled me to use every possible effort to awaken them from their dream of error; and by making them acquainted with their scriptures, enable them to contemplate, with true devotion, the unity and omnipresence of nature's God.'[5] He was naturally vigorously criticised by Hindu Pandits of Madras and elsewhere. In 1817 he published the tract *A Defence of Hindu Theism in Reply to the Attack of an Advocate for Idolatry at Madras.*

Rammohun also did not believe in transmigration of souls and the incarnation of God appearing on earth.

As noted earlier in the discussion on social reforms, Rammohun questioned the religious sanction for the practice of *sati*. He opposed child marriage, stood for the remarriage of widows and for the equal rights of man and woman. While championing all these causes, he maintained that neither Hindu religion nor the ancient history of the country justified the continuation of these social evils.

Rammohun was also opposed to hereditary priesthood and the caste system. He considered the caste system undemocratic, inhuman and anti-national. Under the his guidance the Brahmo Samaj spread these views and its members tried to practise them.

INNOVATIONS IN LITERATURE AND ASSOCIATIONS

Apart from the content of Rammohun Roy's demand for social and religious reforms, his activities indicated that he was making innovations in the nature of conducting an agitation. We have already referred to his attempt to translate the sacred books of the Hindus into vernacular languages, and thus breaking the monopoly of knowledge which the priests and other leisured people had in this field. The importance of his book, entitled *Tuhfat-ul-Muwahhidin*, or a gift to Monotheists, published in 1803 lay not so much in its substance—the ideas he advocated had been preached earlier by other Indian religious leaders like Nanak, Dadu and Kabir—but in the highly original method of reasoning adopted in it. He did not appeal to mysticism or revelation, but with reason and logic tried to demolish the dogmatic structure of religious tradition. The series of pamphlets and books he wrote on social and religious questions in vernacular opened a new way taken up later by others. The priests and the orthodox reacted to this by their own publications and writings in which they criticised Rammohun's interpretation of the sacred books. Further controversy was created when Rammohun published another tract in reply. All these were healthy and new developments in that they introduced the concept of discussion in public, through the means of published writings in a field such as religion.

Then the establishment of organisations like the Atmiya Sabha in 1815, the Mibarian Committee in 1821 and later the Brahmo Samaj introduced the concept of forming associations for religious and social purposes; which was later extended to other fields of activity.

Rammohun Roy, will also be remembered as a maker of modern Bengali prose. The simplicity and directness of his style stood in glaring contrast to that of orthodox scholars and the popularisation of such a style of writing was another step towards democracy.

The next important leader of the Brahmo Samaj was Debendranath Tagore (1817-1905) who openly discarded Vedic infallibility. Under his leadership Brahmaism became a powerful force in favour of economic, social and educational reforms.

DEMAND FOR RADICAL REFORMS

Even when Debendranath Tagore was leading the movement, another dynamic leader who attracted much attention in the Brahmo Samaj was Keshab Chandra Sen (1838-84). During 1850 and 1859 the Samaj was also undergoing some rapid changes. 'When the doctrine of scriptural infallibility was renounced, the younger members of the Samaj tried to broaden the basis of Brahmaism by advocating new social ideals and attempted to critically examine even the fundamental articles of religious faith.'

Keshab Chandra Sen became a symbol and a leader of these new trends in the Samaj. Debendranath was a moderate in matters of social reforms. The younger elements in the Samaj, under the leadership of Keshab Chandra Sen, demanded that the Brahmas must reject the sacred thread and that the custom of allowing only the thread-bearing Brahmin ministers to officiate in the pulpit of the Samaj should be discontinued. They also enthusiastically welcomed the marriage between persons of different castes. Debendranath was unhappy about the quick tempo of these changes and particularly about the encouragement given to the remarriage of the widows. This led to a schism between the orthodox wing of the Brahmo Samaj led by Debendranath and the radical wing led by Keshab Chandra Sen. In 1868, the latter with his followers, broke away from the *Adi* (the first) Brahmo Samaj and founded the Bharatiya Brahmo Samaj.

The new organisation was an active body, and under Keshab's leadership it further spread the ideas of toleration and catholicity. Keshab preached the unity of man. 'While Rammohun's theism was more distinctively Christian, and Debendranath Tagore's more exclusively Hindu, that of Keshab Chandra Sen aimed at comprehensiveness...,... The future Church, he said, was to harmonise prevailing systems of worship, and "the purer elements of the leading creeds of the day, he developed and shaped under the influence of Christianity".[6]

In the field of social reforms also he was very active. Against the violent opposition of orthodox Hindus, the Brahmos, under Keshab's leadership, succeeded in getting the Legislative Council pass a new Marriage Act, legalising Brahma and civil marriages.

In 1870, Keshab also organised the Indian Reform Association with the objectives of providing cheap literature and charity to those who needed them, improving the status of women and spreading education and temperance.

Important as these achievements are, Keshab's unique contribution to modern India was the foundation of an all India Brahmaism. Under his leadership the movement broke provincial bounds and became a national force and a meeting-ground for the new educated middle-class from different parts of India, who subsequently gave the leadership to the political movement of the country.

THEORY AND PRACTICE OF SOCIAL REFORMS

Keshab was not able to maintain his supremacy over all the members of the Brahmo Samaj for long. As a result of the Hindu revivalist and other movements, to which we shall refer later, the hold of the movement upon the younger generation began to decline from the eighteen-seventies. In the same period, Keshab, once the champion of vigorous social reforms, freedom and rationalism, started moving in an opposite direction. Within the Samaj, he became a despot and autocrat. He spread the concept of the *avatar* (incarnation of God) and allowed his followers to roll down at his feet and dance in ecstacy around him. All this gave rise to discontent among the radical sections of the Brahmos who felt that Keshab had deserted them both in his precepts and practices. From 1871 they showed some signs of rebellion against his leadership. The final breach came in 1878 when Keshab's daughter, who was not yet 14 years of age, was married to the Maharaja of Cooch Behar, who was a boy of 15, in accordance with the orthodox Hindu rites. Those who thought that Keshab had violated the principles of Brahmoism left the Samaj and organised another organisation named the Sadharan Brahmo Samaj. Their views were reflected in the following comment in the *Brahma Public Opinion:* 'Are there indeed they who in 1866 fought for a constitution, but who in 1878 baffled every honest effort to bring about a constitution? Are there indeed they who in 1866 eloquently cried down despotism in the Calcutta Samaj but in 1878 support that despotism? Are there indeed they who, while members of the Calcutta Samaj, objected to persons who, notwithstanding that they wore holy thread, a symbol of idolatry, were Brahmos in their conviction to officiate at the marriage ceremony of Baboo Debendranath Tagore's daughter, but who in 1878 as minister and missionaries of the Brahmo Samaj of India, permitted persons wearing the very symbol of idolatry, and who were orthodox Hindus by profession and practice, to officiate at the marriage ceremony of the minister's daughter? Are there indeed they who in 1866 fought for the liberty of conscience, but who call in the aid of police that they may successfully do so? If indeed they are those identical persons, we feel disposed to exclaim with Milton, "Oh how altered! how fallen!".'[7]

This gap between the theory and practice of Brahmo Samajists focusses attention on the obstacles in the way of implementing social reforms of a radical nature in India of the nineteenth century. Those who wanted unconditional application of European ideas to India forgot the hold of the traditions on the people and ignored the difficulties of introducing radical reforms when there were no rapid economic changes which created a change of social patterns. As we noted, some of them had to eat their own words when it came to their own private lives. Others who acted boldly got divorced from the masses of the people and became ineffective in the matter of persuading others to follow them. It is significant that the refusal of the Brahmo Samaj to move away completely from Indian traditions was one of the sources of its strength.

BRAHMO SAMAJ AND INDIAN TRADITIONS

Even when many educated Indians realised that the social systems of the Hindus should be rejected, they did not embrace Christianity. 'Men of the type of Rammohun Roy could not, and did not, shut their eyes to the superiority of Christianity from the ethical point of view. They despised in their hearts the idols, as worshipped by the vulgar; they saw through the pretensions of their priests and had long learnt to doubt the efficacies of their sacrifices. But their social institutions were so intimately interwoven with their religion that it required no small amount of moral courage openly to break with it, and to lose caste, that is, to become estranged from all relations, friends and acquaintances. But while they clearly perceived that their religion was behind the time, and, as a social institution, could not stand long against Christianity, they were by no means inclined to admit that from a philosophical point of view it was inferior to Christianity. Then was the time when Christianity might have stepped forth in its strong armour and gained its greatest victories in India....... Then was the time to act, but there was no Christian ambassador to grasp the hands that were stretched out. Such missionaries as were in India then, wanted unconditional surrender and submission, not union or reconciliation. In many cases they were themselves fettered by superstitions which men of the type of Rammohun Roy had long discarded.'[8]

Raja Rammohun's attitude towards Christianity was: 'I feel persuaded that by separating from the other matters contained in the New Testament, the moral precepts found in that book, they will be more likely to produce the desirable effect of improving the hearts and minds of men of different persuasions and degrees of understanding. For historical and some other passages are liable to the doubts and disputes of free-thinkers and anti-Christians, especially miraculous relations, which are not much less wonderful than the fabricated tales handed down to the natives of Asia, and consequently would be apt, at least, to carry little weight with them. On the contrary, moral doctrines, tending evidently to the maintenance of the peace and harmony of mankind at large, are beyond the reach of metaphysical perversion, and intelligible alike to the learned and the unlearned.'[9]

But this separation between the 'essentials' and 'non-essentials' of the religion of Jesus was not acceptable to missionaries and they attacked Rammohun for his 'heathen' interpretation of, and meddling with, the Christian religion as the orthodox Hindu Pandits did for his unorthodox interpretation of Hinduism.

While this was the reaction of the Christian missionaries to Rammohun's interpretation of Christianity, their attacks against Hinduism continued unabated. But this, in its turn, antagonised the Indian leaders who began to point out the proud achievements of their ancestors. This was the beginning of the assertion of strong, national sentiments in the country. Replying to the arguments of a 'Christian', Raja Rammohun Roy himself wrote: 'If by the 'ray of intelligence' for which the 'Christian' says we are indebted to the English, he means the introduction of useful mechanical arts I am ready to express my assent and also my gratitude; but with respect to science, literature or religion, I do not think that we are placed under any obligation. For by a reference to History, it may be proved that the world was indebted to our ancestors for the first dawn of knowledge... Before the

'Christian' indulged in a tirade about persons being 'degraded by Asiatic inefficiency' he should have recollected that almost all the ancient prophets and patriarchs venerated by Christians, nay even Jesus Christ himself, a divine incarnation and the founder of the Christian faith, were Asiatics.'[10]

Keshab Chandra Sen, whose devotion to Jesus was much more intense than that of Rammohun, considered that. India, in her fallen condition, was destined to sit at the feet of England for many long years, to learn Western art and science. But it is significant that he also felt that India had a reciprocal contribution to make to England. He said: 'England sits at the feet of hoary-headed India to study the ancient literature of this country. All Europe seems to be turning her attention in these days towards Indian antiquities, to gather the priceless treasures which lie buried in the literature of Vedism and Buddhism. Thus while we learn modern science from England, England learns ancient wisdom from India.'[11]

Referring to the impression Keshab Chandra Sen made on the young minds, B.C. Pal writes: 'By his victories over the Christian missionaries, Keshab's countrymen even outside his church and community, felt a genuine pride, which powerfully fed their national conceit. Keshab's English visit and the way he was lionised by the British public and the British press, also reacted very powerfully upon the mind of his people in India. The old paralysing sense of superiority of their new political masters over them was visibly replaced by a new self confidence in our educated countrymen.'[12]

IDEOLOGICAL STRENGTH AND ORGANISATIONAL WEAKNESS

Although there were a few such cases of the Brahmo Samaj and its leaders making the Hindus proud of their traditions, their general approach and total work gave the impression that they were inspired by alien ideologies. The history of the Brahmo Samaj was symbolic of the idiological advance and organisational weakness of a few devoted people who were called upon to popularise ideas which were much ahead of the times. The third schism proved disastrous to the Brahmo Samaj which had never taken deep roots in the country. On an institutional level, the Brahmo Samaj was not a big force when the Indian National Congress began to function. In 1884 there were 173 Samajas, with some 1500 enrolled members and 8,000 adherents throughout the country. In the realm of ideas, however, the contribution of the Brahmo Samaj was much more important than what these figures suggest. It was the first important intellectual movement, which spread the ideas of rationalism and enlightenment in modern India. By taking a cosmopolitan and universal approach towards religious questions, it facilitated the introduction of Western political doctrines into the country. By rejecting dogmas it promoted the spirit of toleration. Its attack on hereditary priesthood, and Raja Rammohun Roy's translation of the sacred books from Sanskrit into a popular language bridged the gulf between the 'learned' few and the rest of the people. This indirectly helped the growth of the democratic spirit. The organisations Rammohun founded and the discussions they organised, introduced into the Indian public life the practice of forming associations and holding debates. In the political field, where they found their most concrete expression, this was a healthy development. It is not an accident that many of the early leaders of the Congress were members of the Brahmo Samaj. By inaugurating a new era in the religious field, the Samaj and its founder Raja Rammohun Roy, laid the foundations of a new political movement in India. The Prarthana Samaj founded in 1867 was often referred to as the Brahmo Samaj of the Bombay Presidency, because it stood for similar, if not identical, views. Its founder was Mahadev Govind Ranade, who was an important leader of the Social Reform Conference in Bombay. The Prarthana Samaj took great interest in the abandonment of the caste, the introduction of widow-remarriage, the encouragement of female education and the abolition of child-marriage. In the religious sphere the members of the Prarthana Samaj were theists and opposed to idolatry. But unlike the Brahmo Samaj, the Prarthana Samaj did not make the rigid loyalty to the exclusion of idolatry and the abandonment of caste a condition of its membership. Its members stood nearer to Hinduism and the Hindu community than the Brahmo Samaj.

OTHER MOVEMENTS FOR REFORM

While the Brahmo Samaj suffered from the fact that many ideas which it propounded were ahead of the times in India, other religious organisations, with less ambitious objectives, succeeded in winning large numbers of people for reforms. The Arya Samaj and the Ramakrishna Mission were striking examples of this. They made greater concessions to Indian traditions than the Brahmo Samaj had done, and were thus in a better position to attract people. But their attempts to bring about social changes were also less radical than those of the Brahmo Samaj, and they did not succeed in introducing any far-reaching changes in many of the social institutions of the Hindus. This aspect of these movements will be discussed in a later chapter. Here we are concerned with those aspects of the Arya Samaj and the Ramakrishna Mission which were departures from traditions and were conducive to the spirit of reform and reconstruction.

ARYA SAMAJ AND THE SOCIAL RECONSTRUCTION ON MODERN LINES

The Arya Samaj, which was founded in Bombay in 1875 and reorganised at Lahore the same year, was often associated with the revivalist, if not reactionary trends in religious reform movements of the country. Although it had this aspect, it cannot be forgotten that in some fields it continued the work of social reconstruction on the basis of modern ideas. Dayanand Saraswati (1824-1883), its founder, was often considered a revolutionary by the orthodox Hindus and attacked as such. He taught the worship of one resplendent, formless God and firmly rejected polytheism. He vigorously criticised idolatry not only as an error, but as positively sinful. He fought against the caste system in the form in which it existed then. The Arya Samajists, under his leadership, questioned the superiority of the hereditary priests who wore sacred threads and maintained the right of every individual to study the sacred scriptures. They also tried to raise the status of the lower caste Hindus by educating them and improving their conditions of life. 'To ensure lasting success for his (Dayanand's) crusade, it was necessary that the restrictions imposed by the ecclesiastical system on the study on the Hindu scriptures—the Vedas—should be removed, and the huge mass of literature, the growth of centuries, which had accumulated as a natural consequence of the system, should be divested of all authority, excepting in so far as it followed the revealed literature. The Brahmins had clothed with divine authority everything written or composed by them; Dayanand exposed the trick and lifted the veil. He called upon all people, regardless of caste and creed, to study the Vedas and he conceded to every human being the right of interpreting the Vedas for himself, provided he gave them their etymological and philosophical meanings and conformed to the ancient and approved canons of understanding and interpreting them. This was verily a revolution which, by a single stroke, broke the shackles which Hindus had worn for centuries.'[13] Dayanand's view of the caste was that it was a political institution made by the rulers at one time for the common good of the society and that it was not a natural and religious institution.

The Arya Samajists also tried to raise the status of women. Before the Samaj became an active body very few women in the Punjab received modern education. Apart from the prejudice against the education of women, the evil institution of child marriage also prevented it. The Arya Samaj was opposed to child marriage. Some of its spokesmen also appealed to the ancient Hindu ideals of womanhood and to the teachings of the ancient Hindu religion to show that there should be complete equality between the sexes. The Arya Samajists helped to raise the status of women by spreading education among them.

The Arya Samaj did very useful work in spreading education among all sections of the people. In the statement relating to the objectives of the Dayanand College, founded by the Arya Samaj, it was stated: 'The reaction towards a national education is asserting itself everywhere, and the demand for the study of national literature is growing... Influenced by these important considerations we propose to establish an educational institution which will supply the shortcomings of the existing systems, and combine their advantages. The primary object will, therefore, be to weld together the educated and the uneducated classes by encouraging the study of national language and vernaculars; to spread a knowledge or moral and spiritual truths by insisting on the study of classical Sanskrit; to assist the formation of sound and energetic habits by a regulated mode of living; to encourage sound acquaintance with English literature; and to afford a stimulus to the material progress of the country by spreading a knowledge of the physical and applied sciences.'[14]

Educational work of considerable importance was undertaken both by the Arya Samaj as a body and by many of its members in their individual capacity. Although one of the proclaimed aims of the institutions they managed was to spread ancient Hindu ideals, *their major function, in actual practice, was the spread of Western humanitarian culture and technical skill.*

Compared to the ideological basis of the Brahmo Samaj and the Prarthana Samaj, that of the Arya Samaj was definitely less advanced and modern. But it was in a position to influence a larger number of people than the other two Samajas through its numerically larger membership and the institutions it controlled. In 1911, it had 243,000 members which was six times larger than in 1891.

PROGRESSIVE FEATURES OF RAMAKRISHNA MISSION AND SWAMI VIVEKANANDA'S TEACHINGS

Like the Arya Samaj, the Ramakrishna Mission, the religious movement connected with Ramakrishna (1836-1886), and his disciple Vivekananda (1863-1902), is also often referred to as revivalist in character. However, its progressive features are unmistakable both in the religious and social fields. Although the Ramakrishna Mission was based on ancient Hindu heritage, it was far from being narrow and sectarian in outlook. It preached the unity of all religions. Addressing the Parliament of Religions held at Chicago in 1893 Swami Vivekananda said: 'The present convention, which is one of the most august assemblies ever held, is in itself a vindication, a declaration to the world of the wonderful doctrine preached into the Gita: "Whosoever comes to Me, through whatsoever form, I reach him; all men are struggling through paths which in the end lead to me." Sectarianism, bigotry and its horrible descendent, fanaticism, have long possessed this beautiful earth. They have filled the earth with violence, drenched it often and often with human blood, destroyed civilisation and sent whole nations to despair. Had it not been for these horrible demons, human society would be far more advanced than it is now. But their time is come; and I fervently hope that the bell that tolled this morning in honour of this convention may be the death-knell to all fanaticism, of all persecutions with the sword or with the pen and of all uncharitable feelings between persons wending their way to the same goal.'[15]

The tolerance towards other religions and catholicity were some of the cardinal principles of the Ramakrishna Mission founded by Swami Vivekananda in honour of his master. It is not an accident that this is the only Hindu mission which has many branches in Western countries with some record of successful work in spreading ancient Hindu ideals on an intellectual plan. Proselytisation is not one of its aims. This is how Vivekananda conceived the objectives of the Ramakrishna Mission: 'The aim of the Association is to preach those truths which Sri Ramakrishna has, for the good of humanity, given out and demonstrated... Hence the spirit of propaganda was established in the doctrine whose essence is "the establishment of fellowship among the followers of different religions, knowing them all to be so many forms only of one undying Eternal Religion".'[16]

With all his pride in ancient Indian traditions, Vivekananda was never unwilling to learn from others. He said: 'Give and take is the law; and if India wants to raise herself once more, it is absolutely necessary that she brings out her treasures and throws them broadcast among the nations of the earth, and in return be ready to receive what others have to give her. Expansion is life, contraction is death.'[17] On another occasion he said: 'My idea is to bring to the door of the meanest, poorest, the noble ideas that the human race has developed both in and out of India and leavc' them to think for themselves.'[18]

Vivekananda gave no blind allegiance to any scriptures as is evident from the following statement: 'Personally, I take as much of the Vedas as agrees with reason. Parts of the Vedas are apparently contradictory.'[19]

The following sayings of Swami Vivekananda indicate how he was aware of the necessity of tackling worldly problems in a realistic manner: 'If you seek your own salvation, you will go to hell. It is the salvation of others that you must seek; and even if you have to go to hell in working for others, that is worth more than to gain heaven by seeking your own salvation.' 'So long as the millions die in hunger and ignorance, I hold every man a traitor who, having been educated at their expense, pays not the least heed to them.' 'So long as even a single dog in my country is without food, my whole religion will be to feed it.' 'Where should you go to seek for God? Are not all the poor, the miserable, the weak, gods? Why not worship them first? Why go to dig a well on the shores of the Ganges? Let these people be your God—think of them, work for them, pray for them incessantly—the Lord will show you the way.'[20]

While these maxims of the Swami gave utterance to his fundamental thought, there are other statements of his which showed how much he was in sympathy with the revolutionary social thought in other parts of the world. A typical one was: 'A time will come when there will be the rising of the Sudra[21] class, with their Sudrahood; that is to say, not like that as at present, when the Sudras are becoming great by acquiring the characteristic qualities of the Vaisya or the Kshatriya; but a time will come, when the Sudras of every country, with their inborn Sudra nature and habit—not becoming in essence Vaisya or Kshatriya, but remaining as Sudras—will gain complete supremacy in every society. The first glow of the dawn of this new power has already begun to break slowly upon the Western world, and the thoughtful are at their wits' end to reflect upon the final issue of this fresh phenomenon. Socialism, Anarchism, Nihilism and other like sects are the vanguard of the social revolution that is to follow.'[22]

All these movements indicate a tendency on the part of Indian leaders to refashion religion and society on new lines. It is significant that these ideas did not emerge in India as a result of the evolution of Indian society, but were received by Indians as a result of Western impact through such agencies as the new administration, education and missionary efforts. This process of receiving ideas, however sound they were, had its weakness. It was not easy to assimilate them in the Indian society without creating some tension and stress. They were evident in some other aspects of these social and religious movements which are discussed in the following chapters.

—*P. Karunakaran*

References

1. Quoted by the Rammohun Roy Centenary Committee in *'The Father of Modern India'*, Rammohun Roy Commemoration Volume (Calcutta 1935), p. 89.
2. *Ibid.*, p. 353.
3. B.N. Seal, *The Universal Man in The Father of Modern India* (Calcutta, 1935), Part II, p. 101.
4. Romain Rolland, *Prophets of the New India* (London, 1930), p. 70.
5. William Theodore de Bary and Others, comp., *Sources of Indian Traditions* (New York, 1958), p. 575.
6. T.E. Slater, *Keshab Chandra Sen and the Brahmo Samaj* (Madras, 1884), p. 69.
7. Editorial in *Brahma Public Opinion* (Calcutta), Vol. I, No. 10, 23rd May, 1878.
8. Max Mueller, *Rammohun to Ramakrishna* (Calcutta, 1952), p. 59.
9. Raja Rammohun Roy, *His Life and Teachings* (Madras, no date), p. 15.
10. Wm Theodore de Bary and others, *Sources of Indian Tradition* (New York, 1958), No. 5, p. 518.
11. *Ibid.*, p. 619.
12. Bipin Chandra Pal, *Story of My Life and Times* (Calcutta, 1932), p. 229.
13. Lajpat Rai, *The Arya Samaj* (London, 1915), p. 73.

14. Quoted by Lajpat Rai, No. 14, pp. 181-183.
15. *The Complete Works of Swami Vivekananda,* Vol. I (Almora. 1932), p. 2,
16. Sarachandra Chakravarthy, ed., *Book of Vivekananda's Dialogues,* p. 483.
17. *The Complete Works of Swami Vivekananda,* Vol. IV, No. 16, pp. 310-311.
18. Quoted by Swami Avyaktananda, *Vivekananda—the Nation Builder* (Patna, 1929), p. 24.
19. *The Complete Works of Swami Vivekananda,* Vol. IV, n. 16, p. 3.
20. Swami Pavitrananda, *A Short Life of Swami Vivekananda* (Almora, 1943), p. 113.
21. On the hierarchy of caste, the Sudras are the lowest representing the menial workers, the *Vaisyas* are the merchants and the *Kshatriyas* the Kings and the warriors.
22. *The Complete Works of Swami Vivekananda,* Vol. IV, No. 16, pp. 401-402.

6

Debendranāth Tagore

THE CONFLICT BETWEEN SANSKRITIC AND WESTERN EDUCATION

Debendranāth tells in his *Autobiography* the story of his search for religious certainty. The following passage relates the way in which he resolved the apparent conflict between the two intellectual traditions in which he was educated.

[From Debendranāth Tagore, *Autobiography,* pp. 9-10]

As on the one hand there were my Sanskrit studies in the search after truth, so on the other hand there was English. I had read numerous English works on philosophy. But with all this, the sense of emptiness of mind remained just the same, nothing could heal it, my heart was being oppressed by that gloom of sadness and feeling of unrest. Did subjection to nature comprise the whole of man's existence? I asked. Then indeed are we undone. The might of this monster is indomitable. Fire, at a touch, reduces everything to ashes. Put out to sea in a vessel, whirlpools will drag you down to the bottom, gales will throw you into dire distress. There is no escape from the clutches of this Nature-fiend. If bowing down to her decree be our end and aim, then indeed are we undone. What can we hope for, whom can we trust? Again I thought, as things are reflected on a photographic plate by the rays of the sun, so are material objects manifested to the mind by the senses, this is what is called knowledge. Is there any other way but this of obtaining knowledge? These were the suggestions that Western philosophy had brought to my mind. To an atheist this is enough, he does not want anything beyond nature. But how could

I rest fully satisfied with this? My endeavour was to obtain God, not through blind faith but by the light of knowledge. And being unsuccessful in this, my mental struggles increased from day to day. Sometimes I thought I could live no longer.

Suddenly, as I thought and thought, a flash as of lightning broke through this darkness of despondency. I saw that knowledge of the material world is born of the senses and the objects of sight, sound, smell, touch, and taste. But together with this knowledge, I am also enabled to know that I am the knower. Simultaneously with the facts of seeing, touching, smelling, and thinking, I also come to know that it is I who see, touch, smell, and think. With the knowledge of objects comes the knowledge of the subject, with the knowledge of the body comes the knowledge of the spirit within. It was after a prolonged search for truth that I found this bit of light, as if a ray of sunshine had fallen on a place full of extreme darkness. I now realised that with the knowledge of the outer world we come to know our inner self. After this, the more I thought over it, the more did I recognize the sway of wisdom operating throughout the whole world. For us the sun and moon rise and set at regular intervals, for us the wind and rain are set in motion in the proper seasons. All these combine to fulfil the one design of preserving our life. Whose design is this? It cannot be the design of matter, it must be the design of mind. Therefore this universe is propelled by the power of an intelligent being.

I saw that the child, as soon as born, drinks at its mother's breast. Who taught it to do this? He alone, who gave it life. Again who put love into the mother's heart? Who but He that put milk into her breast. He is that God who knows all our wants, whose rule the universe obeys. When my mind's eye had opened thus far, the clouds of grief were in a great measure dispelled. I felt somewhat consoled.

One day, while thinking of these things I suddenly recalled how, long ago, in my early youth, I had once realised the Infinite as manifested in the infinite heavens. Again I turned my gaze towards this infinite sky, studded with innumerable stars and planets, and saw the eternal God, and felt that this glory was His. He is infinite wisdom. He from whom we have derived this limited knowledge of ours, and this body, its receptacle, is Himself without form. He is without body or senses. He did not shape this universe with his hands. By His will alone did He bring it into existence. He is neither the Kali[1] or Kalighat,[2] nor the family *Shalgram*.[3] Thus was laid the axe at the root of idolatry.

The Call to Renunciation

Had he followed in his father's footsteps, Debendranāth could have become one of India's wealthiest men. But his innermost desire was to seek salvation through the traditional path of renunciation.

[From Debendranāth Tagore, *Autobiography*, p. 41]

My father was in England. The task of managing his various affairs devolved upon me. But I was not able to attend to any business matters properly. My subordinates used to do all the work, I was only concerned with the Vedas, the Vedanta, religion, God, and the ultimate goal of life. I was not even able to stay quietly in the house. My spirit of renunciation became deeper under all this stress of work. I felt no inclination to become the owner of all this wealth. To renounce everything and wander about alone, this was the desire that reigned in my heart. Imbued with His love I would roam in such lonely places what none would know; I would see His glory on land and water, would witness His mercy in different climes, would feel His protective power in foreign countries, in danger and peril; in this enthusiastic frame of mind I could no longer stay at home.

A Decisive Dream

When his father died, Debendranāth was faced with the choice of performing the customary Hindu funeral rites, in which offerings are made to various gods, or of remaining true to his vow to renounce idolatry. The decision came to him in this dream, whose conclusion gives us a good insight into the Hindu conceptions of religion and filial piety.

[From Debendranāth Tagore, *Autobiography* pp. 48-49]

Which would triumph, the world or religion?—one could not tell—this was what worried me. My constant prayer to God was "Vouchsafe strength unto my weak heart, be Thou my refuge." All these anxieties and troubles would not let me sleep at night, my head felt dazed on the pillow. I would now doze off and again wake up. It was as if I was sleeping on the borderland between waking the sleeping. At such a time some one came to me in the dark and said "Get up," and I at once sat up. He said "Get out of bed" and I got up; he said "follow me" and I followed. He went down the steps leading out of the inner apartments, I did the same and came out into the courtyard with him. We stood before the front door. The durwans[4] were sleeping. My guide touched the door, and the two wings flew open at once. I went out with him into the street infront of the house. He seemed to be a shadowlike form. I could not see him clearly, but felt myself constrained to do immediately whatever he bade me. From thence he mounted up upwards to the sky, I also followed him. Clusters of stars and planets were shedding a bright lustre, right and left and in front of me, and I was passing through them. On the way I entered a sea of mist, where the stars and planets were no longer visible. After traversing the mist for some distance I came upon a still full moon, like a small island in that vaporous ocean. The nearer I came the larger grew that moon. It no longer appeared round, but flat like our earth. The apparition went and stood on that earth, and I did likewise. The ground was all of white marble. Not a single blade of grass was there—no flowers, no fruit. Only that bare white plain stretched all around. The moonlight there was not derived from the sun. It shone by virtue of its own light. The rays of the sun could not penetrate the surrounding mist. Its own light was very soft, like the shade we have in the daytime. The air was pleasing to the senses. In the course of my journey across this plain I entered one of its cities. All the houses and all the streets were of white marble, not a single soul was to be seen in the clean and bright and polished streets. No noise was to be heard, everything was calm and peaceful. My guide entered a house by the road and went up to the second floor, I also went with him. I found myself in a spacious room, in which there were a table and some chairs of white marble. He told me to sit down, and I sat down in one of the chairs. The phantom then vanished. Nobody else was there, I sat silent in that silent room; shortly afterwards the curtain of one of the doors in front of the room was drawn aside and my mother appeared. Her hair was down, just as I had seen it on the day of her death. When she died, I never thought that she was dead. Even when I came back from the burning ground after performing her funeral ceremonies, I could not believe that she was dead. I felt sure that she was still alive. Now I saw that living mother of mine before me. She said "I wanted to see thee, so I sent for thee. Hast thou really become one who has known Brahma? Sanctified is the family, fulfilled is the mother's desire." On seeing her, and hearing these sweet words of hers my slumber gave way before a flood of joy. I found myself still tossing on my bed.

The Brāhmo Samāj and its Relation to Orthodox Hinduism

After Keshab Chandra Sen had seceded from the Samāj, taking the majority of Brāhmos with him, Debendranāth pronounced in 1867 the following message on "gradualism" in matters of social reform.

[From Debendranāth Tagore, *Autobiography,* pp. 152-53].

We are worshippers of Brahma, the Supreme Being. In this we are at one with Orthodox Hinduism, for all our shastras declare with one voice the supremacy of the worship of Brahma, enjoining image worship for the help of those who are incapable of grasping the highest Truth.

Our first point of distinction is in the positive aspect of our creed wherein worship is defined as consisting in "Loving Him and doing the works He loveth"—this at once differentiates us from all religions and creeds which postulate a special or verbal revelation or wherein definite forms, rites, or ceremonials are deemed essential one way or the other.

The negative aspect of our creed which prohibits the worship of any created being or thing as the Creator further distinguishes us from all who are addicted to the worship of avatars or incarnations or who believe in the necessity of mediators, symbols, or idols of any description.

We base our faith on the fundamental truths of religion, attested by reason and conscience and refuse to permit man, book, or image to stand in the way of the direct communion of our soul with the Supreme Spirit.

This message of the Brāhmo Samāj in the abstract does not materially differ from the doctrines of the pure theistic bodies all the world over. Viewed historically and socially, however, the Brāhmo Samāj has the further distinction of being the bearer of this message to the Hindu people. This was the idea of its founder Rammohun Roy, this points to the duty incumbent upon all Brahmos of today, and will serve as the guiding principle in the selection of texts, forms, and ceremonials as aids to the religious life.

We are in and of the great Hindu community and it devolves upon us by example and precept to hold up as a beacon the highest truths of the Hindu shastras. In their light must we purify our heritage of customs, usages, rites, and ceremonies and adapt them to the needs of our conscience and our community. But we must beware of proceeding too fast in maters of social change, lest we be separated from the greater body whom we would guide and uplift.

While we should on no account allow any consideration of country, caste, or kinship to prevent our actions being consistent with our faith, we must make every allowance for, and abstain from, persecuting or alienating those who think differently from us. Why should we needlessly wound the feelings of our parents and elders by desecrating an image which they regard with the highest reverence, when all that our conscience can demand of us is to refrain from its adoration?

The steering of this middle course is by no means an easy task, but during my long experience I have been led greatly to hope for a brighter future by the sympathetic response of our orthodox brethren to the ideal held up before them. The amount of conformity nowadays expected by even the most orthodox, demands so little of us that a little tact and common sense will in most cases be sufficient to obviate all friction.

Nevertheless, great as are the claims of our land and our people, we must never forget that we are Brahmos first, and Indians or Hindus afterwards. We must on no account depart from our vow of renouncing the worship of images and incarnations, which is one of the essence of our religion. It is a sound policy on our part to sink our minor differences, but on matters of principle no compromise is possible. Our Motherland is dear to us, but Religion is dearer, Brahma is dearest of all, dearer than son, dearer than riches, supreme over everything else.

A Farewell Message to His Followers

In 1889, thinking that he was about to die, Debendranāth set down eighteen principles for his followers. Combined in this document we find both the Christian emphasis on brotherly love and the Hindu conception of the relationship between *Ātman* and *Brāhman*. The Sanskrit texts of passages in quotation marks have been omitted.

[From Debendranāth Tagore, *Autobiography*, pp. 191-95.]

Dearly Beloved Brethren

"Be ye united together; speak ye in unity; united know ye each the heart of the other. As the gods of old with one mind received each his offering due, even so be ye of one mind!"

"Harmonious may your efforts be, and harmonious your thoughts and heart, so that beauteous Peace may dwell in your midst!" "Live ye all one in heart and speech." This loving blessing and benediction which I have just expressed in Vedic words, it is meet ye should keep well in view, in the midst of the world's wranglings and jars. If to this end ye follow the way, then shall ye become gainers of your end. This way is the way of unity. If ye follow this way, all contentions shall depart from amongst you. Peace shall reign, and the Brāhmo religion shall have triumph.

1. The Brāhmo religion is a spiritual religion. Its seed-truth is this: By the soul shalt thou know the Supreme Soul. When God is seen in the soul, then, indeed, is He seen everywhere. The dearest dwelling-place of Him who is the root of all this complexity, the One Sovereign of all this universe, is the soul of man. If ye know not the soul, then all is empty. The soul is of the knowledge of God.

2. In this body dwells the soul, and within it, in the pure refulgence of spiritual consciousness, the pure, bodiless Supreme Soul is to be seen. With mind and body subdued, unattached to all outward things, even-minded in sorrow and joy, self-contained, the Supreme Soul is to be viewed. This is spiritual union. When with love ye are united in this spiritual union, ye shall be delivered from all sin and shall attain the steps of salvation. After death, the body will be left here, but, united in this spiritual union, the soul shall dwell with the Soul Supreme for ever.

3. As for the health of the body ye partake of your regular daily meals, so for the soul's health the worship of God must be performed every day. The worship of God is the soul's sustenance.

4. "Loving Him and the doing of deeds pleasant in His sight, this, indeed, is His worship." That Brahma, who is beyond Time and Space, and who yet pervades Time and Space, the Witness of all, Truth Wisdom, and Infinity—knowing Him to be the Soul's Ruler, and the Heart's Lord—adore Him every day with love, and, for the good of the world, be engaged in the performance of works of righteousness which are pleasing in His sight. Never dissever these two ever-united limbs of God's worship.

5. Let only that be done which promoteth well-being. Do no evil to an evil-doer. If any should work unrighteousness, it should not

be requited by unrighteousness. Always be righteous. Evil should be overcome by good, and unrighteousness by righteousness.

6. Contend with no one. Restrain anger; and, imbued with love and charity, behave justly to all. Let love be thy rule of conduct with regard to others.

7. By day and night instruct yourselves—govern yourselves—and accept righteousness as the end of existence. For him who can subdue his heart and senses, there remains no cause for sorrow and suffering. For him who cannot restrain himself there is suffering on every side.

8. He who desireth the good of mankind must look on others as he looks on himself. It behoves thee to love thy neighbour, since it pleases thee to be loved by him, and to avoid giving pain by hatred, since it causes thee pain to be hated by another. Thus in all things shalt thou deal with others by comparing them with thyself; for as pleasure and pain affect thee, so do they affect all creatures. Such conduct alone is the means of attaining well-being.

9. He who adores God and loves man is a saint. Such a man never rejoices in finding fault with men, for man is beloved of him. He is pained by the sight of a fault in others, and lovingly does he labour for its correction. He loves man as man; and owing to that love, is pleased by the sight of good, and grieved by the sight of evil in man. Therefore he is unable to proclaim the faults of others with rejoicing.

10. The satisfaction of the inner spirit, or, in other words, a good conscience, is the unfailing fruit of the practice of righteousness. In this favour of conscience is felt the favour of God. If the inner spirit is satisfied, all sufferings cease. Without the practice of righteousness, the inner spirit is never satisfied. The mind may find enjoyment in the pleasures of the world, but if the conscience is diseased, then even the height of worldly bliss becomes valueless. Therefore, by the practice of righteousness, ye shall preserve a clear conscience, and ye shall abandon all things whereby the satisfaction of the spirit may be marred.

11. Ye shall seek the practice of righteousness to the utmost of your power. If, after the exercise of all your power, ye fail to attain the end, yet ye shall acquire merit thereby. God does not reckon

what portion of His infinite work is performed by individuals. Let every one use the powers given him, without reservation; this is God's ordinance.

12. Ye shall abjure sinful thoughts, sinful speech, and sinful acts. Those who do not sin in thought, word, deed, or judgement—such saints truly practice austerity; not those who mortify the flesh. Therefore, abstaining from sin, engage in good works. Persevering on the road of righteousness, ye shall earn your livelihood.

13. If, by perseverence on the road of righteousness, ye are completely cast down, even then ye shall not turn your thoughts to unrighteous means. Protect dharma with your lives, and dharma will protect you.

14. Not father or mother, nor wife or child, nor friend or relation, remains as our stay in the next world. Righteousness alone remains. Alone a man is born, alone he dies, alone he enjoys the good fruits of his righteous acts, and alone he suffers the evil consequences of his bad deeds. Friends, leaving on the earth his body like a stock or stone, turn away from him; but righteousness follows him whither he goeth. Therefore, ye shall, step by step, acquire righteousness, which shall be your stay.

    Dharma is our friend in this world, and dharma is the guide to the next. "Dharma is as honey unto all creatures."

15. "Not by wealth, nor by children, nor by works, but by renunciation alone, is immortality attained." Renunciation is not the renunciation of the world by becoming an anchorite, dwelling in the wilderness, but dwelling at home, and living in the world, all lusts of the heart should be cast out.

    "When all lusts that dwell in the heart of man are cast out, then the mortal becomes immortal, and even on earth attains God."

16. With all diligence shall ye cherish your wives and children and relations; but, being yourselves free from desire, remain unattached to the fruit of your acts, and then ye shall be able to mount the steps of salvation. God's own love furnishes the most perfect example. See how mindful. He is of the interests of the world. He never forgets to give food even to a single worm or insect. Even in the bowels of arid mountains, He supplies nourishment to living creatures. Yet He keeps nothing for Himself. He is always giving

to all, and never receives. By the light of this example, ye, too, forgetting yourselves, shall be vowed to work for the good of the world. Being united to Him, ye shall perform the duties of life. That which ye shall know to be His command, ye must obey with your lives. That which ye shall know to be against His will, ye shall shun like poison. If thus, forgetful of self, ye perform His work, then be sure He will not forget you, with gratitude receive it as plenty. In whatever condition He may place you, with that be contented. In seasons of prosperity, live in obedience to Him; and, in seasons of adversity, take refuge in Him; and ye shall not be perplexed. At the time of action, act resting in Him; at the time of rest, rest even in Him. This body will move about on earth, but your souls will be united with Him. Even in death there is no dissolution of this union.

17. Blessed is that soul which, self-subdued, freed from sin and impurity like the moon from the shadow of eclipse, and casting off the pride of flesh, can rest in the Supreme Soul. That soul is not cast down by disease, is not frightened by death; it sees from here the abode of God; to it the door of the infinitude of progress is opened, and before it millions on millions of heavens shine forth. On this side is the billowy world of change, on the other side the Peaceful Abode of God; in the middle God Himself, like a bridge, preserves the position of both. Neither day nor night, nor death, disease, or sorrow, nor good or evil deed, is able to cross this bridge. All kinds of sin fall back from there. Sin has no power in the Sinless Abode of Brahma. The liberated soul, leaving behind him the sin and sorrow of this world, attains the Abode of Brahma, beyond this world. There the blind cease to be blind; the sin-stricken become free from sin; for the Abode of Brahma is for ever resplendent; to that splendor there is no end.

18. Following the previous teachings of Brahma-dharma, I make you this offering of my last words. May ye realise it in your lives and attain to everlasting salvation—this is my prayer!

Om—Peace, Peace, Peace.

KESHAB CHANDRA SEN AND THE INDIANISATION OF CHRISTIANITY

The stormy career of Keshab Chandra Sen[5] encompassed both the peak and the later decline of the influence of the Brāhmo Samāj on Indian intellectual life. With his great energy and oratorical skill he brought to fulfillment the openness to Christian inspiration of Rāmmohun Roy and the intuitionist doctrine of Debendranāth Tagore. Yet his very enthusiasm was his undoing, for by the time of his death he had shattered the Samāj into three separate organisations, and damaged its prestige irrevocably.

Keshab's grandfather was a contemporary and friend of Rāmmohun Roy, but did not share the great reformer's ideas on religion. The Sen family was one of the most Westernized in Bengal, and young Keshab grew up speaking English more fluently than Bengali. His career as a student at the Hindu College was marred by his failure in mathematics, but he took great interest in philosophy and ethics. At nineteen his religious spirit found its natural orbit in the Brāhmo Samāj. Within a short time Keshab had become Debendranāth's most beloved disciple. When he was excommunicated by his own family for having taken his wife to a Brāhmo ceremony, Keshab found shelter in the home of his religious teacher.

With unquenchable energy, Keshab threw himself into the activities of the Brāhmo Samāj, founding discussion groups and schools, organizing famine relief, advocating remarriage for widows and education for young women, writing religious tracts, and giving sermons. His fiery oratory in fluent English stirred educated audiences in many parts of India, especially in Bombay, and branches of the Samāj sprang up in cities beyond the borders of Bengal.

Keshab's zeal for social reform carried him far beyond the moderate position taken by Debendranāth. The two finally parted in 1865 over the wearing of the sacred thread and Keshab set up an independent organisation which he named the Brāhmo Samāj of India. From this point on, his faith in inspiration as the guide to action grew more pronounced. In 1878 another and more fatal fission took place within his own movement. Despite his prolonged advocacy of a minimum age for Brāhmo marriages, and his opposition to idolatry, he was persuaded to marry his thirteen-year-old daughter to a Hindu prince, feeling that such was the will of God. Scandalized by this betrayal of his previous principles, most of his followers abandoned him and set up a third group, the Sādhāran (General) Brāhmo Samāj.

In the last years of his life Keshab experimented in synthesizing elements from the world's major religions. Although he borrowed devotional and yogic practices from Hinduism, he drew even more heavily on Christian teachings and practices. The New Dispensation which he proclaimed in 1879 appropriated much from the Christian church which it claimed to supplant, including among other things a direct revelation from God, apostles, missionaries, monastic orders, and the doctrines of sin, salvation, and the divinity of Christ.

Of Keshab's work little remained after his death in 1884 at the age of forty-one. The flaming enthusiasm which had launched him on so many enterprises, and the eloquent oratory which electrified so many audiences, left surprisingly few monuments. But the force of his example was felt in Bengal for decades, and his methods—particularly his oratorical conquests and his synthesizing of Indian and Western ideas—have been imitated by later religious leaders and nationalist politicians alike.

KESHAB CHANDRA SEN

Enthusiasm

Two years before his death Keshab penetratingly summed up his nature and the activities into which it had plunged him.

[From Mozoomdar, *Life and Teachings of Keshab Chandra Sen,* pp. 15-16].

If I ask thee, O Self, in what creed wast thou baptised in early life? The self answers in the baptism of fire. I am a worshipper of the religion of fire, I am partial to the doctrine of enthusiasm. To me a state of being on fire is the state of salvation. My heart palpitates as soon as I perceive any coldness in my life. When the body becomes cold, it is death, when religion becomes cold, it is death also. It may take time to know whether I am a sinner or not, but it is easy to know whether I am alive or dead; I at once decide this by finding whether I am warm or cold. I live in the midst of fire, I love, embrace, and exalt fire. Every sign of heat fills me with joy, hope, zeal. As soon as I feel the fire is losing its heat, I feel as if I would jump into the sea and drown myself. When I find that a man after five years of enthusiasm is getting to be lukewarm, I at once conclude he is on the highway of a sinful life, that before long death will tread on his neck. I have always felt a cold condition to be a state of impurity. Coldness and hell have always been the same to my mind. Around my own life, around the society in which I lived, I always kept burning the flame of enthusiasm. When I succeeded in serving one body of men, I always sought another body whom I might serve. When I successfully worked in one department of life, I always sighed to work in other departments also. When I gathered truths from one set of scriptures, I have longed for others, and before finishing these I have looked out for others again, lest anything should become old or cold to me. This is my life that I am continually after new ideas, new acquirements, new enjoyments.

Loyalty to the British Nation

Keshab was only voicing the sentiments of his time when he declared British rule providential for India. His conviction that India had a reciprocal contribution to make to England was a relatively new idea, and one which was to take on increasing importance in the nationalist era. This speech was delivered in Calcutta in 1877, shortly after Queen Victoria had assumed the title of Empress of India.

[From "Philosophy and Madness in Religion," in *Keshab Chandra Sen's Lectures in India*, pp. 322-26].

Loyalty shuns an impersonal abstraction. It demands a person, and that person is the sovereign, or the head of the state, in whom law and constitutionalism are visibly typified and represented. We are right then if our loyalty means not only respect for law and the Parliament, but personal attachment to Victoria, Queen of England and Empress of India. [Applause.] What makes loyalty so enthusiastic is not, however, the presence of purely secular feelings, but of a strong religious sentiment. By loyalty I mean faith in Providence. It is this faith which gives loyalty all its sanctity and solidity, and establishes it in the individual heart and in society as a holy passion. Do you not believe that there is God in history? Do you not recognise the finger of special providence in the progress of nations? Assuredly the record of British rule in India is not a chapter of profane history, but of ecclesiastical history. [Cheers.] The book which treats of the moral, social, and religious advancement of our great country with the help of Western science, under the paternal rule of the British nation, is indeed a sacred book. There we see clearly that it is Providence that rules India through England. [Applause.] Were you present at the magnificent spectacle at Delhi, on the day of the assumption of the imperial title by our sovereign? Some men have complained that no religious ceremony was observed on the occasion, and indeed opinion is divided on this point. None, however, can gainsay the fact that the whole affair, from beginning to end was a most solemn religious ceremony, and I rejoice I am privileged to say this in the presence of our noble-hearted Viceroy. Was any devout believer in Providence there? To him I appeal. Let him say whether the imperial assemblage was not a spectacle of deep moral and religious significance. Did not the eye of the faithful believer see that God Himself stretched His right hand and placed the Empress' crown upon Victoria's head? [Loud cheers.] And did he not hear the Lord God say unto her: "Rule thy subjects with justice and truth and mercy, according to the light given unto thee and thy advisers, and let righteousness and peace and prosperity dwell in the Empire"? [Applause.]

Would you characterise this sight and this sound as a visionary dream? Is there no truth in the picture? Who can deny that Victoria is an instrument in the hands of Providence to elevate this degraded country in the scale of nations, and that in her hands the solemn trust has lately been most solemnly reposed? Glory then to Empress Victoria! [Applause.] Educated countrymen, you are bound to be loyal to your Divinely appointed sovereign. Not to be loyal argues base ingratitude and absence of faith in Providence. You are bound to be loyal to the British government, that came to your rescue, as God's ambassador, when your country was sunk in ignorance and superstition and hopeless jejuneness, and has since lifted you to your present high position. This work is not of man, but of God, and He has done it, and is doing it, through the British nation. As His chosen instruments, then, honour your sovereign and the entire ruling body with fervent loyalty. The more loyal we are, the more we shall advance with the aid of our rulers in the path of moral, social, and political reformation. India in her present fallen condition seems destined to sit at the feet of England for many long years, to learn Western art and science. And, on the other hand, behold England sits at the feet of hoary-headed India to study the ancient literature of this country. [Applause.] All Europe seems to be turning her attention in these days towards Indian antiquities, to gather the priceless treasures which lie buried in the literature of Vedism and Buddhism. Thus while we learn modern science from England, England learns ancient wisdom from India. Gentlemen, in the advent of the English nation in India we see a reunion of parted cousins, the descendants of two different families of the ancient Aryan race. Here they have met together, under an overruling

Providence, to serve most important purposes in the Divine economy. The mutual intercourse between England and India, political as well as social, is destined to promote the true interests and lasting glory of both nations. We were rejoiced to see the rajahs and maharajahs of India offering their united homage to Empress Victoria and her representative at the imperial assemblage. Far greater will be our rejoicing when all the chiefs and people of India shall be united with the English nation, in a vast international assemblage, before the throne of the King of Kings and the Lord of Lords! [Loud cheers.] May England help us to draw near to that consummation, by giving us as much of the light of the West as lies in her power! That is her mission in India. May she fulfil it nobly and honourably. Let England give us her industry and arts, her exact sciences and her practical philosophy, so much needed in a land where superstition and prejudices prevail to an alarming extent. But we shall not forget our ancient sages and Rishis. Ye venerable devotees of ancient India! teach us meditation and asceticism and loving communion. Let England baptize us with the spirit of true philosophy. Let the sages of Aryan India baptize us with the spirit of heavenly madness. Let modern England teach hard science and fact; let ancient India teach sweet poetry and sentiment. Let modern England give us her fabrics; but let the gorgeous East lend her charming colours. Come then, fellow countrymen and friends, and accept this divine creed, in which you will find all that is goodliest, fairest, and sweetest, based upon a foundation scientific, strong and sound—a creed in which truth and love are harmonised. Let us have only fifty young men from our universities, trained in science and philosophy, and baptised with the spirit of madness, and let these men go forth as missionary-soldiers of God, conquering and to conquer, and in the fullness of time the banners of truth shall be planted throughout the length and breadth of the country. [Loud cheers.]

The Asiatic Christ

Whereas Rāmmohun Roy welcomed only the moral influence of Jesus, Keshab embraced Christ as the fulfillment of India's devotional striving. He also took Roy's assertion that Jesus was an Asian by birth and used it as an argument for better understanding between the rulers and the ruled in India.

[From "Jesus Christ: Europe and Asia," in *Keshab Chandra Sen's Lectures in India,* pp. 33-34]

Europeans and natives are both the children of God, and the ties of brotherhood should bind them together. Extend, then, to us, O ye Europeans in India! the right hand of fellowship, to which we are fairly entitled. If, however, our Christian friends persist introducing our nationality and national character, and in distrusting and hating Orientalism, let me assure them that I do not in the least feel dishonoured by such imputations. On the contrary, I rejoice, yea, I am proud, that I am an Asiatic. And was not Jesus Christ an Asiatic? [Deafening applause.] Yes, and his disciples were Asiatics, and all the agencies primarily employed for the propagation of the Gospel were Asiatic. In fact, Christianity was founded and developed by Asiatics, and in Asia.

When I reflect on this, my love for Jesus becomes a hundredfold intensified; I feel him nearer my heart, and deeper in my national sympathies. Why should I then feel ashamed to acknowledge that nationality which he acknowledged? Shall I not rather say he is more congenial and akin to my Oriental nature, more agreeable to my Oriental habits of thought and feeling? And is it not true that an Asiatic can read the imageries and allegories of the Gospel, and its descriptions of natural sceneries, of customs, and manners, with greater interest, and a fuller perception of their force and beauty, than Europeans? [Cheers.] In Christ we see not only the exaltedness of humanity, but also the grandeur of which Asiatic nature is susceptible. To us Asiatics, therefore, Christ is doubly interesting, and his religion is entitled to our peculiar regard as an altogether Oriental affair. The more this great fact is pondered, the less I hope will be the antipathy and hatred of European Christians against Oriental nationalities, and the greater the interest of the Asiatics in the teachings of Christ. And thus in Christ, Europe and Asia, the East and the West, may learn to find harmony and unity. [Deafening applause.]

An Indian National Church

With characteristic enthusiasm, Keshab saw in the simple theism of the Brāhmo Samāj a platform on which the major religious traditions of India—Hindu, Muslim, Christian—could unite. The resulting faith, he thought, would sustain not only the future church of India, but would qualify India to take part in a world-wide religious brotherhood. Keshab's expectation that Hindus and Muslims would willingly merge into this national church is but one more example of his supreme optimism.

[From "The Future Church," in *Keshab Chandra Sen's Lectures in India*, pp. 155-60]

I have briefly described the general features of the church of the future—its worship, creed, and gospel. Before I conclude I must say a few words with special reference to this country. There are some among us who denounce Mahomedanism as wholly false, while others contend that Hinduism is altogether false. Such opinions are far from being correct; they only indicate the spirit of sectarian antipathy. Do you think that millions of men would to this day attach themselves so devotedly to these systems of faith unless there was something really valuable and true in them? This cannot be. There is, no doubt, in each of these creeds, much to excite to ridicule, and perhaps indignation—a large amount of superstition, prejudice, and even corruption. But I must emphatically say it is wrong to set down Hinduism or Mahomedanism as nothing but a mass of lies and abominations, and worthy of being trampled under foot. Proscribe and eliminate all that is false therein: there remains a residue of truth and purity which you are bound to honour. You will find certain central truths in these systems, though surrounded by errors, which constitute their vitality, and which have preserved them for centuries in spite of opposition, and in which hundreds of good men have always found the bread of life. It is these which form even now the mighty pillars of Hinduism and Mahomedanism, and challenge universal admiration and respect. It is idle to suppose that such gigantic systems of faith will be swept away by the fervour of youthful excitement, or the violent fulminations of sectarian bigotry, so long as there is real power in them. All the onslaughts which are being levelled against them in this age of free inquiry and bold criticism will tend, not to destroy them, but to purify them and develop their true principles. The signs of the times already indicate this process of purification and development; and I believe this process will gradually bring Hinduism and Mahomedanism, hitherto so hostile to each other, into closer union, till the two ultimately harmonise to form the future church of India.

The Hindu's notion of God is sublime. In the earliest Hindu scriptures God is represented as the Infinite Spirit dwelling in His own glory, and pervading all space, full of peace and joy. On the other hand, the Mahomedans describe their God as infinite in power, governing the universe with supreme authority as the Lord of all. Hence the principal feature of the religion of the Hindu is quiet contemplation, while that of the religion of the Mahomedan is constant excitement and active service. The one lives in a state of quiet communion with his God of peace; the other lives as a soldier, ever serving the Almighty Ruler, and crusading against evil. These are the primary and essential elements of the two creeds, and, if blended together, would form a beautiful picture of true theology, which will be realised in the future church of this country. As the two creeds undergo development, their errors and differences will disappear, and they will harmoniously coalesce in their fundamental and vital principles. The future creed of India will be a composite faith, resulting from the union of the true and divine elements of Hinduism and Mahomedanism, and showing the profound devotion of the one and the heroic enthusiasm of the other. The future sons and daughters of this vast country will thus inherit precious legacies from Hinduism and Mahomedanism, and, while enjoying the blessings of the highest and sweetest communion with the God of love, will serve Him in the battlefield of life with fidelity to truth and unyielding opposition to untruth and sin. As regards Christianity and its relation to the future church of India, I have no doubt in my mind that it will exercise great influence on the growth and formation of that church. The spirit of Christianity has already pervaded the whole atmosphere of Indian society, and we breathe, think, feel, and move in a Christian atmosphere. Native society is being roused, enlightened, and reformed under the influence of Christian education. If it is true that the future of a nation is determined by all the circumstances and agencies which today influence its nascent growth, surely the future church of this country will be the result of the purer elements of the leading creeds of the day, harmonised, developed, and shaped under the influence of Christianity.

But the future church of India must be thoroughly national; it must be an essentially Indian church. The future religion of the world I have described will be the common religion of all nations, but in each nation it will have an indigenous growth, and assume a distinctive and peculiar character. All mankind will unite in a universal church; at the same time, it will be adapted to the peculiar circumstances of each nation, and assume a national form. No country will borrow or mechanically imitate the religion of another country; but from the depths of the life of each nation its future church will naturally grow up. And shall not India have its own national church? Dr. Norman McLeod, in expounding last year, in this very hall, his ideas of the future church of this country, said emphatically that it would be a purely Indian church, and not a reproduction of any of the established churches of the West. Though I differ from that learned and liberal-minded gentleman in regard to the doctrines and tenets of that church as set forth by him, I fully agree with him that that church must have a strictly national growth and a national organisation. Neither will Germany adopt the religious life of China, nor will India accept blindly that of England or of any other European country. India has religious traditions and associations, tastes and customs, peculiarly sacred and dear to her, just as every other country has, and it is idle to expect that she will forego these; nay, she cannot do so, as they are interwoven with her very life. In common with all other nations and communities, we shall embrace the theistic worship, creed, and gospel of the future church—we shall acknowledge and adore the Holy One, accept the love and service of God and man as our creed, and put our firm faith in God's almighty grace as the only means of our redemption. But we shall do all this in a strictly national and Indian style. We shall see that the future church is not thrust upon us, but that we independently and naturally grow into it; that it does not come to us as a foreign plant, but that it strikes its roots deep in the national heart of India, draws its sap from our national resources, and develops itself with all the freshness and vigour of indigenous growth. One religion shall be acknowledged by all men, One God shall be worshipped throughout the length and breadth of the world; the same spirit of faith and love shall pervade all hearts; all nations shall dwell together in the Father's house—yet each shall have its own peculiar and free mode of action. There shall, in short, be unity of spirit, but diversity of forms; one body, but different limbs; one vast community, with members labouring, in different ways and according to their respective resources and peculiar tastes, to advance their common cause. Thus India shall sing the glory of the Supreme Lord with Indian voice and with Indian accompaniments, and so shall England and America, and the various races and tribes and nations of the world, with their own peculiar voice and music, sing His glory; but all their different voices and peculiar modes of chanting shall commingle in one sweet and swelling chorus—one universal anthem proclaiming in solemn and stirring notes, in the world below and the heavens above, "the Fatherhood of God and the brotherhood of man." May the Merciful Lord hasten the advent of the true church, and establish peace and harmony among His children! And as His name has been solemnly chanted tonight in this splendid hall by an immense concourse of worshippers of various races and tribes, so may all His children assemble in His holy mansions, and blending their million voices in one grand chorus, glorify Him time without end.

The New Dispensation

The central idea of Keshab's New Dispensation was that the new faith constituted a direct continuation of the Old and New Testament revelations. Implicit in his bold claims lay the assumption that the Hindu religious genius was able to reconcile and harmonise all conflicting creeds. This daring concept of India's spiritual mission to the world has been voiced by many of her thinkers since Keshab's time.

[From "We Apostles of the New Dispensation," in *Keshab Chandra Sen's Lectures in India*, pp. 464-68, 484-85].

Admit, then, that Paul was a necessary logical adjunct and consequent of Christ, as Moses was, indeed, his antecedent. Does the continuity stop here? No. If the New Testament follows the Old in the line of logical sequence, the new dispensation follows as necessarily all the old dispensations which have gone before it. If you cannot separate Paul from Christ, surely you cannot separate us from Paul. Are we not servants of Paul and apostles of Jesus? Yes. You cannot regard us otherwise. When I say the New Dispensation is a sequence of the Christian dispensation you will no doubt admit a chronological succession. You will perhaps go further, and trace a theological connection. But you have yet to discover a logical succession. Students of logic will yet recognise in the present movement a deduction and a sequence resulting from the Christian dispensation. You cannot deny us. We are the fulfilment of Moses. He was simply the incarnation of Divine conscience. But there was no science in his teachings, that science which in modern times is so greatly honoured. Let Moses grow into modern science, and you have the new dispensation, which may be characterised as the union of the conscience and science. As for Christ, we are surely among his honoured ambassadors. We are a deduction and corollary from his teachings. The new dispensation is Christ's prophecy fulfiled. Did not Jesus predict and foreshadow a fuller dispensation of light and grace? Did he not say the Comforter would come after him, and guide the world "into all truth"? Do you not remember those prophetic words?:

"I have yet many things to say unto you, but ye cannot bear them now. Howbeit when he, the spirit of truth, is come, he will guide you into all truth." And touching the subject of synthetic unity, one can hardly conceive a clearer foreboding than is to be found in those words of Paul: "That in the dispensation of the fullness of time he might gather together in one all things in Christ, both which are in heaven and which are in earth, even in him." Inasmuch as the present dispensation sums up all things in a divine synthesis unifying all in God, and seeks new light in the direct inspiration of the Comforter or Holy Spirit, one cannot fail to recognise in it the fulfilment of an ancient prophecy, the realisation of Christian and Pauline anticipations. What do we see before us in India today but the fruit of that tree, whose seed Jesus planted, and Paul watered, centuries ago? The unbeliever may hold that Christ wholly denies us, and is far away from us. But faith points to his spirit in us, and maintains an unbroken continuity of dispensation. Wherever a dozen disciples are gathered in his name, he is there. We in India are imbued with his spirit. If it be true that the faith of our ancient Aryan ancestors has permeated us, it is equally true that Christ has leavened us and Christianised us. The Acts of his Hindu Apostles will form a fresh chapter in his universal gospel. Can he deny us, his logical succession? Surely he cannot. And so Paul too. Wilt thou reject us, Saint Paul? Revered Brother, wilt thou cast us away as thine enemies? Is not thy spirit in us? Let our lives testify. Gentlemen, what was Paul's great mission? To obliterate the distinction between Jew and Gentile. "I speak to you Gentiles," said he; "inasmuch as I am the apostle of Gentiles, I magnify mine office." "There is no difference between the Jew and the Greek; for the same Lord over all is rich unto all that call upon him." Again, in his Epistle to the Corinthians, "By one Spirit are we all baptised into one body, whether we be Jews or Gentiles." Paul was raised by God to break caste, and level the distinctions of race and nationality; and nobly did he fulfil his mission. The Jew and the Gentile he made into one body. The modern Pauls of the new dispensation are carrying on a similar crusade against caste in India. The obnoxious distinctions between Brahmin and Sudra, between Hindu and Yavana, between Asiatic and European, the new gospel of love thoroughly proscribes.

In the kingdom of God there is no invidious distinction, and therefore this dispensation gathers all men and nations, all races and tribes, the high and the low, and seeks to establish one vast brotherhood among the children of the great God, who hath made of one blood all nations of men. Let them that have eyes see that in the midst of the great spiritual revolution and revival going on in this land, Moses and Christ and Paul are gathering through us the many tribes of Israel, and uniting all in the name of the kingdom of heaven....

In all ages devout and godly men have eaten the flesh of saints and been in turn eaten by others. Divinity went into the flesh of Christ. Then Christ was eaten by Paul and Peter. They were eaten by the fathers and the martyrs and all the saints in Christendom, and all these have we of modern times eaten, assimilated, and absorbed, making their ideas and character our own. Thus one nation may swallow another, and be identified with it. Thus one generation may draw into itself the character and faith of another generation. And we too may enter into each other and dwell in each other. We Hindus are specially endowed with, and distinguished for, the yoga faculty, which is nothing but this power of spiritual communion and absorption. This faculty, which we have inherited from our forefathers, enables us to annihilate space and time, and bring home to our minds an external Deity and an external humanity. Waving the magic wand of yoga, we say to the Ural mountains and the river Ural, Vanish, and lo! they disappear. And we command Europe to enter into the heart of Asia, and Asia to enter into the mind of Europe, and they obey us, and we instantly realise within ourselves an European Asia and an Asiatic Europe, a commingling of oriental and occidental ideas and principles. We say to the Pacific, Pour thy waters into the Atlantic; and we say to the West, Roll back to the East. We summon ancient India to come into modern India with all her rishis and saints, her asceticism and communion and simplicity of character, and behold a transfiguration! The educated modern Hindu cast in Vedic mould! How by yoga one nation becomes another! How Asia eats the flesh and drinks the blood of Europe! How the Hindu absorbs the Christian; how the Christian assimilates the Hindu! Cultivate this communion, my brethren, and continually absorb all that is good and noble in each other. Do not hate, do not exclude others, as the sectarians do, but include and absorb all humanity and all truth. Let there be no antagonism, no exclusion. Let the embankment which each sect, each nation, has raised, be swept away be the flood of cosmopolitan truth, and let all the barriers and partitions which separate man from man be pulled down, so that truth and love and purity may flow freely through millions of hearts and through hundreds of successive generations, from country to country, from age to age. Thus shall the deficiencies of individual and national character be complemented, and humanity shall attain a fuller and more perfect standard of religious and moral life.

—A.L. Basham

References

1. *Kālī*—the Great Goddess.
2. *Kalighat*—the temple of Kālī in Calcutta
3. *Shalgram*—the family idol.
4. *Durwans*—Doorkeepers.
5. *Keshub Chander Sen or* Keshab Chandra Sen.

7

Rammohun Roy

Viewed, in reference to native amelioration, the present is perhaps the most interesting and eventful period in the history of this country. It might be properly called the age of enquiry and investigation. The metropolis of British India is now undergoing a remarkable transition. Customs, consecrated by immemorial observance and interwoven with the fibres of Hindu society, are unhesitatingly renounced as incompatible with the laws of God and man. Hinduism is arraigned before the bar of an enlightened reason, and will ere long be swept from the land which had so long groaned under its domination. But in reflecting on the change now being wrought by educational and other instrumentalities on the native mind, we are irresistibly reminded of the impetus originally communicated to it by Rammohun Roy. His name is inseparably connected with the great moral revolution. It is, therefore, peculiarly interesting to trace the history of this extraordinary man, for it is, in a great measure, the history of that revolution.

Rammohun Roy was born in 1774. He was descended from a long line of Brahmans of a high order, who were from time immemorial devoted to the duties proper to their race. Religion was their vocation. They led a purely monastic life down to his fifth progenitor, who, more than a century and a half ago. "gave up," to quote his own language, "spiritual exercises for worldly pursuits and aggrandizement." This change came over the spirit of his family in the reign of that able, emergetic, but tyrannical Mogul Emperor Aurangzeb. Whether this change was voluntary, or the inevitable result of that bitter and fierce persecution to which the sacerdotal order had been subjected by that Emperor is uncertain. The descendants of his fifth progenitor attached themselves to the Mogul Courts, held offices, acquired titles, and underwent the vicissitudes inseparable from a political life, especially under an absolute and arbitrary Government—"sometimes rich," as he himself assures us, "and sometimes poor, sometimes excelling in success, sometimes miserable through disappointment." The grandfather held situations of respectability and emolument at the Court of Murshedabad, the capital of the Soubah of Bengal, owing then nominally allegiance to, but being virtually independent of the Delhi throne. He served under Shurajadowla, who was the Nero of Bengal, and took a particular pleasure in burning and consuming to ashes the houses of his Hindu subjects, in causing boats full of men to be drowned in the middle of the Ganges, and in subjecting even pregnant women to atrocities which we dare not describe. The official career of Rammohun's grandfather was commensurate with that stirring epoch which "Big with the fate of Cato and of Rome" witnessed the struggles of a company of merchants with the Nabob—struggles which ultimately resulted in the establishment of a mighty and magnificent empire. Rammohun's father, Ramkunt Roy, experiencing some ill-treatment at the Murshedabad Court, and not being able to brook the disgrace as most of his countrymen would have done, retired from service, and took up his residence at Radhanagur, in the district of Burdwan, where he had taluks, the patrimony of the family. At Radhanagur Rammohun Roy was born.

Rammohun Roy's mother was a strict and orthodox woman. Though she was wedded to the superstitions of her country, yet her son succeeded in opening her eyes to its monstrous absurdities. She confessed to him a year before her death, that, notwithstanding she had been convinced of the folly of her faith, she had been too long accustomed to the strict observance of its ceremonies to give it up altogether. "Rammohun," said she to him, "you are right, but I am a weak woman, and am grown too old to give up these observances which are a comfort to me."[1] She was descended from Brahmans of the highest respectability who have, up to the present day, uniformly adhered to a religious life—a life of penance and devotion—a life of gloomy asceticism which aims at eternal beatitude through the literal mortifications of the flesh. The maternal ancestors of Rammohun were the prototypes of that class of Brahmans who are essentially and emphatically Brahmans—who conform, to the letter, to all the stringent rules of the *Ahnika Tattiua*—who conduct themselves in the same manner as the great-great-grandfathers of their great-great-grandfathers had done.

Rammohun Roy received the first elements of native education at home in accordance with the system, which universally obtains among the upper classes of native society, of initiating the children in the mysteries of *Subankar* under the paternal roof before sending them to a public school. The initiation takes place under the auspices of that model of an educator, a *gurumahashay,* who, instead of teaching "the young idea how to shoot," takes good care to cramp and check the development of all ideas except such as might be inspired by his example! It must not, however, be supposed that the boys acquire any mastery over the Bengali language. Far from it. They only pick up a few rules of arithmetic and letter-writing. They acquire enough of Bengali to enable them to conduct the duties of a sheristadar and a peshkar, but not enough of it to express their thoughts with correctness or elegance. They acquire enough of it to write a long rubakari, but not enough of it to pen a short decent letter. At the age of eight or nine, they are now generally sent to an English school. It is therefore obvious that the acquisition of the Bengali language—the language of their infancy—the language in which their earliest associations are entwined, forms, properly speaking, no part of their education. Far different, however, was the case with Rammohun. Though he had received his elementary Bengali education from a *gurumahashay,* yet he not only attained, by dint of self-study, a knowledge of Bengali,—which to say the least, was unrivalled by his contemporaries,—but afterwards brought the language itself to a very high state of improvement. We confess that it is, as yet, destitute of a literature; that it may take generations, if not centuries, to bring it to the highest state of copiousness and refinement; that for elegance, flexibility and precision, it cannot be compared to the Sanskrit, which has been cultivated by a Vyasa, a Valmiki and a Manu;—yet it must be admitted that it is far more adapted to be a living *national* language. Sanskrit, so called, because of its being a *finished* language—the language of the Gods, the Mohorshis, and the Rishis,—can never be the medium of imparting instruction to the great mass of the Hindus' as the complexity of its grammar, which Panini and Vopadeva delighted to mystify, renders its acquisition an herculean achievement. All this was known to Rammohun Roy. He therefore undertook to create a

Literature in Bengali, and his exertions were crowned with a success that exceeded the most sanguine expectation. The Bengali has been so vastly improved by his careful cultivation, by his taste and genius, that it can be now successfully devoted to the communication of Western knowledge to the children of this great country. He was evidently the first who consecrated, so to speak, the Bengali language by rendering it the medium of moral and religious instruction. But he experienced the greatest difficulties in embodying in it his elevated ideas on the nature and attributes to God. He found it totally inadequate to the expression of subtle metaphysical distinctions. He found here the same obstacles which Sir James Mackintosh says "Stood in the way of Lucretius and Cicero when they began to translate the subtle philosophy of Greece into their narrow and barren tongue; and are always felt by the philosopher when he struggles to express, with the necessary discrimination, his abstruse reasoning in words, which, though those of his own language, he must take from the mouths of persons to whom his distinctions would be without a meaning." But he obviated these difficulties by the introduction into it of expressive Sanskrit words. To his exertions, therefore, we are largely indebted for the improvement of the Bengali language. He was evidently one of the best, if not the best Bengali writer ever born. He was second to none except it might be to Varut Chandra Roy,—who however prostituted his talents by enlisting them in the cause of libertinism. The court of Rajah Krishna Chandra Roy, of which he was one of the brightest ornaments, and which has been so graphically described by him, afforded the most tempting premiums to such prostitution. The Rajah, who is said to have been the most accomplished gentleman of his time, was a zealous patron of learning.[2] He appreciated the brilliant and caustic wit of Gopaul Bhar, the metaphysicotheology of Buggonundun Srimony, as well as the poetry of Varut Chandra. But, though gifted with a keen appreciation of intellectual excellence, his highness's taste was essentially vicious. A desire to pander to that taste was the cause of the misdirection of the talents fostered by his patronage. The Vida-Sunder of Varut Chandra Roy, the most popular poem in Bengal, and the words of which are as much household words with its people as those of Hamlet and Othello among the people of England, is nevertheless a filthy production. Though it exhibits a rich fancy and almost Shakespearean knowledge of the practical workings of the human heart, yet all its excellencies are marred by that vicious tone which pervades it throughout. Its immoral tendency cannot be too strongly reprobated. But enough of this digression—into which the parallel we have endeavoured to draw between Varut Chandra Roy and Rammohun Roy has betrayed us. Rammohun Roy's Bengali was truly classical. All his vernacular writings are pre-eminently characterised by a chastity of diction, a suavity of style and a felicity of illustration, not to be met with in the writings of older Bengali writers. They are free from that meretricious orientalism which characterises so often vernacular productions. But it must not be supposed that the Bengali language, though thus considerably improved by Rammohun, is yet entirely fitted for the use of the metaphysician or the theologian. It is destitute of a scientific nomenclature, which must be either created or borrowed to enable us to transfuse European science into it. We have no reason, however, to despair of the vernacularisation of Western knowledge. Since the time of Rammohun, the importance of this great work is fully recognised, and the establishment of the contemplated hundred and one vernacular schools in the Mofussil, with other collateral measures, will, we hope, tend to accelerate its accomplishment; since the demand, which it will create for vernacular books, must inevitably bring in a rich supply.

Having received the elements of Bengali education Rammohun Roy was sent to Patna to study Arabic and Persian, the acquisition of which was then what the acquisition of English is now, a passport to wealth and distinction. The study of these foreign languages first opened his eyes to the absurdities of Hinduism. Struck with the simplicity of a faith of which the fundamental doctrine has been pronounced by its prophet to be "God is but *One,*" he instinctively revolted from the unmeaning, frivolous, and disgusting ceremonies of Hindu idolatry. The Maulavis at Patna invited his attention to Arabic translations of the works of Aristotle and Euclid: and it must be easily perceived that the mental discipline thus acquired by the perusal of these works, as well as his acquaintance with the doctrines of the Koran, contributed to cause that vigorous and searching scrutiny into his national faith which soon resulted in his emancipation from its chains, and ultimately led to the great and successful efforts he made to destroy its empire. Rammohun Roy, after finishing his course of study at Patna, went to Benares for the purpose of mastering the aristocratic language of his country. At Benares, the seat of the muses, the Oxford of India, he read the Sanskrit and Vedas. Here it was that, properly speaking, he laid the foundation of his greatness. The zeal and enthusiasm with which he devoted himself to the study of the Sanskrit, and the acquisition of the treasures locked up in it, can alone be conceived from the splendid results to which they afterwards led.

Young as he was, his clear and strong intellect could not fail to discern the absurdities of that superstition which has, from time immemorial, galled and manacled the great mass of his countrymen. Disciplined to the discovery of truth by the process of logical induction and mathematical demonstration, through the writings of Aristotle and Euclid which he attentively studied in Arabic, it revolted from the detestable doctrines of the Puranic system. Saturated with comparatively pure and elevated ideas of God by the study of Mahommedan theology at Patna, it could not hold any fellowship with the puerilities of his national creed. Accordingly, at the age of sixteen, he composed a manuscript calling in question "the idolatrous system of the Hindus." Thus we see that,—at an age, hovering between boyhood and youth, which is seldom devoted to any graver pursuit in this country than playing *Kopoti* and attending school, and which we should deem too premature in any country for so important a decision,—he renounced Hinduism. His renunciation of it, however, to be duly appreciated, must be viewed in connection with the sacrifices inseparable from it. In casting off his allegiance to it, he braved the loss of caste, the loss of ancestral property (for the *Lex Loci* had not then been concocted) and what must have been perhaps more trying to the nerves of the young reformer, the enmity and persecution of his nearest relatives. His composition of the MSS, to which we have adverted, hastened, what could not be long retarded, an estrangement from his father, who was a bigoted Hindu, and could not brook the heresy of his son. It is cheering to contemplate Rammohun Roy at this time. Though literally a boy, and absolutely dependent upon his father for his support, he manfully asserted his principles, despite the obloquy which he knew their assertion must bring down upon him. The tenderness of youth, when associated with such moral courage and such energy and independence of character, challanges our admiration, and exhibits an interesting, we had almost said, a sublime spectacle. It were earnestly to be wished that the educated natives would follow the example of their illustrious countryman much oftener than they now appear to do. Their renunciation of Hinduism must not be lip-deep, but practical. It is not sufficient that they should *talk* of the folly of an observance of the rites and ceremonies enjoined by the shastras, while they conform to them in practice, by performing *shrads*. and marrying their children according to the Hindu mode. It is not sufficient that, when taxed with their inconsistency, they should plead the necessity of bowing to public opinion. The habit of compromising with idolatry, they must know, is incompatible with a sincere and earnest love of God. It is high time, therefore, that they should try to wipe off the reproach so often cast upon them, that their actions clash with their professions.

The coldness which had been produced between Rammohun and his father by his secession from that religion in which the latter had taken so much pains to instruct him, having rendered his home uncomfortable to him, he began to entertain the idea of travelling. Accordingly, at the age of sixteen, he left his paternal roof. He proposed to travel to different parts of the country in order to enlarge his acquaintance with the different systems of religion prevailing there—to watch their practical operation—and to ascertain their effects upon the character of their votaries. The enterprising spirit which led him to fulfil this design cannot be too much lauded, inasmuch as it so seldom characterises the Hindus, who are religiously and constitutionally indisposed to all locomotion except in the cause of superstition. After visiting different parts of the country, he proceeded to Tibet, where he resided two or three years for the purpose of investigating the Buddha creed. The worship of Lama soon disgusted him, and he unhesitatingly ridiculed it before its disciples: the freedom of his remarks gave much offence to them. Prudence might have dictated a different line of conduct, but his frankness and sincerity at this early age gave utterance to his real sentiments. He travelled into other parts beyond the limits of Hindustan till the age of twenty, when his father consented to recall him, and restore him to favour probably through the intercession of his mother.

When he returned, he was met by a deputation from his father and received by him with great kindness. Being domiciled in his father's house, he appears to have devoted himself to the study of the Vedas and the Puranas. With what success he employed himself in these studies, it would be superfluous to inform our readers. From the undivided attention he paid to them, and the zeal and ardour with which he pursued his researches into Hindu theology as developed in the works of Vyas, Manu and Sankaracharya, we are disposed to believe that he had planned, even at this time, that moral revolution with which his name is identified. The evidence on this point is indeed, we confess, hardly sufficient to prove that any systematic scheme should have been so early formed even by so powerful and active a mind. But it is certain that he had been strongly convinced of the debasing and demoralising tendency of Hinduism, and had seriously been thinking of making an attempt at its subversion.

At the age of twenty-two he commenced the study of the English language, but made no marked progress in it for the next six years. This was owing, we are firmly persuaded, to his not having brought to bear upon its study that application and strength of mind which had enabled him to master so many languages. He afterwards addressed himself to it with his characteristic vigour and energy, and acquired so highly respectable a knowledge of it as to be enabled to write and speak it with accuracy. But we would have it distinctly understood that his English writings do not furnish a legitimate criterion of his English knowledge. They were, to a certain extent, the production of his European friends, though the thoughts and sentiments embodied in them owed their paternity to him alone. The matter was his, but not wholly the manner of expression; his acquaintance with the English language was, as we have said, highly respectable, and no more,—though, *for his time,* it might well be pronounced remarkable. In writing his religious and political pamphlets; in drawing up papers or even letters of any importance, he had constant assistance from an intelligent and highly educated friend. He did not send a line to the press without submitting it to his revision. The truth is that Rammohun Roy was exceedingly ambitious of literary fame.

It had been remarked by those who came into contact with him that he wrote English much better than he spoke it. The reason is obvious. What he spoke was really his own. What he wrote was not wholly his own *bona fide* production. In extenuation, if not in justification of this weakness,—for such in part we consider it to be,—we may observe that it was not wholly the result of vanity but of a solicitude to disseminate his sentiments among the European community, for which end it was absolutely necessary that they should be expressed with correctness and elegance. In his own English, unquestionably, they would not have found their way home to the business and bosoms of his friends; and thus a large proportion of the good, which he could alone effect through the co-operation of the intelligent and well-disposed Europeans would probably have remained undone.

To a man of Rammohun Roy's extensive and varied acquirements, it is however no disparagement to say that he was not an elegant English writer. One, who was decidedly the best Bengali writer, who was one of the most profound Sanskrit scholar, who had mastered Arabic, Persian, Urdu, and Hindustani, who had a tolerable knowledge of Hebrew, Greek and Latin, need not take any shame to himself for not having acquired a complete command over the English language.

Rammohun Roy's father, Ramkunt Roy, died in the Bengali year 1210, corresponding to A.D. 1803, leaving another son besides himself, viz. Jugomohun Roy. It has been roundly asserted by the writer of the memoir placed at the head of this article, that Rammohun had been disinherited by his father. This is not true. The assertion owes its origin to the circumstance of his not having accepted any portion of his ancestral property, because of its having been in an encumbered state. As the succession to it would have involved, according to the Hindu Law, liability to the payment of his father's debts, he thought it proper to have had nothing to do with it. The Maharajah of Burdwan, Tejchand, the father, by adoption, of the present Maharajah, instituted a plaint against Rammohun Roy in the Calcutta Provincial Court in 1823, for a balance due from his father on a kist-bundy bond, when his defence was, that inheriting no part of father's property, he was not legally responsible for his father's debts.

The death of his father having developed upon his shoulders the management and maintenance of his family, he was led to seek official employment under the British Government. He was most desirous to obtain a provision which might enable him to devote himself to philosophy and literature. He had been favourably noticed by several civilians. His father and grandfather held responsible and lucrative offices under the Mogul Government. His own talents were such as the English Government might have been glad to enlist in the public service. But the road to official distinction had not then been rendered accessible to the natives. The system of making Hindus, Prime Ministers and Generals, which constituted a redeeming feature of the Mahommedan administration, was swept away with that rule: and they had not yet been allowed to sit on the bench of justice. The enlightened policy of giving them a share in the administration of their country had not been recognised by the British Government. The narrow and mistaken Cornwallis policy of conducting the administration exclusively through European agency, which has since proved such a miserable failure, was then in full operation.

The post of Dewan, since called *sheristadar,* was then the highest to which a native could aspire. Rammohun Roy wished to get it. With this view he entered, as a clerk, the office of Mr. Jhon Digby, Collector of Rungpore. Connected with this subject, it is curious to observe that, on his entering office, a written agreement was signed by Mr. Digby, stipulating that Rammohun should not be kept standing in *"the presence,"* or receive orders as a common Amla from the *Huzur.* This circumstance proves beyond the possibility of contradiction, that the hauteur of the civilian toward the natives, which has since grown into a proverb among them, and which precludes educated, respectable, and high-spirited men from seeking employment in the Company's Courts, was in Rammohun Roy's time, appreciated as now. What a reflection it is upon the official character of the civilian? The sovereign contempt with which many of our English Hukims look down upon the Amla is without a parallel in the annals of servitude, and has in a high degree succeeded in alienating the better portion of the native community. The ranks of the Amlas, being, for this reason mainly supplied from the dregs of that community, their corruption should not be wondered at. That they should sell their official influence to the highest bidder, and convert the Mofussil Courts into dens of inquity and *Joachuiry,* is quite in the course of things. We would, therefore, strongly urge the desirableness and importance of gradually levelling down that invidious line of demarkation between the covenanted and uncovenanted service which an imaginary necessity or a blind self-interest has upreared. We earnestly hope and trust that the discussion which the question of the renewal of the charter will give rise to Parliament in 1854, will result in the abolition of a distinction, which, in the opinion of the Bentincks, the Munros, and the Metcalfes, is not only unjust in principle, but inefficient in practice.

Free from that "insolence of office" against which the agreement entered into by him with the Collector guarded him, Rammohun Roy addressed himself to his duties with a zeal and energy which elicited the approbation of his employer, and soon earned for him the post of Dewan. By serving in this capacity, he is said to have realised as much money as enabled him to become a Zemindar with an income of

Rs. "ten thousand a year." If this assertion be true, it must raise in the mind a strong suspicion of the moral character of this extraordinary man. But we are prepared neither to substantiate nor to contradict it. Whether his integrity was proof against those temptations which are generally irresistible to the Amla, or whether, like another Bacon, he exhibited a melancholy illustration of the union of intellectual greatness with moral littleness, is a problem the solution of which is beyond our power. Whether the apostle of Hindu reform, like the high priest of inductive philosophy, sold justice, is a question which, however, interesting, we are not competent to decide. The evidence on this subject is too inconclusive to enable us to arrive at a decision. It is therefore impossible to ascertain, with any degree of certainty, whether there was any difference between Rammohun Roy the Reformer, and Rammohun Roy the Dewan—between Rammohun Roy seated in his study, and discussing with his friends the means of ameliorating the moral and social condition of his countrymen, and Rammohun Roy located in the collectorate of Rungpore and penning *foisallahs and rubakaries*—between Rammohun Roy thundering against Hindu idolatry, and Rammohun Roy conducting the fiscal duties of his office.

If Rammohun Roy did keep his hands clean, and abstain, as in the absence of all positive evidence to the contrary we are bound to suppose, from defeating the ends of justice for a—consideration,—he must have been a splendid exception. Constituted as human nature ordinarily is, it is preposterously absurd to calculate upon a faithful and conscientious discharge of duties by men who, while clothed with all but an irresponsible authority, are paid a pittance which hardly suffices to meet their pocket expenses. The same causes which led the European functionaries before the time of Cornwallis to be more true to their own interests than to those of their Honourable masters, must inevitably operate in producing the same results among the natives. For the system of small pay and large responsibility, heretofore the pet-system of our Government, makes official corruption the rule, and official integrity the exception. Its inefficiency, however, has been recognised by Government in the late increase of the salaries of the Darogahs. While we rejoice in the adoption of that enlightened policy which has dictated this measure, we would urge its extension to other classes of ministerial officers. The emolument of the Dewan or Sheristadar, the first ministerial officer in the Mofussil Court, is totally inadequate to the responsibility and respectability of the office. We could name several districts and zillahs where the Sheristadar is the *de facto* Magistrate, the *de facto* Collector, and the *de facto* Judge. It is absolutely necessary that the pay of this functionary should be at least doubled before we can have a right to reckon on his integrity.

The more Mr. Digby saw of Rammohun, the more he appreciated him. The esteem which they entertained for each other ripened into a warm friendship which only terminated with the death of the latter. They cultivated oriental and English literature in conjunction—mutually aiding each other. Mr. Digby many years after, while in England, thus bears his testimony to the acquirements and opinions of his quondam Dewan:

> By purusing all my public correspondence with diligence and attention, as well as by corresponding and conversing with European gentlemen, he acquired so correct a knowledge of the English language, as to be enabled to write and speak it with considerable accuracy. He was also in the constant habit of reading the English newspapers, of which the continental politics chiefly interested him, and from them he formed a high opinion of the talents and prowess of the late ruler of France, and was so dazzled with the splendour of his achievements, as to become sceptical as to the commission, if not blind to the atrocity of his crimes, and could not help deeply lamenting his downfall, notwithstanding the profound respect he ever professed for the English nation; but when the first transports of his sorrow had subsided, he considered that part of his political conduct which led to his abdication to have been so weak, and so madly ambitious, that he declared his future detestation of Buonaparte would be proportionate to his former admiration of him.

Rammohun Roy resided alternately in the Zillahs of Rungpore, Bhagulpore, and Ramghur till the year 1814, when he took up his residence in Calcutta. He purchased a garden with a house constructed in the European mode, and furnished in the European style, in the Upper Circular Road at the eastern extremity of this city. Thus we see that, at the age of fifty, he carried into effect his long-cherished plan of retiring from business, and consecrating the latter portion of his life to philosophy and religion. His love of literary retirement amounted almost to a passion. He used to say that a man, after acquiring a competence, should spend his life in the enjoyment of philosophic ease. "Old as I am," said he once to a friend, "I wish I may retire to a solitary cave, and there apply myself to the study of the Vedant and Mesnavi."[3]

To retire from the hurry and bustle of the world—to revel in the luxuries of lettered leisure—to cultivate philosophy and religion amidst the solitudes of jungles—to consecrate his energies to the furtherance of the great work of his country's regeneration,—this was the *beau ideal* of his happiness. Business, which is the "be-all and the end-all" of the existence of the great majority of mankind, whether located in civilized, demi-civilised, or uncivilised countries, was considered by Rammohun Roy as something too low to engross a whole life. He not only knew but felt the great truth, that man is created for higher ends than the acquisition of rupees—that being gifted with moral, and intellectual powers, nothing short of the cultivation of all these powers can promote his happiness—that there is that in man which the things of this world cannot altogether satisfy, which longs after eternity, and after Him of whom it hath been sublimely said that he "inhabiteth eternity."

Rammohun Roy, being permanently located in the City of Palaces, gathered around him many inquiring and intelligent Hindus. He soon became the centre of a circle composed of men in advance of their age. From this time forward his career as a reformer commenced. From this time forward to the last day of his existence he devoted himself, heart and soul, to the mighty work of his country"s regeneration. He laboured day and night, right and left, to promote this great object. All his hopes and aspirations were centred in the prospect of its realisation. It absorbed his energies. It engrossed the whole man.

So effectually has the cruel and demoralising superstition of the Hindus extinguished the religious feelings of their nature, and perverted their ideas of the very fundamentals of divine worship, that they never think of worshipping their God except by means of unintelligible and unmeaning *mantras.* These mantras, which they have been taught to articulate without comprehending their import, are considered to be a passport to heaven. Such lip-deep and mechanical devotion is a mockery of worship, and a downright insult to Him who is *to be loved with all the heart, and with all the understanding, and with all the soul, and with all the strength.*

Rammohun Roy sought to reform the faith and worship of his countrymen. By teaching them to contemplate the natural, intellectual, and moral attributes of God, he proposed to make them worship their

Creator "in *spirit* and in *truth*." The extermination of Hindu idolatry and the dissemination of sound and enlightened views of the Supreme Being—of the unseen and future world—of truth—of happiness—of final beatitude;—this was the great object of his being. And to the furtherance of that object, he unhesitatingly devoted his talents, his time and his fortune. Endowed with an energy of character and strength of intellect of which his age furnished no model, he braved the most formidable obstacles which opposed themselves to the progress of the good cause he had espoused; and the pecuniary sacrifices he made to promote that cause were indeed noble. Though his fortune was anything but princely, yet he gladly consecrated a large portion of it to its advancement. Never did a reformer labour more zealously, more sincerely, more indefatigably. Never did a reformer unite in himself more happily the urbanity of the gentleman and the shrewdness of the man of the world, with the profoundity of the philosopher, and the enthusiasm of the theologian. Of course, it will be understood, that we speak of him *relatively,* as a *Hindu reformer,* rising up, by self-effort, out of the chaos of Hinduism. It would be unfair to judge of him by the highest standard of Christian civilisation.

It is impossible for us to estimate adequately the exertions he made to liberate the Hindu mind from spiritual bondage, and to indoctrinate it with the pure, elevated and living principles of veneration, justice, and benevolence. One of the means he adopted for the realisation of this important end, was the publication and distribution of tracts, on moral and religious subjects. He published them all at his own expense, and distributed them gratuitously among his countrymen.

He first appeared before the public as an author by his translation into Bengali of the celebrated Vedant. It is a resolution of the Vedas, or a compendious digest of the Hindu Scriptures, accompanied with annotations on the more difficult passages. It owes its paternity to that intellectual phenomenon of India, Krishna Dwyiapayana Vyas. Regarding this author and his system, enough has appeared in a previous article to render any additional statements necessary here.

Being written in the Sanskrit language, the Vedant is of course inaccessible to the great mass of the Hindus. By presenting to them a Bengali translation of it, Rammohun Roy did no small service to his cause. The Bengali translation was followed by a Hindustani one. In 1816 he published the English translation of the Vedant, "the most celebrated and revered work of Brahmanical theology." The preface, "addressed to the beleievers of the one true God," is so interesting and so much illustrative of the doctrines he endeavoured to inculcate, that we cannot resist the temptation of quoting it at length:

> The greater part of Brahmans, as well as of other sects of Hindus, are quite incapable of justifying that idolatry, which they continue to practise. When questioned on the subject, in place of adducing reasonable arguments in support of their conduct, they conceive it fully sufficient to quote their ancestors as positive authorities! And some of them are become very ill disposed towards me, because I have forsaken idolatry, for the worship of the true and eternal God! In order, therefore, to vindicate my own faith and that of our early forefathers, I have been endeavouring, for some time past, to convince my countrymen of the true meaning of our sacred books; and to prove, that my aberration deserves not the opprobrium which some unreflecting persons have been so ready to throw upon me.
>
> The whole body of the Hindu Theology, Law, and Literature, is contained in the Vedas, which are affirmed to be coeval with the creation! These works are extremely volumnious; and being written in the most elevated and metaphorical style, are, as may be well supposed, in many passages seemingly confused and contradictory. Upwards of two thousand years ago, the great Vyasa, reflecting on the perpetual difficulty arising from these sources, composed with great discrimination a complete and compendious abstract of the whole; and also reconciled those texts which appeared to stand at variance. This work he termed *the Vedant,* which compounded of two Sanskrit words, signifies *the resolution of all the Vedas.* It has continued to be most highly revered by all the Hindus; and in place of the more diffuse arguments of the Vedas, is always referred to as equal authority. But from its being concealed within the dark curtain of the Sanskrit language, and the Brahmans permitting themselves alone to interpret or even to touch any book of the kind, the Vedant, although perpetually quoted, is little known to the public and the practice of few Hindus indeed bears the least accordance with its precepts!
>
> In pursuance of my vindication, I have to the best of my abilities translated this hitherto unknown work, as well as an abridgement thereof into the Hindustani and Bengali languages, and distributed them, free of cost, among my own countrymen, as widely as circumstances have possibly allowed. The present is an endeavour to render an abridgement of the same into English, by which I expect to prove to my European friends, that the superstitious practices which deform the Hindu religion, have nothing to do with the pure spirit of its dictates!

I have observed that, both in their writings and conversation, many Europeans feel a wish to palliate and soften the features of Hindu idolatry; and are inclined to inculcate, that all objects of worship are considered by their votaries as emblematical representations of the Supreme Divinity. If this were indeed the case I might perhaps be led into some examination of the subject; but the truth is, the Hindus of the present day have no such views of the subject, but firmly believe in the real existence of innumerable gods and goddesses, who possess, in their own departments, full and independent power; and to propitiate them, and not the true God, are temples erected, and ceremonies performed. There can be no doubt, however, and it is my whole design to prove, that every rite has its derivation from the allegorical adoration of the true Deity; but at the present day, all this is forgotten; and among many it is even heresy to mention it. I hope it will not be presumed, that I intend to establish the preference of my faith over that of other men. The result of controversy on such a subject, however multiplied, must be ever unsatisfactory. For the reasoning faculty, which leads men to certainty in things within its reach, produces no effect on questions beyond its comprehension. I do not more than assert that, if correct reasoning, and the dictates of common sense, induce the belief of a wise, uncreated being, who is the supporter and ruler of the boundless universe, we should also consider him the most powerful and supreme existence—far surpassing our powers of comprehension or description! And although men of uncultivated minds, and even some learned individuals (but in this one point blinded by prejudice,) readily choose as the object of their adoration, any thing which they can always see, and which they pretend to feel, the absurdity of such conduct is not thereby in the least degree diminished.

My constant reflections on the inconvenient, or rather injurious rites introduced by the peculiar practice of Hindu idolatry, which, more than any other Pagan worship, destroys the texture of society, together with compassion for my countrymen, have compelled me to use every possible effort to awaken them from their dream of error; and by making them acquainted with their scriptures, enable them to contemplate, with true devotion, the unity and omnipresence of nature's God.

By taking the path, which conscience and sincerity direct, I, born a Brahman, have exposed myself to the complainings and reproaches even of some of my relations, whose prejudices are strong, and whose temporal advantage depends upon the present system. But there however accumulated, I can tranquilly bear; trusting that a day will arrive when my humble endeavours will be viewed with justice—perhaps acknowledged with gratitude. At any rate, whatever men may say, I cannot be deprived of this consolation; my motives are acceptable to that Being, who beholds in secret, and compensates openly.

After the publication of the Vedant, Rammohun printed, in Bengali and English, translations of the Kena Upanishad, one of the chapters of the Sama Veda, according to the gloss of the celebrated Sankaracharya, "establishing the unity and the sole omnipotence of the Supreme Being, and that He alone is the object of worship." The Upanishads constitute the least exceptionable portion of the Hindu scriptures. The Vedas consist of two portions, viz.: the *Karmakand* and *Gyankand*. The former inculcates the worship of the elements and the performance of rites and ceremonies. The latter, to which the Upanishads belong, treats of the existence and attributes of God. The one is the exoteric and the other the esoteric part of the Hindu religion. The object of his translating the Upanishad was to prove that the performance of the absurd rites and ceremonies inculcated by the Karmakand, and the celebration of the Pujahs inculcated by the Purans, far from being sanctioned by, is seemingly repugnant to what appeared to be the real spirit, not of the Vedas themselves, but of *the better and more rational parts of the Vedas,* viz. the *Upanishads.*

He endeavoured to show that *Adwaita,* or unity of the Deity, as contradistinguished from that of *Dwaita,* or plurality of gods, is the fundamental doctrine of the Vedantic system. How far he was correct in holding this opinion, or how far he succeeded in his object is a question which we mean not at present to handle. In the introduction to the Sama Upanishad he says, "this work will, I trust, by explaining to my countrymen the real spirit of the Hindu scriptures, which is but the declaration of the unity of God, tend in a great measure to correct the erroneous conceptions which have prevailed with regard to the doctrines they inculcate. It will also I hope tend to discriminate those parts of the Vedas which are to be interpreted in an allegorical sense, and consequently to correct those exceptionable practices which not only deprive Hindus in general of the common comforts of society, but also lead them frequently to self-destruction, or to the sacrifice of the lives of their friends and relatives."

In conformity with the plan he had proposed to himself of reasoning his countrymen out of their idolatry, by making them acquainted with the contents of the more rational parts of their own scriptures, he published a Bengali, and afterwards an English translation of the Kuth Upanishad of the Yajur Ved, and Mundak Upanishad of the Atharva Ved, and distributed copies of them as widely as possible.

Intense was the sensation which these publications created among the Hindus. Opinions, entirely subversive of the popular and established tenets of Hinduism, had been pronounced by Rammohun Roy in broad daylight. Liberties in thought and action had been fearlessly assumed both by him and his followers, which shocked the bigoted Pandits and the lazy ghee-fed Babus. The injurious effects of those customs and institutions, which had for ages marked the peculiar character of the Hindus, had been exposed to the wonderment of men taught to venerate them from their infancy. The Vedas and the Upanishads, which were sealed books to all but the privileged few, had been shewn, to be decidedly opposed to the worship of the most popular deities, such as Kali and Durga, and Krishna and Shiva. The prerogative of the Brahmans to expound and study the scripture had been set at nought. The great mass of the Hindus, whose belief in their creed was, so to speak, based on *hearsay,* had been called upon to examine for themselves, nay, invited to pronounce the mysteries and pregnant monosyllable Om. Who could therefore assign any limits to the lengths Rammohun might go? The Hindus looked with trembling anxiety on the results of this terrible innovation. The Kali Yug was at hand. In the *Bailtokhanas* of the Babus, as well as in the *Tols* of the Pandits, the heresy of Rammohun Roy was the one great theme of conversation. Both the Brahman and the Sudra united in counteracting the Reformer. The Nyayik, the Mimansik Yogi, and the Puranic, who agree nothing else,—who wage a perpetual polemical warfare among themselves,—who, at a marriage rite, or a shrad shabha, are invariably to be seen seated on a carpet apart from the rest of the company, and engaged in wrangling on knotty points, relieved only by a dip now and then into their snuff boxes;—all agreed to enlist themselves under the banner of opposition.

The publication of the *Kuth Upanishad,* as well as the application of the term "Reformer" to him by the Editor of the *India Gazette,* led to a controversy between him and Sankara Sastri, head English master in the College of Fort St. George Madras. The Sastri, while he admitted the fact contended for by Rammohun, that the doctrine of unity, in a certain sense, was inculcated by the Puranic as well as the Vedantic systems, insisted that Rammohun had no claim to be considered as the "discoverer" of the doctrine. The controversialist, however, justified the idolatry of his countrymen and particularly the worship of the personified attributes of the Almighty, which he considered to have distinct and independent existence. "If a person," says he, reasoning from an analogy more plausible than correct, "be desirous to visit an earthly prince, he ought to be introduced in the first instance by his ministers, but not of himself to rush upon him at once, regardless of offending him. Should a man wish to ascend a flight of stairs, he ought to proceed, step by step, and not to leap up several at a time, so as to endanger the wounding of his legs. In like manner, the grace of God ought to be obtained by degrees, through the worship of his attributes." The indefatigable Rammohun soon published his reply. He disclaims in it the titles of "Reformer" and "Discoverer," —justly observing that he was commonly stigmatised by his countrymen as an Innovator. With reference to the Divine Attributes, he shews, by ample quotations and excerpts from the Vedas, that the doctrine of their independent existence was obviously incompatible with the fundamental principles of the Vedantic system. Soon after, a Bhattacharjya of Calcutta appeared in the field. He published a letter in Bengali and English containing a fierce attack upon his opinions. It elicited a well-penned tract from him entitled, "second defence of the monotheistical system of the Vedas."

But the opposition of his countrymen to his opinions was not confined to literary warfare. A degree of persecution had been excited against him which it required no ordinary moral courage to brave. His name was coupled with obloquy. So utterly incapable were his countrymen of appreciating his labours, or rather so utterly blinded were they by downright bigotry, that they nicknamed him a *nastik* (athcist). That he was an ungodly man, and aimed at the destruction of all religion, was what they firmly believed. He had been several times threatened with personal violence,—so much so, that he made it a point, whenever he went out, to have a kind of guard accompanying his carriage. That he should be called an atheist by the bigoted Hindus is by no means to be wondered at. We know that the charge of atheism, the highest in our opinion which one man can prefer against another, usually proceeds from men who are apt to identify mere theism with atheism. The words *scepticism, atheism,* or *infidelity,* as *generally* applied, mean, when properly analysed, only a departure from national or popular religion. The Mahommedans call everybody an infidel or an atheist who does not believe in the Alkoran. The eduacated native, who dares to disown the doctrines of Hinduism, is called by his idolatrous countrymen a *mlechha* and a *nastik.* Every nation on the face of the earth, and from the dawn of history to the present moment, has branded with the opprobrium of infidelity all those who, persuaded of the absurdities of the national and ancestral faith, embrace purer and more elevated views of religion.

That Rammohun Roy entertained the highest respect for the practical part of the Christian religion does not admit of dispute. No one could more thoroughly appreciate and venerate the code of morality inculcated in the Bible. That it was the purest, the most elevated, the most sublime code in the world, was cheerfully admitted by him. He had acquired the Hebrew and Greek languages in order to be able to read the scriptures of the Christians in the original. He had afterwards studied the Old Testament with a Jewish rabbi and the New Testament with some Christian divines. After having matured the fruits of his researches into the Christian and Hindu scriptures, he published in 1820, anonymously, his celebrated work, "The Precepts of Jesus the guide to Peace and happiness." It consists principally of selections from the first three gospels. In the Preface to this work he says:

> This simple code of religion and morality is so admirably calculated to elevate men's ideas, to high and liberal notions of one God, who has equally subjected all living creatures, without distinction of caste, rank, or wealth, to change, disappointment, pain, and death; and has equally admitted all to be partakers of the bountiful mercies which he has lavished over nature; and is also so well fitted to regulate the conduct of the human race in the discharge of their various duties to God, to themselves and society, that I cannot but hope the best effects from its promulgation in the present form.

The publication of this work brought upon him an attack far more formidable than any he had encountered from his countrymen. In the first No. of the *Friend of India* (quarterly series) there appeared an elaborate and learned article, "Observations on certain ideas contained in the Introduction to the Precepts of Jesus the Guide to Peace and Happiness." This elicited a reply from Rammohun, under the signature of "A Friend to Truth," in "An Appeal to the Christian Public." The Appeal led to a reply from the *Friend of India,* and to a second Appeal in Rammohun Roy's own name, which again called forth an attack upon him from the same journal. The first two appeals had been printed at the Serampore Press, but the proprietor having expressed some conscientious scruples about printing the "Final

Appeal," Rammohun forthwith purchased types, and set up the "Unitarian Press, Dharmatollah." His "Final Appeal," as well as all his subsequent works were printed at this press.

It was amidst the sensation occasioned amongst the European and the enlightened portion of the native community, by the publication of the appeals of Rammohun, and the counter-appeals of the "Friend," that Brojomohun Majumdar, a friend and disciple of the Hindu reformer, published an essay entitled, "Scriptures on the Present System of Hindu Monotheism," in the Bengali language. We are inclined to believe, however, that it owed its paternity, at least in some degree, to an intellect superior to that of the apparent author; and our belief is strengthened by the fact of Rammohun's being in the habit of publishing his works either anonymously, or in the names of his friends. At all events it must have been published under the auspices of the Hindu reformer.

This brochure is evidently stamped with the impress of a strong mind. It is a clever and bold attack on Hinduism. It is "a masterly exposure," as Dr. Marshman in reviewing, justly characterised it, "of the absurdities of the Hindu system." All the arguments brought in support of Hindu idolatry are unanswerably refuted. The tomfooleries of the Hindu mode of worship are held up to merited ridicule and contempt. It displays a profound acquaintance with the Hindu Shastras. In depth of argumentation, energy of diction, and keenness of satire it is surpassed by few Bengali works. But independently of its merits, we hail it as the first production of the kind by a native in his own language. That in the heart of Calcutta, the very stronghold of wealthy bigotry, there should uprise a respectable Hindu to expose the absurdities of Hinduism, was a cheering illustration of the progress of improvement, and an auspicious omen of good things to come.

Though the exertions of Rammohun Roy to subvert Hinduism and disseminate purer and more elavated notions of religion and morality had alienated from him the great mass of his countrymen, and brought down upon him not only unmerited obloquy, but a large amount of persecution;—yet it is comforting to know that they were appreciated by the thinking portion of the natives. The seceders from the ranks of Hinduism daily increased and joined his standard.

Several intelligent, respectable, and opulent natives, in whom we recognise some of the present leaders of the native society, embraced his views. "The ground which I took," says he in one of his letters before us, "in all my controversies was not of opposition of Brahmanism, but to a perversion of it; and I endeavoured to show that the idolatry of the Brahmans was contrary to the practice of their ancestors and the principles of the ancient books and authorities which they profess to revere and obey. Notwithstanding the violence of the opposition and resistance to my opinions, several highly respectable persons, both among my own relations and others, began to adopt the same sentiments." He soon became the leader of a sect, the basis of whose creed was the unity of Deity in opposition to polytheism. It was composed of men who had been taught to think boldly, and who had been strongly persuaded of the evils of that idolatry which had dwarfed the national mind. They therefore readily joined him in establishing a society for putting down that idolatry. The *Brahmo Sumaj* was established in 1828. The Shabha holds weekly meetings on Wednesday evenings, when the Vedas are read and expounded, and discourses in Bengali are delivered. The subjects embraced by the discourses, relate to general principles in morals and religion. The meetings, "open to men of all persuasions," are now attended by considerable numbers. They always conclude with the singing of hymns composed by Rammohun Roy himself and his friends. The other means, adopted by the society for the realisation of its object, are the preparation and publication of Bengali Tracts on moral and religious subjects and the reprinting of Sanskrit works on Vedantism.

The excitement, created by this organisation, was proportioned to the magnitude of the change aimed at by its founder. That the veil of mystery, which had enshrouded from time immemorial, the more sacred portion of the Hindu scriptures should be unceremoniously torn open, and its contents revealed to the irreverant gaze of those who had been studiously precluded, by interested priestcraft, from even a superficial acquaintance with them—that the Gāyatri should be pronounced before not only the sudra, but the *mlechha* —that the sudra and the mlechha should be called upon to participate in the worship of Brahma;—this could not fail to shock the feelings of the Hindus and impel them at last to adopt some strenuous measures for counteracting the efforts of the *Brahma Dol.* They established the Dharma Shabha, with the avowed object of upholding Hinduism in all its integrity, and preserving its laws and institutions from the inroads of the Brahma Shabha. This corporation soon increased in numbers and in strength. The success which had attended its exertions showed that the national character of the Hindus pre-eminently distinguished by a spirit of exclusiveness and disunion, and an apathetic indifference to all but the animal wants of life,—had changed for once. The noise of theological controversy reverberated throughout the country. The Hindu community became divided into two great parties, the Brahma Shabha party and the Dharma Shabha party. The principles of these Shabhas carried on their warfare in every part of native society, in every *Tol,* in every *Baitokhana,* in every Dalan, in every *Chondimundub,* in every *Zenana.* Sometimes the bigotry and fanaticism of the Dharma party, seemed to triumpth over the Vedantism of the Brahma Shabha. Sometimes the Brahma Gyanis seemed to carry every thing before them.

Though the influence, exercised by the Dharma Shabha over the Hindus, was at one time all but omnipotent, yet we rejoice to know that it is now on the wane, and that the days of the Shabha itself are numbered. It has been rent in twain, and ceased to enlist the real sympathies of the Hindu public. Every educated and intelligent native would, we are sure, cordially participate in our wish for the immediate dissolution of a society, which preaches the doctrine of non-intercourse, and aims at the laceration of domestic and social ties. But the Shabha distinguished itself not only by its inquisitorial proceedings but by its opposition to every liberal measure. One of its first movements was, we believe, the presentation of a petition of Government *against* the abolition of the Suttee (Sati) rite, and one of its last movements has been the presentation of a similar petition against the Lexi Loci, in reference to the xi, xii and xiii clauses, emphatically called the *liberty of conscience clauses,*—abolishing that portion of the Hindu law which inflicts forfeiture of ancestral property on persons renouncing the Hindu or Mahommedan religion.

The Suttee rite, in the perpetuation of which the Dharma Shabha had been deeply interested, was one of the monster evils of this country. It had led thousands and tens of thousands of women to an untimely grave. Deluded by the hopes of perennial happiness, they performed the rite of *Sha[ha]maran,* i.e., burnt themselves alive with the bodies of their deceased husbands. The banks of the Bhagirathi exhibited for centuries the horrid spectacle of the *chulli* blazing fearfully, over the dead and the living! Rammohun Roy deeply felt for these infatuated victims of superstition. His heart bled at the horrors of Sha[ha]maran and Anamaran. He had always openly, and in no measured terms, denounced this inhuman and diabolical rite. He published in 1820, for general circulation, a tract both in Bengali and English languages entitled, "A conference between an advocate for, and an opponent of, the practice of burning widows alive." This was followed by a second conference which he dedicated to the Marchioness of Hastings. The object of these publications was to show that the rite of Suttee, though tolerated by Hariit, Ungira and other inferior authorities, was by no means clearly sanctioned by Manu, and decidedly opposed to the tenets of the Vedas. By excerpts from the principal Shastras, he proved that these appeared to assign greater merit to a life of purity and austerity on the part of the widows than to the performance of the *Shahamaran.*

The unanswerable arguments embodies in the "Conferences," silently paved the way for the abolition of this rite. Though the necessity of such abolition had been admitted by the Government as early as 1805, yet nothing was done towards it, because of the interference with the Hindu religion which it was supposed to involve.[4]

The "Conferences" contributed to dispel this error; and towards the close of 1829, Lord William Bentinck—a name enshrined in the hearts of the natives—at once abolished a rite not only horrid and revolting but fraught with incalculable mischief. When the Dharma Shabha got up the remonstrance we have alluded to, Rammohun Roy, in spite of personal outrage, led a deputation who presented an address to the Governor-General, embodying the grateful acknowledgments of the enlightened portion of the native community for this "everlasting boon" conferred on their country. His indefatigable exertions in putting down this rite, as well as in elevating the females of this country from that state of intellectual abasement into which they are sunk, cannot be sufficiently lauded.

In the early part of 1830, an event occurred which signally illustrated his genuine liberality of sentiment. The Founder of the General Assembly (now Free Church) institution, on his arrival in this country, was introduced to him, and propounded those educational views which have since been so largely carried out in practice. Rammohun expressed his warmest approbation of them, declaring that all education ought to be based on religion and that he saw no evil but much good likely to result to his countrymen from the teaching of the Chirstian Bible as a class book in schools. More than this, he practically assisted the Rev. Doctor, in every way in his power, in founding his proposed institution—reserved for the use of it the hall of the Brahmo Shabha, then recently vacated for the one since occupied—attended daily for upwards of a month, and often afterwards, to encourage the boys and reconcile them to the reading of the Bible. He approved of the institution's being daily opened with prayer, and recommended the use of "the Lord's Prayer," as being, in his view, the most compendious, and at the same time, the most comprehensive form of prayer in any book or language. For these and other services we have often heard the Rev. Founder of the institution speak of Rammohun Roy with mingled emotions of affection, gratitude, and respect.

Rammohun Roy cherished for some years a strong desire to visit Europe, and "obtain," as he says in one of his letters, "by personal observation a more thorough insight into its manners, customs, religion and political institutions." He longed especially to see the country to whose keeping the destinies of his own had been entrusted—the country, where philosophy, liberty, and science had achieved their proudest triumphs—the country of Lockes, of Bacons, of Newtons, of Hampdons, and of Watts.

The labours in which he was engaged, tended to postpone for some time the fulfilment of this desire. The success, however, with which they were afterwards crowned (as evidenced in the increase of his party and the spread of his views,) as well as the anticipated parliamentary discussion on the renewal of the Company's charter, induced him to make preparations for his visit. Another circumstance also favoured his design. The emperor of Delhi, considering himself entitled to the revenue of certain lands in the vicinity thereof, had applied to the Court of Directors. The subject had been considered by that body and afterward by the Board of Control: and it was determined that the Mogul received all that he originally agreed to accept, and all that he was entitled to, in law or equity. The emperor, resolved to try the experiment of an appeal to the king of England, had appointed Rammohun his ambassador, with full powers to manage the negotiation, and conferred on him by firman the title of "Rajah."

The announcement of Rammohun Roy's intention of visiting Europe—the land of the mlechas and beef-eaters—excited much speculation among his countrymen. Being incapable of understanding that enlightened curiosity and that disinterested philanthropy which prompted him to undertake the voyage, they ascribed to him several unworthy motives. But the man who had braved their persecutions—who had triumphed over the formidable obstacles which threatened to neutralise his labours—who had set at defiance the thunders of the Dharma Shabha, and the fulminations of the Brahmins, was not to be deterred by the sneerings and howlings of his countrymen from the performance of a resolution he had deliberately adopted. On the 15th November 1830, the Rajah, accompanied by his adopted son Babu Rajaram Roy and two Hindu servants, Ramrutten Mukerjya and Ramhori Mukerjya, left his native land in the *Albion* bound for Liverpool. The particulars of the voyage have been thus graphically described by a fellow traveller who is now among us, and who has been for many years connected with our periodical literature:

> On ship-board Rammohun Roy took his meals in his own cabin, and at first suffered considerable inconvenience from the want of a separate fire place; having nothing but a common earthen *chula* on board. His servants too, fell desperately sea-sick (though, as if his ardour supported him against it, he himself never felt this malady at all) and took possession of his cabin, never moving from it, and making it as may be easily conceived, no enviable domicile; in fact, they compelled him to retreat to the lockers; but still the kindness of his nature would not allow him to remove them. The greater part of the day he read, chiefly, I believe, Sanskrit and Hebrew. In the forenoon and the evening he took an airing on deck, and always got involved in an animated discussion. After dinner, when the cloth was removed, and the desert on table, he would come out of his cabin also, and join in the conversation and take a glass of wine. He was always cheerful, and so won upon the esteem of all on board, that there was quite a competition who should pay him the most attention, and even the sailors seemed anxious to render him any little service in their power. In a gale of wind he would be upon deck, gazing at the foam-crested surges as they roared by the vessel, and admiring the sublimity of the scene. On one occasion I brought on deck the "Ocean Sketches,'[5] and read to him the first piece, entitled 'The Breeze':
>
> 'The distant haze, like clouds of silvery dust
> Now sparkles in the sun. The freshening breeze
> Whitens the liquid plain; and like a steed
> With proud impatience fired, the glorious ship,
> Quick bounds exultant, and with rampant prow,

Off flings the glittering foam. Around her wake,
A radiant milky way, the sea-birds wave
Their circling flight, or slowly sweeping wide
O'er boundless ocean, graze with drooping wing
The brightly crested waves. Each sudden surge,
Up-dashed, appears a momentry tree,
Fringed with the hoar frost of a wintry morn;
And then, like blossoms from a breeze-stirred bough,
The light spray strews the deep,
How fitfully the feeble day-beams pierce
The veil of heaven! On you far line of light,
That like a range of breakers, streaks the main,
The ocean swan—the snow-white Albatross,
Gleams like a dazzling foam-flake in the sun!-
Gaze upward—and behold, where parted clouds
Disclose ethereal depths, its dark-hued mate
Hangs motionless on arch-resembing wings,
As though, 'twere painted on the sky's blue vault.
Sprinkling the air, the speck-like petrels form
A living shower! A while their pinions gray
Mingle scarce-seen among the misty clouds,
Till suddenly their white breasts catch the light,
And flash like silver stars!'

He recognised at once the fidelity of this picture; although not much given to poetical reading.

The *Albion* arrived at her destination on the 8th April 1831. The Rajah landed the same day at Liverpool and took up his lodging at one of the hotels there. His arrival in England, which he had long wished to visit and where his fame had preceded him, excited a considerable degree of interest. His arrival too was at a period of extraordinary political fermentation. The whole nation had been wrought up into a state of overpowering excitement. Reform was then the one great subject which agitated the whole country. Rammohun Roy became a zealous and enthusiastic advocate of it. He saw at once the bearings of the great national measure which was calculated, in his opinion, to "promote the welfare of England and her dependencies, nay of the whole world."

No sooner was the advent of the great Brahmin philosopher known in Liverpool than almost every man of distinction in the place hastened to call upon him. One of the first visits he received was from the three sons of the celebrated William Roscoe. They came, not merely on their own account, but to convey to him the "affectionate greeting" of their distinguished parent. Roscoe had not for years quitted his apartment—being troubled with a paralytic affection which incapaciated him from assuming any other than a recumbent posture. When Rammohun arrived he was confined to his death-bed, and was not allowed to receive any visit. He made an exception, however, in favour of Rammohun, with whom he had before corresponded. The interview was deeply interesting and affecting; interesting, because an event which was the theme of their conversation, viz. Reform, was one to which both had looked forward as a consummation devoutly to be wished for, but as one of those contingencies which was scarcely within the range of early probability; and affecting, because they felt that this cheering interchange of sympathies, this delightful and unreserved expression of sentiments, must soon be terminated by the stern flat of that dread tyrant under whose relentless grasp one of them seemed to be already writhing. This proved, as they had anticipated, their first and their last interview on this side of eternity. Rammohun Roy heard of Roscoe's death while residing in London.

This introduction to the historian of the Medici took place at the well-known house in Lodge-Lane; and though there were none present at the interview except the two great men and one of Roscoe's sons, yet the room below was crowded with the gentility of Liverpool. Many and eager were the enquiries about the stranger's political and religious opinions—his habits, and his object in' visiting England. They were hushed when he returned from the sick chamber, with agitated countenance and moistened eyes. As soon as he recovered from the effects of his interview, he reciprocated the cordial greetings of those around him, and got into a very interesting and animated discussion with some gentlemen. Thus it was that at Mr. Roscoe's house a Hindu was, for the first time in Great Britain, heard zealously and earnestly advocating civil and religious liberty throughout the world—and talking of the *Edinburgh* and the *Quarterly* —the Whigs and Tories—Lord Grey and Reform.

The first public place he attended at Liverpool was Dr. Grundy's Unitarian Chapel. The sermon was, *apropos* to the occasion, in exposition of the duty of unlimited charity in our judgements of the creeds of other men, and of their principles of belief. He listened to it with the utmost attention, and afterwards expressed himself very much pleased with it. When the sermon was over, the scene that ensued was curious enough. The congregation, instead of dispersing, thronged up every avenue to get a near view of the great Brahmin philosopher; and it was not till they had heard him address them in their own language and shaken hands with him, that they could be prevailed upon to allow him to return.

At Liverpool, Rammohun Roy got acquainted with Dr. Spurzheim. Though the great phrenologist and the great reformer met often and were good friends, yet the latter never hesitated to laugh at the science of the former. The bump of good nature being however largely developed in Spurzheim, he used simply to observe when thus attacked, that if his friend would only study the facts on which phrenology was based he would change his opinions. Spurzheim was very anxious to get a cast of the head of Rammohun Roy; and though he was promised that he should be permitted to take one, yet the promise, we know not why, was not fulfilled. One of the visits which Rammohun received in Liverpool is described with great *naivete'* by one of his friends, who was, we believe, present on the occasion:

> While he was at Liverpool he received a call from a gentleman with whom he was much amused; his visitor, a retired Indian officer of the old school, with a squat figure, a jolly face, and a conscious smile of self-satisfaction playing on his features, was much more gifted with good nature than good sense or good taste. As soon as he saw the Hindu philosopher, he began addressing him in that elegant dialect in which Europeans in this country make their coup d'essai in Eastern languages. *Ucha, toom Bengali, hum Bengali, toom Bengali,* well, *Kysa hy Sahib?* Then turning to the young Rajah, who was present, "*Ah Chuckera* (Chokra), well, *Kitna burras?*" (or rather *brass* as he made it) *Kysa Mulk (Moolug) Utcha hy?* and so on; to all which Rammohun gracefully bowed. At length, the gallant officer was informed, that the gentleman he was addressing spoke English as well as he did (in truth he spoke it more correctly.) It appeared that he came as a delegate from no less potentate than the mayor, who, fearful of compromising his dignity by calling himself, had deputed his friend to suggest the propriety of the distinguished stranger's calling upon this high civil functionary, and to hint that if he did, the honour would be acknowledged by an *invite* to a Lord Mayor's dinner; and the intimation was delivered with an air of importance, which seemed to imply, "Think of that, Master Brooke." It happened, however, that the party he addressed, had not formed exactly the same lofty estimate of its importance as his visitor, and therefore declined the invitation with cold ingratitude; and when the Major was gone, he vowed, using an emphatic English expression, that if the mayor

> wanted to see him, he might call upon him as his superiors had done, and as it seemed to me, that hospitality, propriety, and good feeling demanded; but mayors are not always, it must be confessed, possessed of taste,—
>
> 'Unless it be
> For calipash or calipee.'
>
> And so our friend lost the opportunity of making his bow to the Mayor of Liverpool.

Rammohun Roy's stay in Liverpool was not long. As he travelled up to London he was delighted with observing the indubitable and living proofs of wealth, civilisation and refinement which the country exhibited. The splendid villas, the smiling cottages with their well-trimmed gardens, the magnificent prospects, the railroads, the canals and the bridges; all afforded a rich banquet to his eyes, and were eagerly recognised by him as the triumphs of that knowledge, that industry, that energy, that public spirit which had given England her preeminence among the nations of the earth, and the lack of which had rendered his own country the abode of misery and destitution. He stopped at Manchester to visit the great factories. The machinery, which seemed to live, and breathe, and move before him, attracted his attention and admiration; but the scene that ensued at the great metropolis of manufacturing industry was curious and interesting. All the work people men, women and children, left work and rushed in crowds to see the "*great King of Ingee.*" After shaking hands with many of the "great unwashed," he turned round and addressed them, "hoping they would all support the king and his ministers in obtaining reform." His appeal was cordially responded to with loud shouts of "the King and Reform for ever."

The Rajah arrived in London at night and was set down at a filthy inn in a filthy part of the town. He had intended to remain there till morning, but the "abominable odours," that regaled his olfactory nerves in the bedroom allotted to him necessitated him to leave. He ordered a coach and set off to the Adelphi Hotel where he arrived at 10 P.M. When he had retired to rest, and it was nearly midnight, Bentham called at the hotel, and left a laconic and characteristic note for him:— "Jeremy Bentham to his friend Rammohun Roy." The visit of the utilitarian Philosopher to the Hindu Reformer was a compliment which the latter fully appreciated, It was indeed a higher distinction than his subsequent linonisation by the British people. That Bentham—

who had secluded himself as it were from the world—who had made it a point to refuse all invitations to the convivial board, in order that he might "consecrate," to quote his very words, "every moment of his life to the service of mankind"—should have left his hermitage, for the purpose of seeing Rammohun Roy, was an unequivocal proof of his admiration for this enlightened and extraordinary Hindu. They afterward met each other, and it must have been a very interesting sight to have seen these two great men engaged in conversation on the greatest-happiness principle, in reference to politics and morals, on the condition of the natives, and on the administration of the East India Company. "Rammohun Roy," said the venerable founder of the utilitarian school, "has cast off three hundred and thirty millions of gods and has learnt from us to embrace reason in the all-important field of religion." He became so great an admirer of him, that he addressed him as his "intensely-admired and dearly-beloved collaborateur in the service of mankind."

No sooner was his arrival in London announced, than many of the most distinguished men crowded to see him. He had scarcely got into his lodgings in Regent-Street when his door was besieged with carriages, from 11 in the morning till 4 in the afternoon. The urbanity of his manners and the suavity of his disposition, fascinated those with whom he came in contact; and the familiarity he discovered with every topic connected with the institutions, opinions, and religion of England, as well as his liberal views on all subjects, astonished even those who were prepared to find in him an enlightened and extraordinary man.

The recognition of his official relation and title by the ministers afforded an indubitable evidence of the estimation in which he was held by them. When we remember how much the people of England are ordinarily disposed to lionise distinguished foreigners, we should not at all be surprised at the splendid reception he met with from them. He mixed with the first circles. He was courted by the rich and the powerful. Not only the ex-Judges, and ex-Councillors, but ex-Governors sought his friendship. Many of the "nabobs," whose *huzurs* did not condescend to take any notice of him in this country, and who would not have allowed him to wait upon them at their kacharies without being slipshod, were all eager to claim the honour of his acquaintance. Though many of the Earls and Marquisses and Dukes wanted only to lionise him, and turn him to account as an attraction at their *soirees,* yet there were several men who appreciated him, and sought his company with a view to acquire information on India. Among these were Lord Brougham, Sir W. Horton, Sir Henry Strachy and Sir Charles Forbes. With Lord Brougham, or rather with Henry Brougham,—for then this great man was known only as the bold and uncompromising advocate of popular education and the abolition of slavery—Rammohun Roy lived on terms of the closest and most confidential intimacy.

Not only the greatest men in the kingdom, but royalty itself delighted to do him honour. He was presented to the King by Sir J.C. Hobhouse, the then president of the Board of Control, and his Majesty assigned him a place at the Coronation among the ambassadors. On the opening of the London Bridge, he was invited by his Majesty to the dinner which was given in celebration of that event. The Court of Directors, though they refused to recognise his embassy and his title, treated him with honour. They entertained him at a public dinner on the 6th July, in the name of the Company at the London Tavern.

In accordance with the avowed object of his visit to Europe, he frequented every kind of assemblage, religious, political, literary, or social. He was to be seen in the drawing-room of the nobleman, as well as in the study of the humble man of letters—in parliament, listening to the impassioned eloquence of the champions of the Reform bill, as well as in the church, following the preacher in his sublime flights to eternity.

The charms of enlightened Female Society were highly appreciated by the Rajah. The amiability of his manners, and the orientalism and deferential respect of his address, rendered him in return an especial favourite with the ladies. Though born in a country where the females, endungeoned in the Zenana, are sunk in the slough of ignorance and prejudice, yet he knew and felt that humanizing influence which is exercised by female society on European character. It is no wonder, therefore, that he was an ardent admirer of British females. "The particulars of my voyage," says he, "and travels will be found in a Journal which I intend to publish, together with whatever has appeared to me most worthy of remark and record, in regard to the intelligence, riches, power, manners, customs and especially the *female virtue and excellence existing in this country.*"

Besides the society of European females there was another society which he liked, viz. that of pious and enlightened clergymen.

He had seen the generous and heroic sacrifices made by some of the Missionaries in his fatherland. He had witnessed their laudable exertions in promoting the moral and intellectual enlightenment of his countrymen. He had seen them take the lead in every thing that had a tendency to improve and elevate the native character. His intercourse with religious persons in Europe, increased therefore his esteem for a class of men who have done so much to benefit their fellow-beings. "If I were to settle with my family in Europe," he used to say, "I would never introduce them to any but religious persons, and from amongst them only would I select my friends; amongst them I find such kindness and friendship, that I feel as if surrounded by my own kindred."

It was not long before the discussion on the renewal of the charter came on in Parliament. Several individuals who had served under the Company, in their civil or military services, or resided in India as merchants or planters, were examined as witnesses. Rammohun Roy was also called upon to give his evidence before the Select Committee of the House of Commons.

That his knowledge, experience, and patriotism entitled him to speak authoritatively on subjects connected with the government of his country, does not admit of a moment's question. His evidence has been since embodied in a volume entitled, "Exposition of the Practical Operation of the Judicial and Revenue Systems of India and of the General Character and Condition of its Native Inhabitants." His replies to the queries of the Select Committee not only demonstrate an acquaintance with the evils of his country, but contain several valuable suggestions. They are not characterised by any unmeaning vituperation against the Indian Government, but breathe throughout a sincere and earnest with to ameliorate the condition of his countrymen. They are distinguished, above all, by a deep and lively sympathy with the condition of those crushed and prostrate millions of India, known by the name of RYOTS.

The political creed of the Rajah was decidedly that of a liberal. But it did by no means border on ultra-radicalism. He was a reformer, but a moderate and judicious one. In his youth, he was violently opposed to the English Government. But as he saw more of it, and learnt to compare it with the Mahommedan Government, his strong aversion was converted into a warm admiration for its general character. He considered the conquest of this country by the English nation as a providential interposition, calculated to answer important ends in the economy of the moral world. Though he was fully cognizant of the complex organisation of the Government, and of all the wrongs and grievances inseparable from its operation, yet he cheerfully and gratefully admitted the mainfold blessings it conferred on his country; and was strongly of opinion that the English were better fitted to govern it than the natives themselves, and that the withdrawal of the former, under existing circumstances, supposing it were to take place, would prove a curse rather than a blessing.

Rammohun Roy was a bold and enthusiastic advocate of civil and religious liberty. He watched with intense anxiety its progress in Europe, and tried his best to contribute to its advancement in his own country. When the Spanish Constitution was established, he and his friend Dwarakanath Tagore, to celebrate the event, gave a *Burra Khana* to their European friends. He was a great friend of Mr. Buckingham's, and when Governor Adam signed tha death warrant of the "Calcutta Journal," and banished its spirited and philanthropic Editor, he got up, it is well known, the memorable appeal to the King in Council for the liberty of free printing in India.

The influence which the Rajah obtained over the leaders of both the Whigs and Conservatives in England was extraordinary; and it was highly honourable to him that he rendered it subservient, not to his own aggrandisement, but to the political elevation of his country. We shall be able to judge of the extent of that influence, when we observe, that an urgent-letter of his prevented the Conservatives from opposing one of the Indian Bills in the House of Lords; and we are sure that he would have carried many ameliorative measures with reference to this country, but for the influence of the Leadenhall magnates and the weakness of the ministry.

In the autumn of 1832, he paid a visit to France, where the reception he met with, was as splendid as in England. He was received by Louis Philippe with the highest consideration, and dined with his Majesty twice. Literary as well as political men vied with each other in testyfying their regard for their extraordinary guest.

In the beginning of the year 1833, the Rajah returned to the hospitable mansion of Messrs. John and Joseph Hare, brothers of the late David Hare; but he returned with a dilapidated constitution. He had suffered before from bilious attacks. They were aggravated by the climate of Europe, and induced a slight pulmonary affection. In this state he went to Bristol, in the early part of September, to spend a few weeks with Miss Castles, at Stapleton Grove, intending to proceed thence to Devonshire, there to pass the winter.

Nine days after his arrival, he was attacked with a fever. Drs. Pritchard and Carrick attended him. Medicine afforded him, however, only temporary relief. His fever returned with redoubled vigour, and swelled into what the native doctors would call *Bigar*. The delirium was suceeded by a stupor from which he never recovered, and he breathed his last at 25 minutes after 2 A.M. on the 27th September. He had a sort of consciousness that he was approaching his end. He conversed very little during his illness, but was observed to be often engaged in mental prayer. The intensity of his emotions, while thus occupied, was remarkably reflected by his expressive and transparent features.

Just before he had set out for Europe, the Rajah told his friends that, on his death, each sect, the Christian, the Hindu, and the Mahommedan would respectively claim him to be of their persuasion, but he expressly declared that he belonged to none of them. His prediction has been fully realised. No sooner did he depart this life, than the subject of his religious opinions became an apple of discord. A variety of speculations was hazarded by different parties. While some represented him to be a Hindu, others affirmed that he was a Christian. The church-of-England-party said, that he was attached to their church; while the Unitarians claimed him for their own. The Vedantists represented him as literally a believer in their professed revelation; while the Mussulmans contended that he was a follower of the son of Abdullah. We confess, however, that each of these sects had reason enough for wrenching him to its side. From his frequent attendance, while in England, at their chapels, and his known bias to their doctrines, the unitarians had some sort of right to claim him. The especial patronage which he thought it proper to bestow on Vedantism, made it more than probable that he was a Vedantist. The profuse, though not altogether unmerited laudation he was in the habit of lavishing on the Mahommedan creed, was calculated to produce an impression that he was a believer in the Alkoran. But that Rammohun Roy was not a Mussulman in his creed, it requires no lengthened demonstration to prove. Neither was he an unitarian. We would go further and say,—though it may startle some of our readers who have been accustomed to identify Rammohun Roy with Vedantism,—that he was *not* a Vedantist. What then was he? This is not merely a curious, but an interesting and important problem, of which we shall attempt to give a solution, as the religious opinions of the Hindu Reformer appear to be still enveloped in mystery.

All speculations, as to his belief in the abstract truth of any religion, founded on his advocacy of certain doctrines connected with it, or his attendance at its place of worship, are obviously futile. For Rammohun Roy was a religious Benthamite, and estimated the different creeds existing in the world, not according to his notion of their truth, or falsehood, but his notion of their utility; according to their tendency, in his view, to promote the maximization of human happiness, and the minimization of human misery. His patronage, therefore, of any system of creed cannot be construed into a profession of it. He endeavoured to refine all gross and idolatrous systems into a system of pure monotheism. His works on Hindu Theology do not prove that he was a believer in the revelation of the Vedas, but that he aimed at engrafting a kind of universal unitarianism on it. But we have said that he was not an unitarian. To be sure not. At least, his unitarianism was essentially different from that of the Channings, the Carpenters the Priestleys, and the Belshams. His was a sort of Catholic unitarianism. It was philosophical theism. It was Natural Religion. It was the religion of many of the ancient philosophers. His advocacy and support of the doctrines inculcated by religions which are in themselves diametrically opposed to each other, though it might apparently evidence his vacillation, was in fact the result of his religious utilitarianism; for we can confidently assert that, in reference to his religious belief, not the slightest change took place in his mind for the last fifty years of his life. From his first renunciation of Hindu idolatry, at the age of sixteen, to the last moment of his existence, he maintained his religious sentiments, whatever they were nearly unaltered. The real religious sentiments of the Hindu Reformer are embodied in a pamphlet, written in the most choice Persian, with an Arabic preface. Though printed in his lifetime and seen by some of his friends, yet it was not published until his death; for he gave it as his last injunction, on leaving his country for Europe, that it should be published after his departure from this world. This work, which is entitled *Tohufutul Mowahedeen*, or a Present to Unitarians, discloses his belief in the unity of the Diety, his infinite power and infinite goodness, and in the immortality of the soul. It breathes an uncompromising and inveterate hostility to idolatry in all its forms. While due meed of applause is given to the Mahommedan creed, for being based on what he considered as the great doctrine of unity, the prophetical pretensions of the avatar of Mecca are treated with merited ridicule and contempt.

From what has been said, it is obvious that Rammohun Roy was an ecletic philosopher. He was, according to our humble opinion, essentially a theo-philanthropist. To promote love to God, and love to man, agreeably to his own view of both, constituted the practical and most important part of his creed. He had a strong sentiment of natural religion. He was deeply impressed with the necessity and importance of religion to society. He had always cherished, and the longer he lived, became the more confirmed in the conviction, that religion was an ineradicable principle of our nature, and absolutely and indispensably necessary to the welfare of mankind. He had read history, and knew that a godless people could never be a great people. He knew that the social fabric would quake and be shattered to atoms, were the ideas of God, of immortality, of moral responsibility altogether obliterated from every mind. He knew that were men seriously to persuade themselves for a moment that there was no God—that their physical and mental organisations had been the work of chance—that the myriads of suns and planets with which immensity is peopled, had all fortuitously leaped into existence—that, instead of being destined to survive those suns and planets, they were the creatures of a day, and that death was the dissolution of their being—that crimes, perpetrated by them in darkness had no witness;—they would at once plunge into the slough of scepticism, and so relapse into primeval barbarism.

He deeply felt that the idea of God—the great first cause—the primitive and infinite intelligence—is the most sublime and comprehensive of all ideas. The development of this idea he considered to be the great end of education. He was strongly of opinion that the knowledge of God is superior to /389/ every other. All other knowledge dwindles into nothingness before it. It is the source and criterion of man's elevation. It is the foundation of his happiness here and hereafter. To disseminate, therefore, such knowledge among his benighted countrymen, he considered as the object of his being here below.

Rammohun Roy, though he locked upon idolatry as a downright insult to the Supreme Being, and as necessarily and eternally a sin, cherished a stronger aversion towards scepticism. He loathed and abominated it as something worse than idolatry—as something more unnatural—as something more incompatible with the constitution of man.

It has been observed by a writer, who is largely quoted in the Biographical Memoir which we have placed at the head of this article that:

> As he is advanced in age, he became more strongly impressed with the importance of religion to the welfare of society, and the pernicious effects of scepticism. In his younger years, his mind had been deeply struck with the evils of believing too much, and against that he directed all his energies; but, in his latter days he began to feel that there was as much, if not greater danger in the tendency to believe too little. He often deplored the existence of a party which had sprung up in Calcutta, composed principally of imprudent young men, some of them possessing talent who had avowed themselves sceptics in the widest sense of the term. He described it as partly composed of East Indians, partly of the Hindu youth who, from education, had learnt to reject their own faith without substituting any other. These he thought more debased than the most bigoted Hindu, and their principles the bane of all moralitly.

This passage, evidently penned by one who knew the Rajah intimately, reads to us an awful lesson. The progress of circumstances, since his death, has clothed it with terrible import. The party, alluded to by the Rajah, is now a large and increasing party. The Hindu community is very much divided between those who worship Durga and Kali, and those who worship nothing—between those who believe in three hundred and thirty three millions of gods, and those who believe in none—those who think the world under the moral government of multitudinous powers, and those who deny all moral government. It is a humiliating but nevertheless an unquestionable fact, that many of those who call themselves educated natives seldom think of religion, and are known to manifest much indifference to it. We admit that they profess to believe in the existence of one God; but their belief, in nine cases out of ten, is not a living conviction, but a passive acquiescence in a truth forced on them. They oscillate between the creed they have renounced, and that which they profess. In theoretically renouncing the superstition of their fathers, and disembarrassing their minds from the fetters of that antiquated bigotry which still cleave to the great mass around them, they have not, we deeply regret to observe, embraced a purer and nobler religion. We confess, therefore, that there is some truth in the assertion made by even the best friends of India, the several of the educated natives are practical atheists. This practical atheism, however much we may deplore it, is regarded by men whose judgement is entitled to respect in such matters, as one of the natural and inevitable results of that system of education hitherto pursued by the Government—a system, which, though pregnant with results of the last importance to this country, is not sufficiently calculated to realise the great objects of education, inasmuch as it addresses itself more to the *head* than to the *heart*—to the *intellectual* than to the *moral* man. But intellectual cultivation is not identical with moral and religious cultivation. The one does not necessarily imply the other. That the development of our moral and religious feelings and affections cannot be effected by that of the mental faculties alone, is a truth which, though frequently repeated, does not appear to be sufficiently attended to by those, to whose, keeping the interests of our youth are committed.

That Rammohun Roy should think the educated natives of his time, who had avowed themselves sceptics in the "widest sense of the term," as "more debased than the most bigoted Hindu, and their principle the bane of all morality," was quite natural and proper. He thought what Socrates and Plato,—what the sages of his own country, Vyas and Manu,—what, in later times, Bacon had thought—"I would rather believe," says the great apostle of inductive philosophy, "I would rather believe all the fables in the Legend and the Talmud and the Alkoran than that this universal frame is without a mind." It was, therefore, no wonder that the idolatry of the great mass of his countrymen was looked upon by him in a softer and amiable light than the atheism of the *so-called* educated natives. Indeed, so alarming has been the progress of that atheism since his death, that a few Hindu gentlemen, impressed with the necessity and importance of counteracting its pernicious effects have established a society which has been noticed more than once in this Review. The *Hindu Theophilanthropic Society* owes its existence, as mentioned in the preface to the 1st volume of its published discourses, "to a conviction irresistibly forcing itself upon every reflective mind, that the great work of India's Regeneration cannot be achieved without due attention to her moral and religious improvement."

It is evident that Rammohun Roy had to battle with both idolatry and atheism. To wage a war of extermination against the one, and to check the incipient progress of the other, was the work, to the furtherance of which he devoted himself. To say that he had many endowments which eminently fitted him for it would be redundant. He was a man whose genius and energy, under happier circumstances, might have achieved a complete moral revolution among his countrymen. He was by nature one of those who lead, not one of those who follow—one of those who are in advance, not one of those who are behind their age.

Our opinion of Rammohun Roy has already been sufficiently explained. Rammohun Roy was emphatically a great man. His talents were not only varied and brilliant but of an eminently useful kind. He had a sound judgement, a large and disciplined mind. In variety of knowledge, in depth of reasoning, in correctness of taste, he was rivalled by none of his countrymen. Both intellectually and morally he would rank very high among his species. He had not only a strong intellect but a generous heart. No one was more strongly impressed with the conviction, that to do good to man, was among the chiefest of earthly duties and privileges. The golden maxim of doing to others as you would that they should do unto you, was frequently inculcated by him. The exercise of benevolence was associated by him with the greatest pleasure. To relieve the pains and to add to the pleasures of others was considered by him as a source of purest enjoyment. One winter day, as he was returning from his morning walk, he saw a poor sunburnt herb-seller—one of those men who daily cross the river with their basket-load of vegetables—who had alighted him burden from his head to take a little rest. Finding some difficulty in replacing it, as there was none to help him; Rammohun Roy generously gave his assistance and with his own hands helped the man to lift his load. We shall not surely be charged with using the language of exaggeration, if we declare that, among the philanthropists and reformers to whom alone the title of "Great."— too often lavished on tyrants, heroes and conquerors, for building their aggrandisement on the prostration of their species,—should be confined and kept sacred, and who alone should monopolise all the places in the Temple of Fame,—a high place must unquestionably be assigned to Rammohun Roy. With an energy which set at nought the formidable resistance he encountered from the slaves of bigotry—with a perseverence which was unwearying—with a moral courage which triumphed over persecution—with a benevolence which was not exclusive but catholic—with a religious aspiration, which was fervid and impassioned but not impulsive and fanatical—he laboured, according to the light and knowledge which he enjoyed, to liberate the Hindu mind from the tyranny of superstition, and to inoculate it with the elevating principles of a more rational faith.

The life of Rammohun Roy was commensurate with one of the most important and stirring periods in the annals of this country. Its embraces the commencement of that great social and moral revolution through which she is now silently but surely passing. When Rammohun Roy was born, darkness—even the darkness of ignorance and superstition—brooded over his fatherland. When he died, the spirit of enquiry was abroad in high places, and was triumphantly exploding antiquated errors. He lived to see a line of demarkation, which, since his death, has been considerably deepened, strongly drawn among the Hindus between the enlightened few and the benighted many. Rammohun Roy was the author of a great religious schism, which is destined to spread and widen. He helped to break the crust of that rigid and unbroken superstition, which had braved the formidable attacks of the Buddhist, and the fierce persecution of the Mahommedan. No native had before been enlightened and bold enough to do any thing of the kind. He was the first who opened the eyes of his countrymen to the monstrous absurdities of their national creed. He was the first who thundered forth into their ears—which had been for ages accustomed to the invocation of *mantras,* and hermetically sealed against all true religion—the great truth that, "*God is One and without a second.*" But, as yet, we have only seen the dawn of a better and more promising era. The number of those, upon whose taste and feelings, and sentiments, education has effectually told, is comparatively very limited. And even in their minds there is hitherto a strange mixture of light and darkness, truth and error. The great mass still grope in moral and intellectual night. But the light that is to travel eastward and westward, and northward and southward, has already begun to illumine the horizon. The days of Hinduism are therefore numbered. The time is coming (and oh, may it approach with lightning speed!) when the millions of Hindustan, who now exhibit a heart-rending spectacle of the prostitution of all that is sublime in religion and divine in worship, shall,—liberated from the thraldom of ignorance, and bigotry and superstition,—learn to love, and obey, and adore the one, true, and living God!

—K.C. Mitter

References

1. This was said by her before she set out on her last pilgrimage to Juggernaut, where she died. With such self-denying devotion did she conform to the rites of the Hindu religion, that she would not allow a female servant to accompany her to Juggernaut, or any other provision to be made for her comfort or support on her journey. When at Puri, she occupied herself in sweeping the temple of the uncouth idol. One-eighth of the infatuated pilgrims who crowd to Juggernaut at Dol and Rathjatras every year meet with untimely graves. They fall victims to the fœtid air of the place and the extraordinary hardships of the journey.

2. The great grandson of this Rajah, Srish Chandra Bahadur, seems to have inherited his ancestor's liberality. He has subscribed Co.'s Rs. 3,000, to the New College at Kishnaghur.

3. The Mesnavi is a work of Maulano Rum, a celebrated Persian poet. It treats of religion, morality and politics. "It is an astonishing work," says Sir W. Jones, "and the highest flights of sublimity can be found in it."

4. Mr. Secretary Dodswell, in writing to the Register of the Nizamut Adawlut, of the Suttee rite, says, "*Should* this practice be not grounded on any precept of their law, the Governor-General would hope that the custom, which at present prevails among Hindu women of burning themselves with the bodies of their deceased husbands, might gradually but not immediately be altogether abolished."

5. By. D. I,., R.—a signature too well known in our Indian Literature to require any further explication here.

8

The Mission of the Brahmo Samaj

I. THE CHURCH IDEA

The Mission of the Brahmo Samaj or the Theistic Church of India in the modern world is unique; and the work it has undertaken to do is altogether new; *viz.*, to organise a system of religious culture and to build up a Church on the basis of natural and Universal Theism.

Now there are many amongst modern thinkers who are of opinion that natural Theism, having no firmer basis than human thought, is quite insecure for the purpose of starting a system of effective culture or for keeping up an active religious organisation. It is too open to the inroads of modern science and speculation. The doctrine of a Supreme Being, endowed with wisdom and love, on which alone it can be lastingly founded is, according to these thinkers, yet far from being established by human reason. All the ancient religions were safer, because they were supported by two well-known props, *viz., (I) special and miraculous revelation* and *(II) infallible authority.*

In the face of such doubts the Theistic Church of India has undertaken to organise itself as a spiritually effective body. It is for this reason that we have called its mission unique. But what is our reply to these objections? First, our reply is very simple. Men must live according to their faith; they must abide by it, and they must preach it. They must propagate it if they truly believe that it leads to the good of man; and if they are wise, they should start social organisations for its effective propagation. Secondly, it is not simply from an inward conviction of truth that our adherence is due to the

Theistic Church; but we believe that by the providence of a wise and merciful Being, this church has been brought into existence to furnish guidance to the people of this country and of the world at large during a period of crisis in the world's spiritual history. The Supreme Being is using the Theistic Church as a new blow-pipe, like the one in a goldsmith's hand, to strengthen and divert and spiritual energies of the race into new directions by joining it, we fulfil His purpose and co-operate with Him in His great work.

The Theistic Church is not merely a system of new philosophy. Philosophy, as such, is meant for a few advanced thinkers; it engages their attention for sometime and then disappears in course of the evolution of human society and becomes a matter of historical opinion. But Modern Theism is not such. It is organising itself into a church or community of fellow believers, with definite ideas and courses of action. As a living seed falling into the ground at once proceeds to gather round itself a crust of earth as a sort of protection against the wear and tear of conflicting natural forces, and to allow itself time for development, so by Divine ordination, a recreated saving energy, coming into operation in human society, gathers round itself a number of sympathetic souls who form something like a crust round it and help it to carry out its object. Thus is the formation of a church natural and universal.

THEISM DEFINED

The faith of the Brahmo Samaj is Natural and Universal Theism and not the Deism that was prevalent in the western world during the latter half of the eighteenth and the first half of the nineteenth century. Nor is it that poor and helpless faith, known to modern philosophy, which represents the Supreme Being only as the first link of a long chain of causation, as if he has, once for all, surrendered the government of the world to blind forces and to the silent but steady operation of natural laws working through a process of evolution no longer needing his personal guidance. The Theistic Church believes in Theism *i.e.* the doctrine of a Supreme Being endowed with wisdom and love.

In inunciating such a thing as an Infinite Being endowed with wisdom and love, I render myself open to the charge of raising a great philosophical difficulty; for personality, some argue, means limitation and distinction, whereas infinitude, by its very nature, is undetermined and all-inclusive. To some thinkers, an Infinite Person may seem to be something like 'a golden cup of stone', to use a familiar Bengali expression. But think deeply, and you will find that there is both unity and difference; room for both the infinite and the personal. The external world and the internal spirit of man are both *from* Him, *in* Him and *of* Him, manifestations of His supreme energy, wisdom and love, yet they are different—different not only from each other in their manifested selves, but also different from the supreme in their manifested natures and proportions. The supreme is *in* all, *includes* all, but transcends all. The relation is something like the one existing between the speaker and his speech. The word is ushered into existence by the will of the speaker and can be justly said to be *from* the speaker, *in* the speaker and *of* the speaker, yet it is not the speaker, but is only, an infinitesimal manifestation of the energy of the speaker. Similarly we have been launched into life by the will of the Supreme and may justly be said to be *from* the Supreme, *in* the Supreme and *of* the Supreme yet *not* the Supreme, being only infinitesimal manifestations of His energy. He pervades us, He includes us, He ingulfs us, He upholds, He is immanent in us and in the world; yet transcends both and is thereby distinct *from* both.

This conception, it will be found, is vastly different from the current Christian idea of an anthropomorphic and extra-cosmic Being called God, residing in a certain place called Heaven, knowing the affairs of men by reason of his Omniscience and ruling the world by reason of his almightiness. To us, Hindus of the East, such a conception is childish. To conceive an extra-cosmic Being is to give up his Infinitude; from which our Eastern minds shrink in disgust.

The Supreme Being has so constituted the soul of man and has so endowed it with spiritual instincts, that it naturally tends to mingle with Him in loving communion as the river runs to mingle with the sea. The Bhagavat defines loving communion, as "that incessant flowing of the soul into the oversoul, as flows the Ganges into the Sea." In Him is the full satisfaction of our spirit. To know him as truth is the greatest joy to its knowledge, to love him as the Supremely loveable is the highest satisfaction of its love and to exercise the active powers in obedienee to His guidance is the highest fulfilment of its aim in life.

Accordingly, it will be seen that loving communion with the supreme is the second great point in that natural and universal Theism which the Theistic Church of India has adopted for itself.

THE UNIVERSAL AND THE LOCAL IN RELIGION

The laws of the spiritual world like those in the domain of nature are marked by uniformity and universality. Certainly there is revelation. As heat in any form is a revelation of the sun, and has its source in the sun, so spiritual life in any form, whether garbed under the misleading cover of oriental Panthism or occidental Anthropomorphism, is revelation from the Supreme Being. There has been groping and finding for eternal truth in all lands and in all ages; and human search under certain condition has been blessed by such revelation. The study of a series like the "Sacred Books of the East" has convinced even the narrowest and most sectarian minds of the west, that there has been no monopoly in divine truth for any race. This discovery of the universality of Divine revelation has brought into the operation a new spirit in the modern world. (i) The old spirit of sectarianism which took pleasure in dividing and sub-dividing men into conflicting sects is receiving a check. (ii) Men's eyes are turning to the distinction between the universal and the national or local, in popular religions. We cannot deny that there is such a distinction in all religions. Why in religiön alone, there is such a distinction in all human institutions, nay, in human nature itself. The manner in which family and society are regulated may be different in different countries but the spirit is the same everywhere. The differences are but the local aspects of the same guiding principle.

Religion or man's attitude towards the Infinite can be viewed in many aspects. Some may regard Him from the standpoint of the knowing mind and may feel Him to be the *Supreme Truth*; others who view Him from the side of the emotions may regard Him as the *Supremely Loveable*; whereas a third class may view Him as the Supreme Regulator of human conduct. Thus the Supreme Reality may reveal Himself to some minds as an abode of peace, to some as a benign master, to others as a friend, to some as a loving father, whilst perhaps to others He may reveal Himself as a loving consort of the soul. Different men approached Him from different standpoints and were differently enlightened. There is an element of truth in each point of view as we can plainly see. The error of sectarianism lay in conceiving its own point of view as the only true one and in contemptuously disregarding and at times carrying on mortal warfare with all others. The second error was that among the sects, the beliefs and practices which were purely local and national assumed in the eyes of their followers all the importance of universal principles and were accepted as the effects of the Supreme Being's special and miraculous revelation. It was under this conviction that endless wars were carried on among the sects.

Time has now come for discriminating between the universal and the local or national in religion and also for accentuating its universal aspects more than its local differences. The modes of expression of the piety of different races may be different but we cannot ignore the fact that these are local manifestations of the same fundamental truth, *viz.*—Natural and Universal Theism.

Let us now put briefly and in a concise form our ideal of the future religious life of mankind. Loving communion with the Supreme Being will be the guiding principle in which all sects, all parties, all communities of religious believers will unite, all other things being held may be national, local, traditional and sectional. Individuals also will have as much voice in their religious ideas and their local national and personal preference as their material and spiritual constitutions vary. Religious bodies will also differ in their modes of church organisation, their social usages, their means of spiritual culture, their modes of propagation and active ministry, their rites of private and public service and in their domestic and social ceremonies; but they will agree in the main principles of the universal religion—namely in the Fatherhood of God and the Brotherhood of man, in the freedom of the human soul, in love and reverence for the great and the good of all races, in the final triumph of righteousness, in the purity and elevation of domestic and social like as a stepping-stone to man's spiritual and social progress, in the love and service of man as the best way of serving the Supreme Being.

LOVING COMMUNION WITH THE SUPREME THE ESSENCE OF SPIRITUAL LIFE

As rivers have their fruition and perfection in mingling with the ocean, so the human soul has its fruition and perfection in loving-communion with the Supreme. Accordingly the Theistic Church of India lays all the insistence, that is possible with its limited energy, on living and loving communion with the Supreme as the chief spiritual aim of its members. It is not simply a theological body delighting in clever expositions of nice points of liberal religion; nor is it merely a reformatory organisation, seeking to reform the many social abuses by which our dear country is afflicted. Of course social reform forms an important part of the programme of its work; but that is only its secondary aim, a part of the conscientious and consistent operation of its principles, but its main effort is directed towards enabling men and women themselves to the contemplation and loving communion with the Supreme.

Such loving communion is the spring from which flow all the streams of pure and elevated life. All rightiousness, all unselfishness, all deeds of duty and sacrifice, all ennobling thoughts of the mind or impulses of the heart, all philanthropy, spring out of this fountain.

The exercise of loving communion with the Supreme Being is a source of peace and strength for the tempted, buffeted and careworn souls of men. The lovers of God, in all ages and all climes, have borne testimony to this fact. What the solitary nest is to the frightened bird, what the shady bush in the forest is to the arrow-stricken deer, what the safe harbour is to the passengers of a tempest-tossed ship, what the mother's bosom is to the suffering child, the same is the peaceful shelter at the feet of the Supreme Being. This abode of peace is ready at hand within the reach of all. Retire, O man, in your moments of trouble to the feet of this indwelling Power, in a spirit of resignation, and rest and refreshment, hope and strength, peace and joy, will be your portion.

Thus to enable men and women to hold loving communion with the Supreme and thereby raise and ennoble them, and to lift them above their sins and temptations, is the *first,* the grandest and the most spiritual part of the mission of the Theistic Church of India.

IMMORTALITY

In this loving communion lies the germ of another faith which is also a marked feature of the faith of the Theistic Church of India, namely, the faith in the immortality of the soul. In the state of loving communion with the Supreme, there comes an inwork conviction to the soul that such communion knows no limitations of space or time and that it is for all time. In ascending to the Highest we ascend above death. The soul refuses to believe that after having drawn us into His closer embrace and after having awakened in us such spiritual aspirations, He will doom us to destruction. The joys of that spiritual relationship bear an internal evidence that they would be ever-lasting. Thus far we are certain; all other speculations, such as the form in which we shall live, the place or sphere whither we may be transported after death, or the new relations into which we may enter & c., are more or less in uncertainty and individual believers are left free to arrive at conclusions that seem most reasonable to them.

THE SOCIAL MISSION OF THE THEISTIC CHURCH

Next after this comes the social and moral part of the Church's work. We in India have been taught to look upon pure and spiritual Theism as anti-social under the influence of Vedantism, the theory of *maya* or illusion has been invented which looks upon society and its relations as so many snares, the greatest wisdom of an aspirant for final deliverance lying in shunning them. This anti-social philosophy has done an incalculable amount of harm in this country. It has drawn away into the life of mendicancy hundreds of spiritually disposed persons, and has thereby robbed society of their personal influence and example and has led many others, whom circumstances prevented from adopting that life, but who yet believed in their hearts the prevalent theory, to pine away in life by looking upon the world as a prison-house. It has checked the spirit of philanthropy as a part of religious exercise and has made the cast of Hinduism sombre and melancholy. It is the mission of the Theistic Church of India to raise Hinduism and Hindu Society from this sombre and gloomy view of life and this trainting touch of Vedantism by teaching that human society is a Divine dispensation and all its relationships are sacred and spiritual. The Supreme Being has placed individual man in this world in the midst of other individuals, tied together by various loving relationships. Each of those relationships has duties apportioned to it which are sacred and important and cannot be neglected without degrading man or without degrading human society. The proper direction of the relationship between husband and wife or between parent and children, or between brothers and sisters or between neighbour and neighbour or between the citizen and country, or between man and society, is an essential and important condition of the growth and development of the human soul. Hence is morality an essential part of man's true spirituality.

Accordingly, the second feature of modern Indian Theism is that it is essentially social and moral. Being social, it seeks to reform and improve human society, to remove those abuses that afflict communities of men and interfere with their true spiritual progress; and being moral, it directs its efforts to the improvement of human character as the best means of holding loving communion with the Supreme. Thus it will be seen that every domain of social reform whether it be the abolition of caste, or the lifting-up of the depressed classes, or the education and emancipation of women, or the discontinuance of child-marriages, or the allowance of widow-remarriages, legitimately comes within its scope and is a necessary part of its programme of reformatory work.

This social side of Theism also necessarily leads it to look upon philanthropy as a part of its spiritual culture. It was a pet saying of Raja Rammohun Roy,—"Brother, brother, the service of man is the service of God." The religiousness of the Hindu race has ever been a marked trait of their national character from the earliest times. But that religiousness has always had two characteristics, first, it has been largely coloured by their pessimistic view of life engendered by the Vedanta; secondly, it has had its play largely in external ceremonial forms, penances and austerities. Religion as the voice of a loving father, and as a messenger to suffering humanity, had never occurred to our teachers. Now has come the time to give religion that turn in India—*to divert the religiousness of the people to philanthropy*. It is something like diverting the currents of our mighty rivers into new channels, for irrigation purposes, by digging canals.

A significant aspect of the social side of this modern Indian Theism is the importance it attaches to home-life. Of all the dispensations of the Almighty for the education and perfection of man, the evolution of home-life has been the most far-reaching in its effects. What the shady retreat or the nursery is to the young plant, that has been the home to the human child; a refuge of rest and protection without which human society would have crumbled away. Not only that, such a refuge of rest and protection is extremely useful to men and women for the growth and cultivation of their higher faculties, which go a great way to ennoble human nature and to improve human society. A good and orderly home is the best institution under which the moral and spiritual progress of society can be attained, and the best of places where an altar of the Supreme Being can be raised.

Hence the Theistic Church attaches considerable importance to the duty of creating good and orderly homes. But the question of creating good and orderly homes necessarily involves the question of raising the present social position of woman in India. As long as woman is degraded, despised and down trodden, so long the improvement of our home life is difficult of attainment. The best way of raising woman from their present state of degradation is to give them education and social liberty. I have no time to enter here into a detailed discussion of the objections that are generally put forward by a class of critics in this country against the elevation and social emancipation of woman. Suffice it to say that the conviction is daily strengthening in me, that no race that consents to keep its women in bondage and degradation can ever attain to true national greatness. The backbone of a nation's true worth is to be found in its homes and in its women.

The *Third* prominent feature of this Theism is the abolition of caste. The hereditary caste-system in India has been productive of many social evils. It has given undue prominence to the priestly caste, leading to all the evils of unrestrained sacerdotalism; it has depressed the lower ranks of society thus degrading them to a most abject condition; it has divided and sub-divided the Hindus of the country, till all feeling of the unity of the race is almost dead; it has brought in a most abject form of social slavery, which has altogether repressed individual independence, and has thereby extinguished all real manhood in our men; it has checked foreign travel, national enterprise and the industrial development of the country. But to the theist it is objectionable, because it is based on the virtual denial of the brotherhood of man. He cannot countenance it in his own person, nor can he tolerate it in society. To speak truly, most of the present prejudice of the orthodox Hindu community against the Brahmo Samaj is due to two causes—1st, its advocacy of the abolition of caste, second, its advocacy of the social emancipation of woman.

The *fourth* feature of this social side of the Church's Mission is the great importance it attaches to the purity of man's moral conduct. It is essentially moral. It holds that man's spiritual progress depends on the moral purity of his mind and character, that righteousness in thought and action is an essential condition of man's communion with the Supreme. This feature is highly important in this country; because here there has been, in many sects, something like a divorce between religion and morality. Not to speak of the followers of certain schools of the sect called *Tantrics,* who openly indulged in wine and promiscuous intercourse with women, and raised ordinary forms of bestiality into forms of religious culture, or of the Vattabhacharyas of Guzrat, whose priests made undisguised indulgence in immorality a mark of their religious prominence, there have been and still are many mystical sects in this country with whom the practice of immorality is not incompatible with the attainment of high degree of spirituality:—a view from which the Theistic Church turns away in disgust. According to its principles, purity in thought and deed, utter unselfishness in pursuit of truth, strict observance of the moral law, honesty in thought, speech and action, courage to shun the wrong and do the right and unfailing adherence to the rules of justice, are the basal principles on which alone can be raised the superstructure of a truly pious life. That being its principle, it seeks to carry on an unceasing war against such social evils as intemperance, the encouragement of prostitution, of dancing girls, of the native theatres where professional public women are actresses and have an opportunity of freely mixing with young men belonging to respectable middle-class families, and all other forms of secret or open social vice to which modern India is a prey by reason of the unsettling effects of modern education.

RECAPITULATION

Let me now sum up by recapitulating some of the leading features of this Theism of ours, which I have put forward in the forgoing pages.

(i) In the first place, a prominent feature of our faith is its *universality*. It stands on the common element in all religions, and therefore has a word of sympathy for all. It is true that in one sense it is eclectic; but its eclecticism is not a many-coloured robe of an Indian Fakir, produced by mere patch-work, but is a spiritual organic fusion produced by natural evolution; it is an intellectual and spiritual attitude, born of a conviction of the universality of religion.

(ii) The second great feature is its *spirituality*. In point of spirituality it turns to the East and to the Rishis of India, who have taught us to hold living and loving communion with the In-dwelling Presence and it also teaches the practice of contemplation and meditation as an effective means of promoting that communion. In this respect it is essentially Hindu.

(iii) The third feature is its *Sociality*. It is not anti-socialism of Vedantism, which teaches man to look upon life with

all its relations as a bondage and a snare, but teaches that those relations are Divine ordinations for the education and perfection of man. It looks upon the human home as a sacred institution, and the position of woman in it as sacred and important. From its sociality arises another important feature, namely, *morality.* It makes morality an essential part of its spirituality. It looks upon purity of mind and conduct as necessary conditions of loving communion with the Supreme. Besides the elevation of society being within the range of its aims and purposes, the promotion of morality comes legitimately as a part of its mission. In this respect it is rather Western.

(iv) The fourth is an important feature, namely, its *independence.* We believe in Divine Revelation; we believe that man, by reason of his spiritual endowment, can rise to the contemplation of the Supreme Being and can establish direct relationship with Him, and as a result of that communion can receive spiritual and moral revelations from the Supreme. At such moments spiritual and moral truths may intuitively and instinctively come within the range of his spiritual vision and he can become a seer. Truths similarly revealed by the seers and sages of all lands have been treasured up in the scriptures of all races. Accordingly, we honour all scriptures, but yet do not believe in infallible authority. We know that Divine truth has been mixed up with human error in the sayings of all teachers and we try to sift them with the aid of the Divine light within us. Human independence in this matter is sacred and inalienable. So the character of our faith is essentially free. There is harmony between reverence and freedom, conservation and progress.

(v) The fifth feature is its immediacy. As every morning the earth looks directly to the sun and in that direct looking are its life, its energy, its beauty and is fruitfulness, so in direct loving communion with the Supreme lies its life and light. What the air is to the bird, what the water is to the fish, that is the light of the Divine Presence to the soul. It truly lives, moves and has its being in Him. And

that the human soul may be able so to move, it has been spiritually endowed with the power of loving communion. We see no place of mediation in that great act of soul-communion with the Supreme. The doctrine of mediation has done one great moral and spiritual harm. It has thrown up a screen, as it were, between man and God, and has taught man and woman to give to man the thanks that are due to the Almighty, and has forged chains of bondage that have bound down human thought to the errors of individual thinkers.

(vi) The last and perhaps the greatest feature of modern Theism is its *Catholicity.* It arises directly from its naturalness and its universality. We believe there is no monopoly in religious truth. Of course, in the course of historical development, some races have shown special aptitudes for certain elements of human character. Such difference was due to various natural causes. The Hindus, who lived in a mild and genial climate and were comparatively free from struggles with nature for subsistence, and who were surrounded by stupendous mountains and large rivers and extensive fields, naturally became contemplative. And their contemplation led them into deep researches into the spirit and they became possessors of mines of spiritual wisdom and became accustomed to see God in the soul. The Greeks, who lived in the midst of natural beauty and had a light heart in their struggle for existence naturally came to regard God as the supremely beautiful. To them virtue was beautiful conduct and vice was another name for ugliness in life. The Jews, who had a chequered history, who were wanderers over the earth always feeling the bitterness of foreign dominion and always aspiring for a return to their favoured land, naturally attached great importance to the facts of history and naturally regarded their leaders who promised to lead them to deliverance, as Divinely appointed and viewed them as rescuers and liberators. Thus every nation developed its spiritual instincts according to its inheritance and its environment. Along with the universal element of faith there came to be

mixed up many local and peculiar national beliefs. We, who keep our eyes on the universal in religion, are more sympathetic towards what is good in all and can more truly honour the spiritually good and great in every land. We often pass by their local prejudices and peculiarities, their erroneous notions and doctrines, and fix our eyes upon the lessons of love of God and man that they bear witness to in their lives. Thus is our faith Catholic in its spirit.

—Mahes Chandra Ghosh

9

The Brahmo Samaj

Personally ever ready to stand up to any challenge, Rammohun directed his institutional activities to preparation for active social work rather than for such work itself. His single experiment of vigilance committees to fight sati yielded magnificent results but it also revealed that more work was needed before it could be expanded. He looked to education to bring about a receptive atmosphere to new ideas. He wrote text-books in Bengali and he extended his generous support to all movements and organisations which had even a remote bearing on education. It was his inspiration that started the move for the Hindu College, though he had to withdraw from it because of the antipathy of interested Hindus. And it was his active support which enabled Dr. Alexander Duff to carry on despite the opposition that faced him on his arrival in India. Rammohun allowed him the use of his old Brahmo building, brought him students and even attended his religious classes in order to win over critics or silence them. The Hindu College became later the Presidency College, and Dr. Duff's institution grew into the Scottish Churches College—the two institutions of higher learning which provided Bengal its leadership for the next century. Apart from this, Rammohun maintained an English school in Calcutta from 1817, the Vedanta College for Sanskrit studies from 1826, and personally conducted a Bengali and a Persian Journal for the diffusion of scientific, historical, literary and political knowledge. In his latter to Lord Amherst, he strongly urged the cause of Western education—a letter which failed at the time to receive the attention it merited but which played a decisive role later in determining policy.

Rammohun had always been interested in religious discussion. Since his residence in Calcutta, he had experimented with forming religious societies—the Atmiya Society (1815), the Unitarian Committee (1822), and the Brahmo Samaj (1828). In all three, weekly meetings were a regular feature. For various reasons it was not a popular movement, and the excommunication of Rammohun by his brother's son restricted its appeal even more. There were regular attenders who had been with Rammohun through all three experiments. These accepted the worship of Brahma (monotheistic) as the true religion. Others without avowing their faith in monotheism were drawn by Rammohun's personality. But, on account of his incessant attacks on Hindu idolatry, most of these gradually dropped out. The Unitarian Committee which consisted of Indians and European missionaries, entered troubled waters when Rammohun extended his rationalisation to Christianity. So with the Brahmo Samaj there was left a devoted but small band. Many came to the weekly meetings out of curiosity. He was opposed to caste distinction but even he refrained from admitting any but Brahmins to the recitations of the Vedas and the Upanishads. His staunchest supporter was Dwarakanath Tagore who looked after the affairs of the Samaj. The first minister, Ram Chandra Vidyavagis, brother of Rammohun's ascetic friend, had in a weak moment joined the orthodox in their petition against the suppression of sati, but he returned to the Samaj. Until Devendranath Tagore entered the Samaj, he carried on the work with single minded devotion. With Devendranath's entry into the Samaj began a period, from 1843 onwards, when the issues that troubled Hindu society were fiercely agitated in the Samaj itself, separating its members and giving rise to schisms. Religious differences there were, the pull of Christian ideas and the force of Hindu thought working in different directions. But the parting of the ways invariably came over social issues. And it is interesting to note that almost in every instance the seceding or protesting element was formed by men who sought to make practice conform to profession. Thus the theories propounded by Rammohun Roy were taken up by those who followed him.

Improving the condition of widows, the education of women and the removal of caste restrictions were natural lines of practical work rising out of the Raja's writings. Yet there is an interesting suggestion that the intense work for women's education started in 1863 under Keshab Chandra Sen followed on the criticism of Dr. Bhau Daji, the Bombay scholar, who rebuked the Brahmo Samaj during his Calcutta visit for emphasising contemplation at the expense of practical social work. Dr. Daji commended the work of the Bethune Society and called upon the Brahmos to imitate it. As early as 1840, a society, "Founded somewhat on the principles of freemasonry had been formed in Bombay by the first generation of educated Hindus, having for its object the abolition of caste." On June 13, 1848, they formed a society called the Students' Literary and Scientific Society which ran classes and schools for the education of girls. By 1862, the principle of equal education for men and women had been fully accepted in Western India.

The enabling measure which permitted the remarriage of Hindu widows, is remarkable for the speed with which it was enacted. In October 1855, Pandit Iswarchandra Vidyasagar, Principal of the Sanskrit College, Calcutta, presented a petition to the Government of India demanding legislation on this subject. In November, Mr. J.P. Grant, member of the Legislative Council, Presented a Bill "to remove all legal obstacles to the marriage of Hindu widows." It was referred to Select Committee and in July 1856 the Bill suitably amended was passed into law. The proceedings of the legislature which, of course, consisted mainly of English officials, reveals how at all stages the general attitude was to ensure the permissive nature of the measure and to meet the "legitimate" fears of the reactionary about the consequences to Hindu social life.

In moving the Bill, Mr. Grant revealed how Pandit Iswarchandra Vidyasagar had worked for it, how he had wide support from all over the country, and how attempts had been made in the years intervening between its presentation and the suppression of sati to bring about widow marriages in Hindu Society. The one success, he reported, came from Poona where "a large assembly of Pandits actually gave permission to the widowed daughter of a Hindu of high caste to remarry and the permission had been acted upon." The largest number of petitions came from Bengal, but Mr. Grant referred to representations from Nagpur and Madras and petitions from parts of Western India.

There were many more representations from reactionary Hindus, whose signatures outnumbered those of the reformers by twelve to one. Mr. Grant, however, declared emphatically that everyone of the 5,000 signatories for the reform had a personal interest concerning the domestic happiness of his family. He insisted that for everyone signatory there would be a hundred in favour of the reform. He disclosed that the Law Commissioners in framing the penal code had considered a law to enable widow remarriage. He quoted a paragraph which read:

> The Law Commissioners are sensible that a mere alteration in the law will immediately and directly effect little towards remedying the evil. But they are not without expectation that an alteration of the law would induce an alteration of feeling in this matter; and, if that could be effected, more would be dome towards repressing child murder than could be done by the most severe laws. They are now collecting information on this point, the result of which will duly be laid before the Government.

The provincial governments had been silent, except for the strong support of the Lieutenant-Governor of Agra. But in the Legislative Council in 1856, there was general support for the Bill. "If I knew for certain that but one little girl will be saved by this Act from the horrors of *Brahmacharia*", said Mr. Grant, "I would pass it for her sake; if I believed, as firmly as I believed the contrary, that the Act would remain wholly a dead letter, I would pass it for sake of the English name." And he appealed to the house to pass it, though the petitioners against it were ten times the number of those in its favour, because the latter "had an interest in the bill which was personal."

The expectation entertained by Mr. Grant that those who had braved Hindu orthodoxy in petitioning for the Act, would make good use of it, was fully borne out in the beginning. The first widow remarriage has been described by Pandit Sivanath Sastri in his sketch on Pandit Vidyasagar:

> I shall never forget the day. When Pandit Vidyasagar came with his friend, the bridegroom, at the head of a large procession, the crowd of spectators was so great that there was not an inch of moving space, and many fell into the big drains which were to be seen by the sides of Calcutta streets those days. After the ceremony, it became the subject of discussion everywhere; in the bazaars and the shops, in the streets; in the public squares, in students' lodging-houses, in gentlemen's drawing-rooms, in offices and it distant village homes, where even women earnestly discussed it among themselves. The weavers of Santipore issued a peculiar kind of women's sari which contained woven along its borders the first lines of a newly composed song which went on to say "May Vidyasagar live long".

Twelve years later, the indefatigable reformer was less optimistic. Attending a window remarriage, he blessed the nine-years old daughter of a friend with the words, "May you live long, may little daughter, may you be united to a suitable bridegroom, but then become a widow, and may I have the opportunity of getting you married again." He explained that if the daughters of his friends did not become widows, how was he to carry out his pet idea!

Iswarchandra Vidyasagar had argued the cause purely for the sake of child widows. Though he had delved deep into the sacred texts to establish that widowhood was not enjoined by the shastras, the Government throughout refused to declare an opinion on the subject. In this it diverged from Lord Bentinck's concept of "legislator for the Hindus." It legislated for that section of the Hindus which held that widow marriages were permissible, safeguarding in matters of inheritance the customs of the orthodox. One important concession was made to the reformers—that the marriage ceremony for a widow should be the same as the ceremony for a first marriage.

In the five years following the enactment of the Widow Remarriage Act, 25 such marriages were performed through the efforts of Pandit Iswarchandra Vidyasagar who was liberal with offers of monetary help. Because of this, some of the marriages led to complicated situations, the bridegrooms coming forward with a view to obtaining financial assistance and sometimes even threatening to leave their wives if further money was not forthcoming. The five years from 1864-1869 saw eight widows remarried under the auspices of the Brahmo Samaj under very different conditions. "Many a widow", observes Pandit Sitanath Tatvabhushan, "had literally to be stolen from their parents' house, and the history of their rescue will ever remain as a great monument to the moral enthusiasm and devotion to the causes of suffering humanity of the early members of the Samaj."

One of these, Sasipada Banerjee, began his long life of public service with the promotion of the marriage of his widowed niece (1868) in the face of reactionary opposition which did not stop short of kidnapping and assault. The story is told at length by Pandit Tatvabhushan who had it from Sasipada Benerjee himself. The young widow and her mother had taken refuge at Barahanagar with the Brahmo Samajist whose unorthodox ways had roused the enmity of the community. But during Sasipada Banerjee's absence from home the girl was forcibly removed and the mother was dragged out on the public road, and pressed to go back to the family home. After a hundred days, Banerjee rescued them from Benares, evaded pursuit by pressing on to Allababad and finally brought them to Calcutta. He resolved to have the niece married to a Brahmo colleague who had lost his wife, a decision which left even some of his Brahmo colleague aghast because the bridegroom was of lower caste. After facing many difficulties in securing a house, and amid hostile demonstrations, the ceremony was performed.

When Sasipada Banerjee returned to his Barahanagar home, he found the doors and windows of his house broken. A sustained campaign was started to punish him for his temerity in flouting orthodoxy. But Banerjee's house became a refuge for widows, and some 40 remarriages took place from his home. "In those early days, specially in the seventies," observes Pandit Tatvabhushan, "the reform activities of Brahmo young men often found expression in the zeal with which they helped young widows among their friends and relations to come out of their homes and join the Samaj, for purposes of remarriage: and in the absence of any public institution where these widows might find shelter and education, they had generally to be accommodated in Brahmo families, whence, as opportunities arose, they were married out. The work of rescuing young widows was always undertaken from the purest of motives, and in no case was marriage permitted between a young widow and her rescuer, the inevitable result of which was that these widows had to live in some Brahmo family for years before they could be married."

Recounting the death of his widowed mother and the absence of timely medical aid or even elementary concern on the part of the other members of the joint family, Pratapchandra Mazumdar ovserves:

> I do not care whether all or many widows remarry; but I do feel that they should be more loved, nursed and cared for, more humanity shown to them. It is not true that they are always persecuted, not true at least in Bengal. They willingly court the miseries under which so many, like my loved an honoured mother, die. But, if men were more compassionate, and society recognised their right to the commonest necessaries of life, perhaps they would be less hard on themselves, and many a heart-stricken son would be spared the misery I felt when I found my mother's beloved life sink under the load of the world's neglect and indifference.

Mazumdar's cry has the advantage of perspective. But improvement in the general attitude called for wider spread of education, and, since the problem concerned women in the home very closely, the education of women was essential. Moreover, for the widow who was to live, whether remarried or not, a training of some sort seemed very important. But how was this to be expected?

Strong prejudice prevailed against girls' education in Bengal. It was feared that by teaching the girls to read and write, the curse of widowhood would be brought down on them. "There is absolutely nothing in the law-books and scriptures of the Hindus", says Pandit Tatvabhushan naively, "That might engender or foster such a notion. But popular prejudice and prevailing custom wield infinitely greater influence over the life and thought of the degenerate Hindus than either the voice of reason or the injunctions of the scriptures." In 1821, the Calcutta, School Society approved of women's education but it felt that the time had not yet arrived to set up girls' schools. Accordingly when an Englishwoman came out as a teacher to India on a project to train Indian women teachers, she had to offer her services to the Church Missionary Society. She was up against not only the prejudice against girls' education but a strong objection to having girls taught by a European Christian women. All her persuasions, from house to house, presents and enticements failed to work. And finally she gave up the task and confined herself to teaching Christian girls.

She had not, however, failed completely. In 1824 there were 24 schools with 400 pupils under her charge and the Christian Missionary Society handed over the management and direction of these schools to a new organisation, the Ladies' Society for Native Female Education. This society did a great deal of pioneering work but as the education imparted was mostly religious and Christian, it made little headway. It was in 1849 that the first schools for Hindu girls of the higher castes was founded in Calcutta. The Hindu Balika Vidyalaya which owed it origin to Mr. Drinkwater Bethune and Pandit Iswarchandra Vidyasagar, had great difficulty in securing its first batch of students. The parents who sent their daughters they were subjected to persecution and even excommunication.

But the Hindu Balika Vidyalaya, later named the Bethune Female School, was in fact the beginning of a general movement for women's eduction. Pandit Vidyasagar who was inspector of schools with jurisdiction over certain districts, had started a number of girls' schools and run them at his own expense. Assurances of support had been given by the Lieutenant-Governor of Bengal but Vidyasagar had certain differences with the Director of Public Instruction. As a consequence, the charge of running these schools, about a hundred in all, fell on Vidyasagar; and he did this for some years after he had retired from the Education services. With all this, however, education made slow progress, and in 1860 the Bethune School had only 70 pupil on its rolls.

This was the general picture when Sasipada Banerjee, often described as the last great Bengal reformer; began his energetic career. The son of a teacher and educationist, Sasipada, unlike the other reformers, came from the middle class. Barahanagar where he was born, was an industrial suburb of Calcutta, with several mills, factories and workshops. He had married a Brahmin girl from an orthodox family at the age of 20, and his own advanced views tended to isolate him in his own ancestral home, whose inmates extended to seven generations both by the male and female line.

The education of women was little thought of in 1860. But Sasipada first broke down the prejudices of his own wife and then proceeded with her assistance to turn his home into a school. In 1865, Sasipada established a girls' schools to which women from the neighbouring families also came. Its was uphill work for, after he openly joined the Brahmo Samaj, his students left him and even the pandit in charge of it deserted the school; and the landlady drove Banerji out. But he started again with one pupil, and by giving dolls and other prizes everyday to those who came, and paying a commission to the woman in charge of the premises for every new student she brought, he brought the number up to 57 a year later. He also conducted zenana classes until his new faith forced him to leave his family house. Another girls' schools was launched by him in 1871, and in 1873 an institution for higher education for women was established in Ballygunge with which he was connected as the most active member of the committee. He started the first women's journal in Bengali, conducted by his two daughters and exclusively run by women. In 1887, he founded the Home for Hindu Widows, and in 1894 he experimented with a project to educate women in their homes, where students making good progress were helped with stipends.

In most cases, it was an individual effort, the main assistance coming from the women he had educated and from his own family; sometimes specially in his broader schemes he encountered opposition from old Brahmo reformers like Iswarchandra Vidyasagar and Keshab Chandra Sen. The one feature common to all his efforts was the close association in every detail of his wife and himself. Sasipada Banerjee's work inspired others in Bombay and Madras to similar effort.

There is another sphere in which Banerjee played the role of pioneer. Night schools and working men's clubs were first launched in Barahanagar, to be followed up in other parts of Calcutta and its suburbs. Banerjee promoted temperance and thrift among the workers and organised excursions and lantern-lectures. In the schools, the attempt was to impart education quickly and intelligently. Nor in this work did Sasipada neglect the working class women. He was above all caste prejudice and he had the vision to see that the temperance movement which was so necessary in the conditions then prevailing in his own city, needed a positive content no less than resolute opposition to drink. When in 1871 he sailed for England, he was accompanied by his wife, the first Hindu women to cross the seas. On her death in 1877, he married a widow himself. In Barahanagar, he often mediated in quarrels between Hindu and Muslim workers, and among his experiments was the Sadharan Dharma Sabha, a form of fellowship of faiths, which failed because there were no active workers to keep it going in his absence. His own staunch Brahmoism was unquestioned; he had suffered persecution on that score. Yet he ran a section of his widows' home on orthodox lines and, when failing health forced him to consider handing it over, the Brahmo Samaj was unable to take it up because it entailed concessions to orthodoxy.

It was the opposition of the Brahmos to idolatrous observances in the Hindu ceremony that led to Brahmo marriages in Bengal being celebrated differently and to the adoption of a special marriage law in 1872. The Brahmo Marriage Act which made child marriages illegal, sanctioned inter-caste and widow marriages, and forbade polygamy, was restricted to reformed groups. It had been four years in the making, and it called for a declaration from the contracting parties that they did not belong to the established religions. Though it was brought about by the active interest of the Brahmos, it was not made a purely Brahmo Marriage Act because of dissensions amongst the Brahmos who had divided into two groups, one continuing as part of Hindu society, the other insisting on a separate identity.

The reason for the long delay in passing the marriage act was twofold: In the first place, the intervening revolt of 1857 was looked upon by some English officials as a consequence of measures like the Remarriage Act. The opposition to the Widow Remarriage Act after its enactment was much stronger and more violent than the opposition to the suppression of sati. Even liberal-minded Hindus held that remarriages should be permissible only to child widows. The strength of the feeling against remarriage in India can be gauged by the comments of the Begum of Bhopal (1912) on her mother's remarriage. She observed:

> Second marriages and the remarriage of widows are contrary neither to Muslim custom nor to Muslim religion. For a considerable number of years, however, the Muslims of India had adhered rigidly to the customs of the Afghans, and this had taken such a hold on society that any breach of it was regarded as a heinous sin. This feeling was shared by men and women alike; even those whose ideas had been modified by Western education, never permitted a second marriage in their families, and up to the present day the practice is viewed with disfavour by nearly all Muslims of Afghan descent.

Secondly, even among Brahmos it was not possible to arrive at agreement on the terms of the law desired. For some years, a group had grown within the Brahmo Samaj with progressive ideas. Devendranath Tagore who headed the Brahmos from 1844 onwards, favoured a cautious policy. With the entry of Keshab Chandra Sen in 1858, the Progressive group gained in strength. For ten years, the two sections were held together, mainly on account of the personalities of Devendranath Tagore and Keshab Chandra Sen. The vanguard of the reformers in fact came in for strong criticism from Keshab Chandra Sen because of their insistence on bringing women into social life. Finding that the customary dress of women in Bengal did not suit their going out, these enthusiasts evolved a new dress, half European and Indian, for their wives and began to take them out publicly to visit friends; private tutors for their education were engaged, in which they were generously helped by their educated men friends. The roused criticism even in Brahmo circles. The breach that divided the Brahmos into Adi Brahmos and Brahmo Samajists of India, occurred, however, over questions regarding conformity with Hindu practices. And as soon as the Brahmo Samaj of India came into existence in 1866, a new marriage ceremony was introduced from which many Hindu features of the ritual adapted by the Adi Brahmo Samaj were expunged and a new ritual framed. Between 1861, when the daughter of Devendranath Tagore had been married under modified Hindu rites and 1868, a number of marriages had taken place—some of which were inter-caste and widow marriages—under the auspices of the two Brahmo Samaj. Their validity was questioned by the Advocate-General on a reference. It was felt that a law providing for civil marriages was urgently needed, and Keshab Chandra Sen moved the Law Member of the Council. The strength of his representations, however, was considerably weakened by dissensions between the Adi Brahmo Samaj and the Brahmo Samaj of India over the question of the relation of Brahmos to Hindu Society.

The final passage of the Brahmo Marriage Act in 1872, while it was a gain for the Brahmo reformers in that it insisted on monogamy, forbade child marriages and permitted widow and inter-caste marriages, was a set-back in that it separated the Brahmos from the Hindus and insisted on a declaration that the contracting parties were neither Hindus, Muslims, Parsis, Christians nor Jews. And, when Keshab Chandra Sen, acting against the spirit of Act, consented to the marriage of his thirteen-years old daughter to the young Maharaja of Cooch-Bihar, in 1878, the leadership in the reform movement finally passed out of the Samajes. The Brahmo Marriage Act did not apply to Cooch-Bihar but Keshab Chandra Sen had been instrumental in getting the 14-year limit inserted in the Act, and he had publicly declared that he himself preferred the limit of 16 years in conformity with medical opinion as the marriageable age for girls. Because, in the second schism that rent the Brahmo Samaj, the issue became confused with observance of Hindu ritual, with the new orientation of the Samaj, and with the growth of the personality cult, this blow to the cause of reform was not appreciated in Bengal. But Keshab Chandra Sen had expanded the work of the Samaj—from 12 institutions he had built up some 124 throughout the country. And, while the ideas of reform had spread through the country, the controversies had been kept to Bengal.

—Natrajan

10

The Brahmo Samaj and Indian Civilisation

In this age of exaggerated emphasis on the political and economic factors in the evolution of man, one risks a good deal by attempting to demonstrate that religion is not less, probably more, important a factor in the development of humanity. This is particularly true of the ancient and mediaeval periods, when religion served as the main channel through which flowed the creative energies of the nations, fertilising the banks of history, from century to century, with the immortal contributions of man, such as literature, art, philosophy, ethics, rituals, etc., reflecting the poetry of social life. In fact, all that went to characterise, in the permanent sense, the real assets of a nation grew out of a pervasive religious experience. This experience may come by accident to an individual, to a special clan or group, or to a vaster concourse of humanity developing a mass movement. But in every case, religion, in its creative stage, has elevated individuals, clans, and groups above the limitations of the immediate present to build enduring structures of human civilisation having reference to the Ultimate and the Eternal. This applies particularly to Indian history and the Indian people. We too have, recorded in our annals, the facts of political conquest and economic exploitation like those of any other country. But the real mass movements in India were the direct outcome of the promulgation of a new truth embodied in a new religion. This has been admitted so far as our ancient and mediaeval periods are concerned, which show a unique record of philosophical and spiritual research as well as of charity and philanthropy through Jainism and Buddhism, Vaisnavism and Saivism, down to the various Bhakti cults of medieval India, immortalised by Ramananda and Kabir, Nanak and Caitanya.

In the case of modern India, however, it was supposed by many indigenous as well as foreign investigators that India was modernised by shedding many of her social and historiçal habits, which were summarily disposed of as antiquated traditions or noxious superstitions. In the sudden invasion of the 'modern', India was supposed to have surrendered at discretion, relinquishing her past and prostrating herself before the innumerable challenges of the present. A deeper study of the personalities and events of the dawn of modern India, however, convinces us of the fact that the break of the present with the past was more apparent than real. While the age of 'illumination' was inaugurated in Europe with a temporary negation of religion, in the case of India such an epoch was inaugurated by Raja Rammohun Roy, in the last quarter of the eighteenth century, following our traditional method of revitalising decaying society through a new religion, by founding Brāhmo Dharma, based on our age old principle of unity underlying the Vedāntic monism.

THE NATION AT THE BIRTH OF RAMMOHUN

In those early days of the foundation of British power in India, the Indian people, Hindu or Mohammedan, had very little to boast of in the domain of politics and economics, both being equally dominated by the aggressive and efficient occidental nations who came to dictate the pace of our modern history. But even in that age of abject degradation, the Indian people as a whole, not only the unlettered millions of our villages, but also the *elite,* clung tenaciously to their ancestral faith and traditions, and faced successfully the deadly onslaughts of outlandish modernism. The Hindus and the Muslims, chastened by common suffering, the great equaliser, came to forget the political disparity that existed between them as rulers or the ruled. Only the consolation of spirit, that never failed the nation, percolated the Hindus as well as of the Muslim through innumerable *ṭols* and *muktabs* (village seminaries), so wonderfully efficient and pervasive in character as to put to shame the record of our bureaucratic primary education a century later Sanskrit and the various vernaculars derived from it were cultivated side by side with Persian and Arabic. The court of Maharaja Krishna Chandra was adorned by notable writers from both communities. Bharatchandra was an adept in composing gems of literature in Bengali, as well as in Persian; and when, during the last quarter of the eighteenth century, Christianity was slowly assuming a proselytizing character, Ramram Bose showed a remarkable adaptability by co-operating with the Christian missionaries and by composing the earliest hymnology in vernacular for the Christian churches, although he remained himself a Hindu till the last day of his life.

The first thirty years of the life of Rammohun Roy are more or less veiled in obscurity. The stories of his early life depicting his preoccupation with religious reforms and consequent conflict with his family, a stronghold of orthodoxy, and of his wanderings in different parts of eastern India, and even as far as Tibet, may or may not be true. But this much is certain that in his intellectual and spiritual make-up Rammohun showed all the traces of indigenous influence which were found in his immediate predecessors. He had a liberal education, which then meant a mastery of Sanskrit, Persian, Arabic, as well as a critical study of Hindu and Islamic law, literature and philosophy, which prepared him wonderfully well for the role of the first prophet of progressive reform in our religion and society, during the first quarter of the nineteenth century.

CONTRIBUTIONS OF RAMMOHUN AND HIS CONTEMPORARIES

Raja Rammohun Roy says in his *Autobiographical Sketch*: 'When about the age of sixteen, I composed a manuscript calling in question the validity of the idolatrous system of Hindus. This, together with my own sentiments on the subject, having produced a coolness between me and my immediate kindred, I proceeded on my travels and passed through different countries, chiefly within, but some beyond the bounds of Hindustan.' The authenticity of the *Autobiographical Sketch*, however, is admitted by some and disputed by others, and for that reason, we cannot affirm that Rammohun composed the manuscript above referred to. In any case, the manuscript was probably never printed, nor has it yet been traced. What has been traced up to now, which is in the form of court records, relates to his ancestral property and to his own independent sources of income before the death of his father in 1803, when Rammohun was past thirty. But it is a significant fact that his earliest writing so far traced—*Tuhfat-ul-Muwahhidin* (A Gift to Deists)—introduces Rammohun to us in his well-known historical role of a free thinker in religion, if not as a religious reformer. This valuable treatise was composed in Persian with an Arabic introduction, which confirms the tradition attested by many of his contemporaries that Rammohun was deeply read in Persian and

Arabic literature. Yet, not a single document has so far been traced to indicate the steps leading to his mastery in those languages. Nor has anything definite been found as yet to show how he managed to gain that mastery in handling Sanskrit and Bengali, his mother tongue, as we find him doing in his published works between 1815 and 1832. Let us hope that intensive research will bring out more positive facts relating to the formation of that wonderful personality. What we do not know as yet about the early life of Rammohun should not prejudice our appreciation of that illustrious pioneer, who left an indelible mark on the history of our national progress, during the early days of the nineteenth century. Very characteristically Rammohun inaugurates the new century with these significant lines in his *Tuhfat-ul-Muwahhidin*:

'I travelled in the remotest parts of the world, in plains as well as in hilly lands, and found the inhabitants thereof agreeing generally in the personality of one Being, who is the source of all that exists and its governor, and disagreeing in giving peculiar attributes to that Being and in holding different creeds consisting of the doctrines of religion and precepts of *harām* (forbidden) and *halāl* (lawful). From this induction it has been known to me that turning generally towards one eternal Being is like a natural tendency in human beings and is common to all individuals of mankind equally.

This generalisation surely was the result of years of study and intensive thinking, and Rammohun was to some extent anticipating many of his remarkable thoughts and activities when he expressed himself in the following lines of his first published work:

The followers of different religions, sometimes, seeing the paucity of the number of believers in one God in the world, boast that they are on the side of the majority. It is to be seen that the truth of a saying does not depend upon the multiplicity of the sayers, and the non-reliability of a narration cannot arise simply out of the paucity of the number of the narrators. For it is admitted by the seekers of truth that truth is to be followed, although it is against the majority of the people.

It is strange to say that after the lapse of hundreds of years from the time of these religious leaders, with whom the prophetic mission is said to be closed. Nānak and others, in India and other countries, raised the flag of prophetic mission and induced a large number of people to become their followers and were successful.

'O God! Notwithstanding implicit faith in the orders of the *mujtahid* or the doctors of religion, there is always such an innate faculty existing in the nature of mankind that if any person of sound mind, before or after assuming the doctrines of any religion, makes an impartial and just inquiry into the nature of the principles of religious doctrines of different nations, there is a strong hope that he will be able to distinguish truth from untruth and true propositions from fallacious ones, and also that he, becoming free from the useless restrains of religion, which sometimes become sources of prejudice of one against another and causes of physical and mental troubles, will turn to the one Being, who is the fountain of the harmonious organisation of the universe, and will pay attention to the good of society.

Two fundamental principles or laws have been discovered and repeatedly emphasised by Rammohun: the basic unity of mankind as the goal of human research on the intellectual plane and the welfare of society as the dominant consideration and the ultimate goal of our moral endeavour. Thus the philosopher-theologian, as well as the great social reformer, who came to vindicate the honour of modern India amongst the progressive nations of the world, stands clearly before us, even while we read his earliest treatise. Perfect free lance and free-thinker that he was, Rammohun was not free from a legitimate pride in his Brāhmaṇa heredity which, amidst a thousand persecutions, held aloft the touch of *Brahmavidyā,* the divine knowledge, which alone leads to immortality. There is a touching note of autobiography in the lines we quote below:

'The Brahmins have a tradition from God that they have strict orders from God to observe their ceremonies and hold their faith forever. There are many injunctions about this from the divine authority in the Sanskrit language, and I, the humblest creature of God, having been born amongst them, have learnt the language and got those injunctions by heart, and this nation (the Brāhmaṇas) having confidence in such divine injunctions cannot give them up, although they have been subjected to many troubles and persecutions and were threatened to be put to death by the followers of Islam.'

Yet rarely could we find a greater admirer of Islam and of other historic religions than Rammohun, who formulated, at that early age the profound truth that 'social laws depend on an understanding of each other's meaning'. That is why, even in the midst of heated controversies, religious, social, or political, Rammohun ever showed that phenomenal lack of personal bitterness, that enlightened tolerance, and that profound sympathy which lend an epic grandeur to his personality. He found 'contradictory precepts' clouding the cardinal truths of all religions, and he wanted to test them as to how far they were 'consistent with the wisdom and mercy of the great, generous, and disinterested creation'.

PUBLICATION OF THE UPANIṢADS AND VEDANTA

Twelve years after the publication of *Tuhfat-up-Muwahhidin* from Murshidabad, we find Rammohun finally established in Calcutta and publishing, almost simultaneously in Sanskrit, Bengali, and English, his studies on the Upaniṣads and Vedānta (1815-19). His was the earliest published study on those valuable texts of Brāhmaṇical philosophy and religion. There were few good libraries in those days, excepting the libraries attached to the Asiatic Society of Bengal and to the Fort William College, where rare books and manuscripts were being collected, through the noble endeavours of Sir William Jones, Colebrook, Carey, and others. Rammohun is now known to have possessed a house of his own in Calcutta as early as 1792 and, consequently, might have frequented some of those libraries; and we find him writing with deep appreciation whenever he referred to the works of pioneer orientalists like Jones and Colebrooke.[1]

DEBATES AND CONTROVERSIES

But before settling down in Calcutta, Rammohun came into intimate contact with the representatives of various sects, such as Vaiṣṇavas. Tāntrikas, Jains, Mohammedans, etc. He frequently arranged discussion-meetings among them, during his residence at Rangpur (1809-14), where he is said to have made a careful study of Tāntrika works with the help of a Bengali mendicant named Hariharananda Tirthaswami. Rammohun's appreciation of the *Mahānrvāṇa Tantra* is an important link in this chain of evidence. He is also reported to have entered into discussion with another great scholar. Utsavananda Saraswati. But the discussion soon developed into downright controversy, from 1817 onwards, when we find Rammohun publishing the tract. *A Defence of Hindoo Theism in Reply to the Attack of an Advocate for Idolatry at Madras.* Side by side with the pundits of Madras appeared stalwarts from Bengal, the Bhattacharyas and the

Goswamis, joining issues with Rammohun, who was showing a real flair for enlightened controversy on recondite topics. At the same time (1817-20), he was vindicating the moral conscience of his people by pleading for the abolition of the cruel rites of suttee (*satī*, making most touching appeal to his countrymen, reminding them of the glory of Indian womanhood, the real *śaktis* of our nation. Between 1820 and 1823, we find him engaged in the historic controversy with the missionaries on the fundamentals of Christian religion.

It, is now generally admitted that Rammohun did not make serious study of English till the very end of the eighteenth century, when he was approaching thirty. But how quickly and efficiently he mastered that difficult tongue was clearly demonstrated through his remarkable English compositions. His capacity for mastering foreign languages was phenomenal, as has been attested by eminent foreigners like Abbé's Gregoire, James Buckingham, and Victor Jacquemont. But through language, Rammohun always drew spiritual nourishment, strengthening his cosmopolitan personality, as has been clearly demonstrated by Brojendra Nath Seal in his remarkable study, *Rammohun, the Universal Man.*[2] So, when the Christian controversialists met this pagan Brāhmaṇa philosopher, they soon discovered that he deserved more than a mere patronising attention. Rammohun was already pre-eminent in theological controversies with his own compatriots, ever attempting to disentangle the eternal foundations of Hindu faith and culture from the debris of later centuries; and if he engaged now in a prolonged controversy with the Christian missionaries, it was because they totally misunderstood the inner significance and the abiding grandeur of Hindu spiritual idealism. India of the Upaniṣads and Vedānta need not feel the least humiliated before the champions of any other religion, so the Raja maintained, and the exposed the fallacies and weaknesses of the overbearing polemists of early Christian missions of India. His legitimate pride in the spiritual heritage of his ancestors was clearly expressed through the following memorable lines:

By a reference to history, it may be proved that the world was indebted to our ancestors for the first dawn of knowledge, which sprang up in the East, and thanks to the goddess of wisdom, we have still a philosophical and copious language of our own, which distinguishes us from other nations who cannot express scientific or abstract ideas without borrowing the language of foreigners.'

CONSTRUCTIVE STATESMANSHIP

It would be doing, however, great injustice to this pioneer of our national progress, if by constant references to his controversies with his own countrymen, as well as with foreigners, we exaggerate the apparent destructive side of his genius; for Rammohun left a record of constructive statesmanship, rarely paralleled by any other in that epoch of our history especially in the two vital departments of national education and national politics. In modernising our antiquated and effete system of education, he shines as one of the founders of the Hindoo College, as the intimate friend and co-worker of David Hare and Rev. Alexander Duff, and, above all, as the most enlightened co-operator with every champion of science and modernism, official or non-official, who then came over from Europe to work in India. His letter on English education to Lord Amherst is a veritable landmark in the educational history of modern India; for he urged therein for the promotion of a more liberal and enlightened system of instruction, embracing mathematics, natural philosophy, chemistry, anatomy, and other useful sciences, and for the establishment of a college with necessary books, instruments, and other apparatus. This was in 1823, more than a decade before the foundation of the first medical college in India, and more than a quarter of a century before the foundation of the first university in India.

ORIENTALISM VERSUS OCCIDENTALISM

Rammohun has been frequently misunderstood, because of his zealous advocacy of occidental sciences and vigorous criticisms levelled against the mummified oriental systems of education. He yielded to no one in his admiration for the deathless treasures of ancient philosophy and religion, both of his own country as well as of other oriental nations, including even the Chinese, not to speak of the contribution of the Greeks and the Hebrews, the Persians and the Arabs. His rich mind has well been compared by Brojendra Nath Seal to a universal encyclopaedia, embracing all that is best and enduring in the culture of the major branches of the human family. He was a veritable pioneer in collecting and publishing the texts of the Upaniṣads and Vedānta at that early age, and, not satisfied with that scholastic achievement, Rammohun ever strove to convey to common men and women the significance of those texts by means of lucid translations in the vernaculars. Some of his translation in Hindi are unfortunately lost. The Bengalis will ever remember Rammohun as their first grammarian (of course, he had his missionary predecessors like Halhead and Carey), and as their first inspiring prose-writer. Thus Rammohun's contributions, as an orientalist, both in the department of language and literature as well as in Hindu law, were undisputed; and that is why, long before his visit to Europe, Rammohun had the honour of being nominated (July 1824) by the Asiatic Society of Paris as its first Hindu honorary member.

Why the orientalist Rammohun so vigorously championed the cause of the occidentalists in our educational history would be clear from his significant remarks that the natives of Europe have carried (the sciences) to a degree of perfection that has raised them above the inhabitants of other parts of the world. He wanted to instruct the natives of India in mathematics, natural philosophy, chemistry, anatomy, and other useful sciences', because those sciences as he was convinced, were responsible for the predominant position of the Europeans in the world. The conclusion is therefore intervitable that Rammohun was longing to see his countrymen in the same position of eminence and efficiency in the family of nations as the Europeans had achieved following one and the same method—the conquest and control of nature through the sciences.

NATIONALISM AND INTERNATIONALISM

Another characteristic symptom is his instinctive *penchant* for politics and publicity. He was not satisfied with quiet meditation or mere metaphysical debates within his own self. He was ever bringing all his grievances and complaints, no less than his positive programmes and patriotic dreams, before the open forum of the public, challenging and being challenged, but always fighting a clean fight. The politics of Rammohun was but another aspects of his humanism, as we clearly find in his noble words, penned a few months before his death, protesting to the Ministry of Foreign Affairs of France against the restrictions imposed on foreigners desiring to visit France:

'It is now generally admitted that not religion only, but unbiased common sense as well as the accurate deductions of scientific research lead to the conclusion that all mankind are one great family, of which the numerous nations and tribes existing are only various branches. Hence enlightened men in all countries feel a wish to encourage and facilitate human intercourse in every manner by removing as far as possible, all impediments to it, in order to promote the reciprocal advantage and enjoyment of the whole human race.'

The last phrase of this valuable document, dated December 1831, was nothing but an amplification of the same theme discussed in his earliest published treatise, *Tuhfat-ul-Muwahhidin,* of 1803. Everything that arrests and denaturalises the healthy relations of the whole human race must be opposed and fought to a finish. This was what politics meant to him, and his politics of perfect candour and constitutional rhythm was but another name for philanthropy. That was, probably, why Jeremy Bentham, the great English philosopher, greeted him as 'his intensely admired and dearly beloved collaborator in the service of mankind. In his report submitted before the judicial Committee of the British Parliament. Rammohun concluded by 'beseeching any and every authority to devise some method of alleviating the miseries of the agricultural peasantry of India and thus discharge their duty to their fellow creatures and fellow subjects'. This friend of the poor ryots of India also befriended, with rare courage and tact, the last unfortunate-Mogul emperor of Delhi. Akbar II, whose cause he started championing as early as 1828. This led to this being sent out to England as the ambassador of the Mohammedan emperor, for whom Rammohun pleaded eloquently and secured the redress of his grievances.

In his bold agitation against the Press Regulations of 1823, we find the same grasp of general principles which elevates his 'Petitions' high above the level of occasional writing, so much so that those were supposed to have the dignity and conviction of an *Areopagitica.* The attachments of the natives of India', the Raja observed, 'to the British Government must be as permanent as their confidence in the honour and justice of the British nation. Resistance of a people advanced in knowledge has ever been not against the existence, but against the abuses of the governing power.'

His specific observations on the value of the freedom of the Press equally remarkable:

> 'A Free Press has never yet caused a revolution in any part of the world, because, while men can easily represent the grievances arising from the conduct of the local authorities to the supreme Government and thus get them redressed, the grounds of discontent that excite revolution are removed; whereas, where no freedom of the Press existed, and grievances consequently remained unrepresented and unredressed, innumerable revolutions have taken place in all parts of the globe, or if prevented by the armed force of the Government, the people continued ready for insurrection.'

Freedom was resorted to the Indian Press by Sir Charles Metcalf five years after the death of Rammohun, but in the Free Press Dinners given to Sir Charles Metcalf at the Calcutta Town Hall (February 1838), Mr. Leith, an Englishman, proposed a toast 'to the memory of Rammohun Roy', which was sconded by Prasanna Coomer Tagore, a friend and colleague of the Raja in the foundation of the Brāhmo Samāj.

RELIGIOUS REFORMS

As early as 1803, in his preface to *Tuhfat-ul-Muwahhidin*. Rammohun recorded in unmistakable terms his convictions about the unity of Godhead, and his life thereafter seemed to be but an improvisation on that theme. Almost simultaneously with his settling down in Calcutta, we find him establishing the Vedanta College, in 1816, for the 'propagation and defence of Hindu Unitarianism'. Shortly before, Rammohun founded the Ātmiya Sabhā with some of his illustrious contemporaries as members: Dwaraka Nath Tagore, Prasanna Coomar Tagore, Nanda Kishore Bose (father of Rajnarain Bose). Brindaban Mitra (grandfather of Dr. Rajendra Lal Mitra), and others, Two renowned Sanskrit scholars, Pandit Sivaprasad Misra and Hariharananda Tirthaswami, joined the Sabhā. Pandit Sivaprasad signed some of the controversial writings actually composed by Rammohun. Hariharananda was the mendicant friend of the Raja from the days of his religious discussions with him at Rangpur. The Swami not only contributed substantially to the philosophical make-up of the Sabhā, but gave his own brother, Pandit, Ramchandra Vidyavagish, who became the first minister of the Brāhmo Samaj, founded by the Raja. For the first two years (1815-16), the Ātmiya Sabhā held its weekly meetings in the garden-house of Rammohun at Manicktolla. There were recitation and expounding of sacred texts and the singing of hymns composed by Rammohun and his friends. In 1819, a memorable debate took place between Subrahmanya Sastri of Madras and Rammohun , when the latter is reported to have completely vanquished the former in a discussion on idol-worship in the presence of the leading citizens of Calcutta including Radhakanta Dev, who was the leader of the orthodox Hindus and who later on, in 1830, promoted the foundation of the Dharma Sabhā, the rival organisation of the Brāhmo Samāj. Between 1815 and 1819, most of the important texts and translations relating to the Vedānta and the Upanisads were published by the Raja, who simultaneously started his campaign of social reform with the anti-suttee agitation. These publications not only created a stir in his own country, but roused the attention of his European contemporaries; for we find that, in 1816-17, the *Monthly Repository of Theology and General Literature* published a lengthy and appreciative review of the Raja's *Abridgement of the Vedānta.* About the same time, Abbe' Gregoire, Bishop of Blois, wrote a striking pamphlet in French in which we read: 'The moderation with which he repels the attacks on his writings, the force of his arguments, and his profound knowledge of the sacred books of the Hindoos are proofs of his fitness for the work he has undertaken; and the pecuniary sacrifices he has made show a disinterestedness which cannot be encouraged or admired too warmly.'

In 1817, Mr. John Digby arranged for the publication of the first volume of the Raja's work in London, and between 1823 and 1824, his *Precepts of Jesus* was published by the Unitarian Society of London and was reprinted in America in 1828. From far-off America. Rev. H. Ware of Cambridge (Mass.) corresponded with the learned Raja on the prospects of Christianity in India. The famous controversy with the Christian missionaries of Serampore, in 1821, was the result of the Raja's converting Mr. William Adam, the Baptist missionary, to his Unitarianism. The Trinitarian Christians made violent and often undignified attacks on the Raja through the pages of the *Friend of India* and the Bengali *Samacara Darpana.* The Raja published at this time his *Brāhmanical Magazine,* and when the Baptist Mission Press refused to print his *First Appeal to the Christian Public,* the Raja started his Unitarian Press (1823). The Ātmiya Sabhā meetings were discontinued after 1819, but the Calcutta Unitarian Committee was formed by the Raja in 1821, who raised a large sum to support Mr. William Adam, as well as to maintain the Anglo-Hindu School. Along with a few British barristers, attorneys, and merchants, we find, as members of the Unitarian Society, Dwaraka Nath Tagore, Prasanna Coomar Tagore, and Radha Prasad Roy, the eldest son of the Raja, standing by his side. But occidental Unitarianism did not take root in Indian soil, and the Raja soon thought of establishing an indigenous institution based on the bed-rock of Upanisadic idealism. On the 20th August, 1823 (6th Bhādra, Śaka 1750), at 48 Chitpore Road, Jorasanko, Calcutta, was founded the Brāhmo Sabhā, with Tarachand Chakravarty as its Secretary. Two Telugu Brahmins used to recite the Vedas in a side-room, screened from the view of the congregation, where non-Brahmins would not be admitted. Utsavananda would read texts of the Upaniṣads, which were afterwards explained in Bengali by Pandit Ramchandra Vidyavagish, who would then preach or read the sermons, some of which were written by Rammohun Roy, Singing of hymns terminated the ceremony.'' The services of the Brāhmo Sabhā (the popular name of the Brāhmo Samāj) began to attract a large number of sympathisers, so that within two years Rammohun was able to raise sufficient funds for the purchase of a house to serve as the permanent place of worship for the members. Mr. Montgomery Martin in his *History of the British Colonies* gives the following account of the opening ceremony of the Brāhmo Samāj at this new house at 55 Upper Chitpore Road (at present occupied by the Ādi Brāhmo Samāj of Maharshi Devendra Nath Tagore):

> The institution was opened by the late Raja Rammohun Roy accompanied by the writer (the only European present) in 1830. There were about 500 Hindus present and among them many Brahmins who, after the prayers and singing of hymns had been concluded, received gifts in money to a considerable extent.'

That Rammohun devoted a considerable part of his fortune to the propagation of the cause was attested by another European contemporary, James Silk Buckingham, the editor of the *Calcutta Journal:*

> He has done all this to the great detriment of his private interests, being rewarded by the coldness and jealousy of all the great functionaries of Church and State in India, and supporting the Unitarian Chapel, the Unitarian Press, and the expense of his own publication... out of a private fortune of which he devotes more than one-third to acts of the purest philanthropy and benevolence.

Rammohun's religion was the crowning glory of his career as a scholar, a statesman, and a patriot. We can easily understand why he laid so much emphasis on unity in this land, where man and man, sect and sect, community and community were weakened and degraded through irrational and interminable wranglings resulting in disunion. The success of his pioneer activities in connection with the unification (cultural as well as spiritual) of India inhabited by persons of so many races and religions, should not be judged by the numerical strength of the congregation which he founded. It is rather the fundamental truth of human fellowship and unity underlying the memorable trust deed of the Brahmo Samaj (dated 8th January, 1830) that should be cherished as a priceless legacy of the Raja to posterity:

'And that in conducting the said worship of adoration no object, animate or inanimate, that has been or is, or shall hereafter become, or be recognised, as an object of worship, by any man or set of men, shall be reviled or slightingly or contemptuously spoken of or alluded to either in preaching, praying, or in the hymns, or other mode of worship that may be delivered or used in the said messuage or building.

'And that no sermon, preaching discourse, prayer, or hymn be delivered, made, or used in such worship but such as have a tendency to the promotion of the contemplation of the Author and Preserver of the Universe, to the promotion of charity, morality, piety, benevolence, virtue, and to the strengthening of the bonds of union between men of all religious persuasion and creeds.'

MAHARSHI DEVENDRA NATH TAGORE

The relation of Rammohun Roy with the personalities and movements of the subsequent epochs was to intimate that a learned Christian writer, Dr. H.G.E. Zacharias, in his famous book *Renascent India* observes:

'Of such personalities—good, bad, and indifferent—who have become prominent in this Indian renascence, the number is very great indeed and ever swelling; but, in the last instance, all really can be said to go back in their spiritual parentage to one man—Rammohun Roy.

'Rammohun Roy and his Brāhmo Samāj form the starting point for all the various reform movements—whether in Hindu religion, society, or politics—which have agitated India during the past hundred years and which have led no her wonderful renascence in these our own days.'

When Rammohun passed away in distant Bristol, fighting till the last days of his life to vindicate the rights of his countrymen, his Brāhmo Samaj, here in India, was little more than an aspiration and a dream. For years after his death, Pandit Ramchandra Vidyavagish kept the lamp burning and it was only in 1843 (7th Pauṣa, Śaka 1765) that Devendra Nath Tagore, son of Dwaraka Nath Tagore, brought a new inspiration and strength to the Samaj. He underwent a formal ceremony of *dīkṣā* (initiation) at the hands of Vidyavagish, who lived to pass the torch, as it were, to his spiritual successor of the Raja. Born in 1817, Devendra Nath Tagore, endowed with an inborn hankering for things spiritual, as we read in his remarkable *Autobiography,* came across, accidentally, the opening verse of the *Iśa Upanisad:* 'God is immanent in all things, in whatsoever lives and moves in the universe: enjoy therefore without being attached; covet not the wealth belonging to others.'

This spark of ancient Indian wisdom would have had a poor chance of blazing forth into conviction, had it fallen on the damped religious spirit of early nineteenth-century Europe, convulsed with the stormy competition for material wealth engendered by the Industrial Revolution. But to Devendra Nath, the young mystic, it brought a different kind of revelation. Born and brought up, as he was, in the lap of luxury, he felt the imperious call of the Essential drowning the clamour of gaudy unessentials. In October 1839, he established, with some of his friends and relatives, an association which grew into the Truth-teaching Society or Tattva-bodhini Sabhā, which marked an epoch in the literacy and spiritual history of eastern India. Starting with only ten members, whose number later rose to five hundred, the Sabhā attracted some of the leading men of that period, including the Raja of Nadia, the Maharajadhiraja of Burdwan, and others.

Being an association formed by young men, it spontaneously took to the idealistic training up of our youth under that eminent scholar Akshoy Kumar Dutta, who is one of the rare writers of early Bengali prose and who gave us a famous study on the 'Religious Communities of India' (*Bhāratavarṣīya Upāsaka-sampradāya*). He was also the first editor of the monthly journal of the Society, *Tattva-bodhini Patrikā,* which marked an epoch in the history of Bengali literature. Some of the outstanding literatures of that age Pandit Iswar Chandra Vidyasagar, Dr. Rajendra Lal Mitra, and others, were amongst its contributors. It began to publish a translation of the *Rig-Veda* in 1847, when Max Mueller was studying the same Veda in Paris under the great French Sanskritist. E. Burnouf. Starting the translation of the Upaniṣads, Devendra Nath found that a knowledge of the Vedas was indispensable, and therefore he sent a student from his Sabhā to Banaras in 1844. Before long, in 1845, a controversy on Vedic infallibility cropped up in the Sabhā, and three more students were sent to Banaras to bring authentic information on the Vedic texts. That was nearly twenty years before the initiation of Swami Dayanand Saraswati by his master Virajananda, who enjoined upon him the solemn task of propagating the truths of the Vedas. While, in 1845, the Brāhmo Samāj under Devendra Nath was publicly proclaiming the Vedas and Vedāntism as the basis of its faith, the very same year the rival faith from the occident claimed a respectable Hindu, Umesh Chandra Sarkar, as a convert to Christianity. This threw the public of Calcutta into convulsion. A meeting of the leading Hindu citizen was called by Devendra Nath, and a sum of rupees thirty thousand was raised, with a view to stemming the tide of conversion. The controversy between Dr. Alexander Duff and the members of the Sabhā, represented by Rajnarain Bose, would be read with interest by those who have followed similar controversies between Rammohun Roy and the Baptist missionaries, a quarter of a century earlier. But there was perfect tolerance and openness to conviction amongst the members of the Sabhā many of whom did not believe in Vedic infallibility, especially the rationalistic group headed by Akshoy Kumar Dutta. Devendra Nath paid a personal visit to Banaras in 1847, while the four Brāhmaṇa students returned with positive information on the Vedas. The inevitable rejection of the creed of Vedic infallibility led to the formulation of the fundamental principles of natural and universal theism through the *Brāhma Dharma,* a compilation from the Upaniṣads published by Devendra Nath.

Rationalism thus triumphed over creeds and cults and, quite in keeping with the tradition of Rammohun, it refused to remain as a mere intellectual pastime. On the contrary, it began attacking some of the fundamental iniquities and abuses of society. Intemperance, polygamy, etc. were denounced; widow remarriage and female education were strongly advocated by the Brāhmo Samāj of Devendra nath, expressed through his famous *Patrikā* (1850-55). A little tired with rationalistic debate, in the course of which some members proposed to settle their belief in God by counting votes, Devendra Nath retired to the Himalayas and for a couple of years (1856-58) remained absorbed in studies and meditation. When he returned from the hills, he rejoiced to find a new recruit in Keshab Chandra Sen, the grandson of Dewan Ramkamal Sen, the first Indian Secretary to the Asiatic Society of Bengal. Keshab, a talented young man, was born in 1838 and was then barely twenty. We turn a new leaf in the history of the Brāhmo Samāj with the Devendra Nath-Keshab episode.

DEMOCRATIZATION AND EXPANSION

Keshab was drawn to the Brāhmo Samāj by a chance study of *What is Brahmoism,* a tract of Rajnarain Bose who, along with Akshoy Kumar Dutta and Iswar Chandra Vidyasagar, continued to be a literacy and intellectual exponent of Brāhmoism. The Brāhmo Samāj was managed by the Tattva-bodhini Sabhā, and the Secretary of the Samāj was the illustrious Vidyasagar, who resigned the post in 1859, owing to some differences of opinion regarding administrative details, and Devendra Nath and Keshab Chandra became the Joint Secretaries of the Samāj, which took over the printing press, the library, and other properties of the Sabhā, then dying a natural death. To inaugurate, as it were, a new period of expansion, the two leaders, young and old, undertook a voyage to Ceylon in September 1859, which must have opened a new perspective to them. On his return, Keshab developed a youth movement, delivering addresses and publishing tracts such as *Young Bengal, This is for You* etc., which attracted a large number of young men and college students to the Samaj. Vidyasagar had retired, but his noble championing of the cause of the poor Hindu widows inspired this leader of the younger generation, for we find Keshab utilising the stage to rouse public sympathy, through the performance of the sensational drama *Vidhavā-vivāha.* The enthusiasm was irresistible, especially after 1861, when Keshab gave up a lucrative government post in the Bank of Bengal and, with his young idealistic friends and colleagues, organised a spiritual fraternity, the Sangat Sabhā. Here, by the side of the Hindu scriptures, we find the works of Theodore Parker, Hamilton, Victor Cousin, and Prof. F.W. Newman studied with rare zeal. But it was not a group of book-worms or theologians indifferent to the conditions around them. For we find Keshab publishing *An Appeal to the British Nation,* for the promotion of mass education in India, which was circulated in England, through his learned correspondent Prof. F.W. Newman, Such a progressive programme was more remarkable, as it came within three years from the foundation of universities in India (1858). In 1861, Keshab also organised relief funds to mitigate the sufferings of millions in the then North-Western Provinces, ravaged by a terrible famine. Thus social service came to be a part of the work of the Samāj, and in the same year, which witnessed the birth of Rabindranath, Keshab started, with the financial backing of Devendra Nath, the influential journal, *Indian Mirror,* which, along with the *Hindoo Patriot,* edited by Harish Mookerjee and Kristo Das Pal, came to be the harbinger of social and political reform in our country. In 1862, Keshab delivered his memorable address 'The Destiny of Human Life' and was elevated by Devendra Nath to the post of the Ācarya or miniter of the Brāhmo Samāj, when he was barely twenty-four. In 1863, just thirty years after the death of Rammohun, Keshab was driven to defend the Samāj against the attacks of the Christian missionaries led by Rev, Lal Behari Dey. His brochure, *The Brāhmo Samāj Vindicated,* proved what fibre Keshab was made of. The miserable condition of our womenfolk, imprisoned in our homes by age-long custom, did not fail to rouse the reforming zeal of Keshab and his associates, who started the first journal for women, *Vāmā-bodhinī,* in 1863. Courting persecution and social ostracism, these young reformers defied caste, celebrated intermarriages, and tried in many ways to remove the barrier between man and man and man and woman.

The apostolic zeal of the younger group carried the message of the Brāhmo Samāj to the remote villages of Bengal, and very soon to places beyond the limits of Bengal, as a result of Keshab's first preaching tour through Madras in 1864. The Prārthanā Samāj of Bombay was organised in 1867, on the lines of the Brāhmo Samāj, under the inspiration of eminent reformers of western India like Ranade and Bhandarkar. From an article in the *Indian Mirror* (January 1866), we find that there were then 54 Samājas; 50 in Bengal, 2 in North-Western Provinces, 1 in the Punjab, and 1 in Madras. Quite a large number of boys' and girls' schools were maintained by the Brāhmos, and there were 37 periodicals devoted to the propagation of Brāhmoism, most of them in Bengali and English, 1 in Urdu from North-Western Provinces, and 1 in Telugu published by the Veda Samaj of Madras. Thus it assumed the character of an all-India movement. But, unfortunately, in the course of the years 1865 and 1866, the differences between the old conservative party and the party of youthful reformers came to be so serious that a schism was inevitable. The old party shrank into the Ādi Brāhmo Samāj, and the new party formed the Brāhmo Samāj of India (1866). The attitude of Devendra Nath during this party struggle was as calm as it was dignified and, till his last days, he continued to welcome and support every earnest Brāhmo who cared to seek his advice. Laying the foundation of Santiniketan Ashram, which was later to be the principal seat of activity of Rabindranath, Devendra Nath Tagore, the venerable patriarch of the Samāj of Rammohun Roy and revered and loved by all sections of the community as Maharshi, passed away in 1905.

He was without so long; but now He revealed Himself to my spirit within; I beheld Him in my soul. Such profound lines from the pages of his *Autobiography* go to prove that modern India was not all mad for modernism, but that the eternal search of India for immortality, instead of material wealth, was still being expressed through the lives of our modern mystics.

THE BRĀHMO SAMĀJ OF INDIA

When, on the 24th January, 1868, Keshab laid the foundation of the Mandir of the Brāhmo Samāj of India (Bhāratavarṣīya Brāhma Samāj), a big *saṅkīrtana* party went round the city signing the memorable song:

'To grant salvation the merciful God has sent His new faith of Brāhmoism. Lo! the gates of salvation are wide open; He calls one and all; entrance through His gate is free; no one ever returns disappointed; the rich and the poor, the wise and the ignorant, all are equally welcome there.

'Men and women of all classes have an equal right; whoever truly loves God, the same shall be saved, there is no caste distinction here'.

Henceforth, in most of the utterances and writings of Keshab, we find a great spirit of catholicity and earnest endeavour to harmonise the apparently conflicting creeds of all religions. But he was misunderstood, for his lecture 'Jesus Christ: Asia and Europe' (1866) encouraged a Christian preacher, Mr. Tinling, to hope for the conversion of the Brāhmos into Christianity. His introducing devotional exercise through *saṅkīrtana* branded him, in the eyes of radical Brāhmos, as a backslider to Vaiṣṇavism, as a result of the influence of his devoted friend Vijay Krishna Goswami. With the same curious logic, some may consider him to be a Śākta, because in a prayer included in his *Śikṣā-saṅgraha* (1866) Keshab cries out passionately, 'Oh Thou Mother Divinel bind me with Thy mercies'.

The fact is that the deep sentiments of *bhakti* surged in his soul, and he evolved a new mysticism of his own based on the reconciliation of all faiths, which found its culmination, in January 1881, in his announcement of the New Dispensation (Nava Vidhān). Eleven years earlier, when Keshab visited England, he had a phenomenal success as a spiritual ambassador of India, no less than as a great social reformer, who promoted inter-caste marriages in this caste-ridden country, who waged the early campaigns for temperance, and who, by his unrivalled eloquence, could make the heart of an Englishman as well as of an Indian pulsate with equal sympathy.

The East and the West spoke simultaneously their profound spiritual messages through the harmonious voice of Keshab, who was admired by his countrymen no less than by eminent foreigners, like the Very Rev. Dean of Westminster, Dr. Martineau, John Stuart Mill, Prof. Max Mueller, Grant Duff, Louis Blanc, and others. He showed that there was no conflict between the Hindu instinct of spirituality and the deeper spiritual experiences of Christianity or Islam.[4] At the same time, Keshab commanded that penetrating vision which enabled him to discern and respect the revelation of truths in the orthodox Hindu religion, as manifested in the careers of Swami Dayanand Saraswati and Sri Ramakrishna Paramahamsa. The former met him in 1870, shortly after Keshab's return from England. The probable date of the meeting of Keshab with Ramakrishna was 15th March 1875, and are read in the *Indian Mirror* (28th March, 1875) the following touching lines:

'We met one (a sincere Hindu devotee) not long ago and were charmed by the depth, penetration, and simplicity of his spirit. The never-ceasing metaphors and analogies, in which he indulged, are most of them as apt as they are beautiful. The characteristics of his mind are the very opposite to those of Pandit-Dayanand Saraswati, the former being so gentle, tender, and contemplative, as the latter is sturdy, masculine, and polemical. Hinduism must have in it a deep sense of beauty, truth and goodness to inspire such men as these.'

While sectional and denominational controversies would raise a thousand questions to cloud the main issues, no sane man will doubt that Keshab's contribution as a reconciler of apparently contradictory creeds was considerable, and that his, communion with the unlettered sage of Dakshineswar forms one of the sweetest chapters of spiritual kinship. Towards the end of his short, yet brilliant career, Keshab was getting more Indian and more Asiatic, as we feel from his prophetic lines in 'Asia's Message to Europe' (20th January, 1883):

'I am a child of Asia; her sorrows are my sorrows, her joys are my joys. From one end of Asia to the other, I boast of a vast home, a wide nationality, and an extended kinship. Upon Asia's soil have flourished and prospered those feet at whose the world lies prostrate. The great religions which have given life and salvation to millions of men owe their origin to Asia'.

THE SĀDHĀRAN BRĀHMO SAMĀJ

Keshab died prematurely when he was about forty-six, only three years after his proclamation of the New Dispensation. A man of masterful personality, Keshab had many difficulties as regards the financial and administrative aspects of the Samāj. As early as 1871-72, we find that some of his junior contemporaries were becoming impatient, owing to the lack of a rational and constitutional procedure in the Samāj, which they thought was more or less dominated by one individual. This constitutional party, moreover, did not like certain conservative tendencies among the *entourage* of Keshab. The radical group organised itself, in 1874, as the Samadarsi party, counting among its leaders. A.M. Bose, a Cambridge wrangler and one of the earliest leader of the Indian National Congress, D.M. Das, the uncle of C.R. Das, and D.N. Ganguli, who risked his life investigating the pitiable condition of the coolies of the tea-plantations in Assam. They were soon strengthened by the comradeship of Nagendra Nath Chatterjee, the biographer of Rammohun Roy, and pandit Sivanath Sastri, the life and soul of the Sādhāraṇ Brāhmo Samāj. A temporary reconciliation between this radical group and the conservative group of Keshab was effected through his granting a sort of a representative assembly composed of the members of both parties. But the unfortunate controversy growing out of the marriage of his eldest daughter with the prince of Cooch Behar, in contravention of act 3 of 1872 which fixes the marriageable age for girls at fourteen completed the rupture. On the 15th may, 1878, the new party held a public meeting in the Town Hall and formally organised the Sādhāraṇ Brāhmo Samāj. The venerable Maharshi Devendra Nath sent his message of blessing to the new Samāj. At the time of this second schism, there were 124 Samājas: 80 in Bengal, 8 in Assam, 6 in Bihar, 11 in North-Western Provinces, 5 in South India, 5 in Outh, 7 in Bombay Presidency, and 2 in Sind. Altogether they conducted 21 periodicals in English. Bengal, Marathi, Urdu, and Hindi.

The foundation of the Sādhāraṇ Brāhmo Samāj Mandir was laid on the 11th Māgha, Śaka 1800 (A.D. 1878), the building fund of which received generous donations also from sympathisers in other parts of India, to mention among others, the Maharaja Scindia and Sirdar Dayal Singh of Amritsar. The anniversary celebration, in January 1879, was memorable for two other events: a meeting organised by the new Samāj in honour of Raja Rammohun Roy was held at the house of Devendra Nath, while another meeting was organised by Keshab's party. Secondly, the foundation was laid of the City School, which soon developed into the City College of Calcutta under the able guidance of Ananda Mohun Bose, who met the initial expenses, and of Surendranath Banerjea who, though not a member of the Samāj, offered to be one of its first teachers. Another noticeable institution was the Students' Weekly Service, arranging for the growing student community of Calcutta lectures on religious, social, moral, and political topics, preceded by a short divine service. In quick succession followed the establishment of a society for the progressive ladies, who used to meet the discuss and read papers. A library and printing press also gradually developed with the two organs of the new Samāj, *Tattva-Kaumudī*, in Bengali, and *Brāhmo Public Opinion*, English. The year 1881 saw the completion and consecration of the Mandir and, though the renewed activities of the missionaries of the Samāj, 15 new Samājas were founded in different parts of the country in 1883. Maharshi Devendra Nath and Rajnarian Bose bless the congregations by preaching from the pulpit, and the same year we find a lady occupying the Samāj pulpit.

In 1884, the famous Bengali weekly, *Sanjīvanī*, edited by Krishna Kumar Mitra, started its career, and a regular social service centre was organised to bring relief to the famine-stricken people of Birbhum. In 1888-89, the Brāhmo Girls' School was opened and missionary activities were carried into the Khasi Hills, Assam. In 1896, Rev. J.T. Sunderland visited the Samāj as the representative of the British and Foreign Unitarian Association and succeeded in bringing together the leading men of the three sections of the Samāj to form a committee for the purpose of selecting a candidate to receive theological training in the Manchester College, Oxford. A second representative, Rev. James Harwood, from the same Association visited the Samāj in 1897, presented a whole set of the Hibbert Lectures to the Samāj library, and strengthened further the ties of the Brāhmo Samāj with the Unitarian Societies abroad. By the end of the nineteenth century, the Samāj, unfortunately, lost many of its valiant workers; D.M. Das, Rajnarian Bose, D.M. Ganguli, Ramtanu Lahiri, Sib Chandra Dev and others. But a new generation of workers, under the inspiring guidance of Pandit Sivanath Sastri, stepped into the breach and started their work in a spirit of service to the motherland.

Thus, from the very beginning of our national awakening, this numerically small family of social-radicals have ever tried through their best representatives, like J.C. Bose and P.C. Ray, Aurobindo Ghosh and Bepin Chandra Pal, Lord Sinha and C.R. Das, and Sarojini Naidu and Sarla Devi Chaudhurani, to further the cause of social, educational, and political advancement of India.

It is a matter of sincere congratulation that both during the cerebration of the centenary of the Brāhmo Samāj in 1928, as well as during the death centenary of its illustrious founder, Raja Rammohun Roy, in 1933 representatives of Islam, Christianity, Buddhism, Sikhism, Ārya Samāj, the Ramakrishna-Vivekananda Movement, and various other denominations of Hinduism participated in a most laudable spirit of fraternal co-operation. In the Parliament of Religions in Chicago, Swami Vivekananda sat side by side with Pratap Chandra Mazumdar, and in the one held at the Senate Hall, Calcutta University, under the auspices of the Brāhmo Samāj Centenary, the spirit of fellowship through religion, which was the basic principle of Brāhmoism, came to be gloriously vindicated by the delegates and representatives of the various religious denominations of the East and the West. The incarnation of this spirit of tolerance and fellowship was our national poet Rabindranath Tagore, the son of Maharshi Devendra Nath and the spiritual grandson of Rammohun Roy. The deathless truths of the Upanisads, on which the Raja and his noble successors based the Brāhmo Samāj, found their universal expression through the creations of Rabindranath, the poet laureate of Asia, who was, during his lifetime hailed by the republic of letters as a world-poet. His *Naivedya* and *Gītānjali, Sādhanā* and *Creative Unity,* and *Personality* and *Religion of Man,* to mention only a few of his immortal creations have won for India a permanent place in the world of beauty and truth. And in this age when Mahatma Gandhi has opened a new chapter in the history of modern India, with the solemn declaration of rights of all individuals, high or low, Brāhmana or pariah, we feel that the struggles of the Brāhmo Samāj in the vindication of the principles of equality and unity have not been in vain and may have lessons of permanent value in our national history as well as in the general progress of humanity in the orient.

References

1. *Vide* his Preface to *Essay on the Rights of Hindus over Ancestral Property (1830).*
2. Rammohun Death Anniversary Address at Bangalore on the 27th September 1924.
3. Pandit Sivanath Sastri, *History of the Brahmo Samaj,* 1.
4. Under Keshab's inspiration and direction. Babu Giris Chandra Sen prepared and published the first complete translation of the *Quran* (with commentaries) from the original Arabic into Bengali.

Appendix

BRAHMO SAMAJ

Founded in 1828 by *Rajas Rammohun Roy* in Calcutta, the Brahmo Samaj is a religious movement. At its centre is the belief that there is one God, who is omnipresent and omniscient. It initially evolved in India where it differed from existing practice as it did not believe in idol worship or the caste system. The Brahmo religion is now practised in many parts of the world.

The Brahmo Samaj has played a significant role in the renaissance of India, and the roots of much of modern thinking in India can be traced back to the Brahmo movement. *Rabindranath Tagore,* the Noble Laureate, was one of the illuminaries of the Brahmo Samaj.

BELIEFS OF THE BRAHMO SAMAJ

Fundamental Principles of the Brahmo Religion and Universalism

The fundamental principles of the Brahmo Samaj, founded by *Raja Rammohun Roy* in 1828 are:

1. There is only one God, who is the creator, and the saviour of this world. He is spirit, infinite in power, wisdom, love, justice and holiness, omnipresent eternal and blissful.
2. The human soul is immortal and capable of infinite progress, and is responsible to God for its doings.
3. Man's happiness in this and the next world consists in worshipping God in spirit and in truth.
4. Loving God, holding communion with Him, and carrying out His will in all the concerns of life, constitute true worship.

5. No created object is to be worshipped as God, and God alone is to be considered as infallible.

To this, Raja Rammohun Roy added "The true way of serving God is to do good to man. " Since no one person is considered to be infallible, the Brahmos hold all the great religious leaders of the world in respect, and believe that truth is to be gleaned from all the scriptures of the world. To that extent, the Brahmo religion is truly eclectic. Universalist in nature, it is "dogmatically undogmatic".

The Brahmo Samaj has a great deal in common with the other free churches of the world, and is one of the founding members of the "The International Association for Religious Freedom". Rationalist in everything, it does not deny the possibility of Divine Revelation, but reserves the right to test the validity of what is supposed to be revelation. The connection between the Brahmo Samaj and the liberal churches of the world is best understood when we considered the basics of Universalism, which are dealt with in the following paragraphs:

Duncan Howlett has aptly described Universalism as a doctrine of

"Testing, Questing and never Resting, with Open Mind and Open Heart."

Each of these items bears detailed examination. The root question is how can we be sure about the truth of our beliefs? After all, there is no doubt that we human beings are fallible. The only way we can surmount our human fallibility is by continually testing the validity of our assumptions. We have to accept that we are prone to making mistakes and deceiving one another all the time. Even in the age of computers, there is always the possibility of mistakes being made in programming or worse still, valuable data being lost on account of viruses deliberately planted by misguided souls. We must therefore check everything by all the means at our disposal. This is true even in the case of religion, where we can no longer be certain of the infallibility of scriptures or prophets.

If our human capacity for error is a severe limitation, then our imagination and probing curiosity are surely among our greatest assets. It is the human spirit of inquiry and questing, in other words, seeking for the truth, which is behind all advances in Philosophy or Religion. The enquiring mind pushes beyond ideas that we already have, in order to discover new perfections. In this process of Questing, we are never really satisfied until we feel that we have gone as far as is humanly possible. This is what is meant by "never Resting". On the path of discovery we are bound to meet like-minded souls also engaged in the same search for truth. We must be open to dialogue with them, and at least listen to them even if we do not agree. The spirit of the "open mind" is a safeguard against dogma, which has no place in Universalism.

While the open mind enlarges our own frontiers, it is not enough to merely be open to other ideas. Acceptance of the other person as a brother and a comrade makes religion truly universal. Merely accepting that "In the Father's house there are many mansions" does not better our human lot the way "Love they neighbour as thyself" does. True Universalism is based on the "Fatherhood of God and the Brotherhood of Man" more than anything else.

Universalists believe that religion should be dynamic and not static. Everything in this world is evolving and religion too, changes with time. Any religion that adheres to a set of unchanging beliefs is a dead religion. Of course, any change has to be tested for validity by applying our God given powers of logic and reasoning, and must be acceptable to our conscience. The Brahmos believe that God reveals Himself in His own creation, and speaks to man through his conscience. The relationship between God and man is one of loving and giving. Our life is a gift from God. What we do with our life in our gift to God.

HISTORY OF THE BRAHMO SAMAJ

As British rule consolidated in India during the 18th century, two factors contributed to the formation of the Brahmo Samaj in the following century. Firstly the Hindu social system had begun to stagnate and placed too much of an emphasis on traditional rituals. Secondly an English educated class of Indians began to emerge to fulfil the administrative and economic needs of British rule. Raja Rammohun Roy, a Bengali, was a product of the latter trend.

What made Raja Rammohun Roy stand out from his peers was his questioning mind. Apart from knowing several languages he was a Sanskrit and an Arabic scholar, and studied several religions. He campaigned for social reform and women's education. He founded the Brahmo Samaj at Calcutta in 1828 which was initially known as the

"Brahmo Sabha." Later in 1868 it was changed to the "Adi" (Original) Brahmo Samaj. It rejected idol worship and the worship of multiple gods and goddesses of the traditional Hindu beliefs.

Raja Rammohun Roy was much influenced by western thought, especially Christianity. He was one of the first Hindus to visit Europe, where he was much admired by the intellectuals. He died in Bristol.

He was friendly with another famous Bengali Dwarakanath Tagore. Prior to his departure to Europe, Raja Rammohun Roy had asked Dwarakanath Tagore's son. Devendranath Tagore to continue his work in his absence. Devendranath Tagore took an active interest in the Brahmo Samaj, and began to transform the Brahmo Samaj into a spiritual fraternity. He formulated the "Brahmo-upadesa" which were a set of readings from the ancient Hindu book, the "Upanishads."

Devendranath Tagore's successor was Keshab Chandra Sen. He sought to incorporate Christian ideals into the Brahmo Samaj movement. He began the compilations of a scripture including passages from the Holy Books of many religions—Hindu, Buddhist, Christian and Muslim.

Gradually, due to differences in certain areas of religious beliefs, three institutors arose.

- The Adi (Original) Brahmo Samaj—founded by Devendranath Tagore
- The Naba-Bidhan (New Dispensation) Samaj—founded by Keshab Chandra Sen
- The Sadharan (Common) Brahmo Samaj—founded by Pandit Shivanath Shastri.

The Sadharan Brahmo Samaj sought to provide a more rational and monotheistic interpretation of the Upanishads. A "mandir" (prayer house) was built in Cornwallis Street, (now re-named "Bidhan Sarani") Calcutta. Eventually these three Samajes united to form the "Brahmo Sammilan Samaj," and a "mandir" was built in Bhowanipour, Calcutta. This celebrated its century in 1997.

The Brahmo Samajes grew in several Indian cities and abroad. There are records of one being present in Rangoon and in London as far back as 1911.

SOCIAL WELFARE

Removing the Caste System

The caste system has been a part of Hindu society for hundreds of years. Its inherent divisive nature and social injustices were abhorrent to the early Brahmos. Therefore an important reform that the early Brahmos campaigned for was the removal of the caste system.

Many of the early Brahmos came from the Brahmin caste, who wore a sacred thread around their body to signify their caste superiority. From the 1850's onwards the renunciation of the sacred thread came to symbolise this break with tradition.

The equality of all men and was fundamental to the Brahmo movement, and to them it did not matter what caste or indeed religion someone was born into. For example even in 1865 there was a case of a Muslim boy being attracted into the religion. Given the polarization of society between Hindus and Muslims at the time, this was revolutionary in those days.

Widow Remarriage

Despite Iswar Chandra Vidyasagar's campaign that led to the legalisation of widow remarriage (1856) in India. Hindu society had many reservations on this issue. The Brahmos campaigned against such prejudice. To reinforce their commitment to this many young men of the Brahmo movement made a positive point of marrying widows.

Saving of Upper Caste Unmarried Women

It wasn't just the lower caste who suffered in the caste system. Despite their caste status, the girls from the upper caste families suffered because of their position. If a suitable bridegroom could not be found for such a girl in their caste, their options were limited as marriage to lower caste men was not permitted. These girls often found themselves being married off to very old men who were already arrived several times over. Of worse still, sometimes these girls would be poisoned to death. Again the Brahmos campaigned against such unjust practices and saved the lives of any such girls.

Women's Education and Status

Traditionally education had been primarily for the men. However, during the 1860s and the 1870's the attitude of the Brahmos started to change. Education was encouraged among the Bramho women. At the same time their equal status in society was emphasised by allowing women to pray with men at the prayer halls. In 1881 the Brahmo Samaj at Barishal (Bengal) appointed the first women Brahmo preacher (Manorama Mazumdar).

BRAHMO WEDDING

In a Brahmo wedding, the bride and the groom, as adults, declare in an open house that each is willing to accept the other as a partner for life. Thus a Brahmo wedding has no tradition of "giving away" the daughter by her parents. The bride and the groom pray to God together and take their nuptial vows. The minister and the other fellow Brahmos pray for their welfare and future happiness. The bride and groom typically exchange garlands and rings, and the prayers are complemented by singing of hymns.

FAMOUS BRAHMOS

Ever since its inception in 1828, the Brahmo Samaj has included several famous people. The list below contains links to various biographical www pages.

- Jagadish Chandra Bose
- Prasanta Chandra Mahalanobis
- Satyajit Ray
- Raja Rammohun Roy
- Rabindranath Tagore

MILLENNIUM SERMON

London Brahmo Samaj Maghotsav-30 January 2000

On the first Maghotsav of this century and in the new millennium I would like to share with you some thoughts that have crossed my mind.

The word January comes from the Roman God Janus, who had two heads—one pointing to the past, and one pointing to the future.

As we are celebrating Maghotsav in January at the beginning of the century, it is befitting that we first take a look at the past, and then into the future. A look at the past takes us to the Renaissance in India, and in Bengal in particular. In 1823 the Brahmo Samaj was established by Raja Rammohun Roy, who was followed by other leaders like Keshab Chandra Sen and Shivanath Shastri. It was a time of great spiritual social reforms against casteism and the emancipation of women. It was a period when superstitious and evil customs like the suttee were abolished. It an era when great educational institutions were established in Calcutta. That era has also seen the birth of men like Ramakrishna and Rabindranath and preachers of a non-violence like Mahatma Gandhi. We have seen the birth of the largest democratic nation when India achieved independence in 1947.

During the last century we have seen tremendous advances in the field of science and medicine. We have made great strides in developing transport—faster cars, trains and planes. Men have landed on the moon and we have watched it sitting in our own homes on TV. The past century has made enormous progress in the field of computers and satellite communication—the mobile phones and telecommunications by way of videoconferences in distant lands has brought the world closer. The world has become smaller and closer. Countries no longer think individually. They take a global view of trade and commerce.

However, in spite of all the scientific achievements and material comforts have we made any real progress in moral and human values? Are human hearts and minds now closer to each other than 500 years ago? The 1900s have seen two World Wars—the people of the past century have experienced fighting and bloodshed and the horrific destruction of Nagasaki with the atom bomb. In spite of modern communications system, communities seem to have grown apart and divided as we have seen in Bosnia and very recently in the atrocities of Kosovo and now in Chechnya. At present and there are many wars going on the Africa and Asia with the devastating consequences of land mine injuries long afterwards.

Our social structure and family life has also changed. The extended family is on the brink of extinction. The advances in medicine have increased longevity, but are we able to provide a reasonable quality of care? Can we spare a little time for visiting elderly friends? Do we as human beings care for other humans and the plants and animals of this beautiful world?

Today at the beginning of the 21st century let us attempt to try to look at the future. We do not know what the future holds for us but we can hope that the world will be a better place for all of us. The world, we can hope, will be a peaceful place—not only will there be peace among nations, but also in the hearts all men who will fulfil their duties towards the old, the sick and hungry. Societies and nations will not just think of their own survival but will work for the benefit of others, which is one of the ideals of the promise of the Brahmo Samaj, and that the other principles—"truth, justice and love" shall prevail in the hearts of men and women of the 21st century. We hope that the hearts and the minds of all the people in the world will be untied and the century will be a happier place for all of us. It may seem like a dream but it is up to each one of us to make an effort, however small towards achieving this dream—and making this place a better place. May we find the world in the 21st century as Tagore has described in one of his poems:

> "Where the mind is without fear and the head is held high;
> Where knowledge is free;
> Where the world has not been broken up into fragments of narrow domestic walls.
> Where words come out from the depths of the truth;
> Where tireless striving stretches its arms towards perfection
> Where the clear stream of reason has not lost its way into the dreary desert sand of dead habit."